KU-466-399

An Occasion of Sin

Andrew M. Greeley

PIATKUS

412129
MORAY DISTRICT COUNCIL
DEPARTMENT OF
LEISURE AND LIBRARIES
F

Copyright © 1991 by Andrew Greeley Enterprises, Ltd

This edition first published in
Great Britain in 1992 by
Judy Piatkus (Publishers) Ltd of
5 Windmill Street, London W1

**The moral right of the author
has been asserted**

*A catalogue record for this book is available
from the British Library*

ISBN 0–7499–0137–3

Printed and bound in Great Britain by
Butler & Tanner Ltd, Frome and London

An Occasion of Sin

Can one be a saint without God? That is the only problem I know of today.

ALBERT CAMUS

Many of the insights of the saint stem from his experience as a sinner.

ERIC HOFFER

Saints should always be judged guilty till they are proved innocent.

GEORGE ORWELL

Grace is indeed needed to turn a man into a saint and he who doubts it does not know what a saint or a man is.

BLAISE PASCAL

It is easier to make a saint out of a libertine than out of a prig.

GEORGE SANTAYANA

The only difference between the saint and the sinner is that every saint has a past and every sinner has a future.

OSCAR WILDE

The story of a saint is always a love story. It is a story of a God who loves, and of the beloved who learns how to reciprocate and share that "harsh and dreadful love." It is a story that includes misunderstanding, deception, betrayal, concealment, reversal, and revelation of character. It is, if the saints are to be trusted, our story. But to be a saint is not to be a solitary lover. It is to enter into deeper community with everyone and everything that exists.

KENNETH L. WOODWARD
Making Saints

PROLOGUE

Two groups of anxious young men faced one another across the narrow mud plaza at the heart of the jungle village. Save for their automatic weapons they might have been two teams about to enter a closely matched game. Men on both sides fingered their weapons, not sure whether to shoot first and risk casualties or not.

A tall, handsome man in a white shirt and black trousers stepped ahead of his group. A woman and a man on either side of him reached out to restrain him. Gently he shook them off and, holding a jeweled cross in his hand, slowly walked across the plaza.

Suddenly, with a sound like popping firecrackers, a volley of shots was fired. The tall man turned slightly to the right, as if he was executing a soft-shoe dance step, and then pitched over in the mud, his body as limp as a rag doll.

Both sides now opened fire, wildly releasing the nervous tension that had been building up.

The man and woman who had been standing on either side of the tall man rushed to him. The man pulled out a small vial of oil and made a sign of the cross on the wounded man's forehead.

"Through this holy anointing and His most tender mercy may God forgive all your sins."

The woman cradled the man's head in her arms. His shirt was now red with blood and black with mud.

"John!" she screamed, as if trying to summon him back to life.

The man opened his eyes. "God, how I love you," he murmured.

Then he died.

|| 1 || "In all candor," the Cardinal said, shaking his head regretfully, "the miracles are embarrassing."

My Cardinal has not uttered a candid statement for at least twenty years. When he purports to be candid, he is being more devious than usual. Since the subject of our discussion in his office on this glorious late summer day was his martyred predecessor, I assumed that truth would be wrapped in several layers of ecclesiastical evasion and euphemism.

"You saw 'Walter Jacobson's Perspective' on Channel 2 last night?" He extended his arms in a gesture of helplessness which used to fool most priests and still fools some of them. "If the late Cardinal is really a saint, why is the Archdiocese afraid to say so?"

I poured myself another cup of tea from the Belleek teapot which had been placed on the Cardinal's solid oak coffee table in my honor. His refreshment was a glass of water (with his coat of arms embossed on the side) and three ice cubes. He hadn't touched it.

The Cardinal's office is a smooth blend of ecclesiastic traditional and Swedish modern: light oak instead of dark, functional rather than ornate furniture, broad windows with a view of men and women in swimsuits hurrying to and from the lake instead of heavy red drapes. But cardinal red still abounds in the desk set, upholstery, and framing the pictures of Popes on the wall. His coat of arms was emblazoned, it seemed, on every flat surface. I often alleged that it could even be found on the toilet paper in his private bathroom, though in true candor, I've never checked.

Though he is of Eastern European origins, the Cardinal looks like a hungry medieval French peasant in a Robert Bresson film. He is tall, bushy-haired, and gaunt, with thick iron gray eyebrows and a long, thin face that looked haggard even before he was given the second toughest job in the Catholic world. Maybe it's the toughest. At least in Rome they don't measure you against the Mayor at every turn.

"Did you see the TV special three nights ago?"

Although I was loath to own up to so much TV watching, I had to admit that I had.

"And you found it?"

It was so like my Cardinal not to venture an opinion first. "I would say I found it persuasive," I said after a considered pause. "In terms of the cure, at least," I added, not that the Cardinal could have mistaken me as one among the make-Johnny-a-saint camp.

It had been a damned powerful spot. Sitting along with Channel 5's Carol Marin were Mary Elizabeth Quinlan, her daughter Nancy Quinlan Epstein, Nancy's husband Noah Epstein, an MD, their little son, Brendan, and Monsignor Leonard Carey, secretary to the late Cardinal. Young Brendan had suffered from retinoblastoma—a very aggressive carcinoma in the optic region. There had been no known cases of remission with this particular form of cancer. None, at least, before young Brendan. The cause of his cure had been ascribed to the late Cardinal's cross, the same cross he had held aloft just moments before his murder.

Resorting to the cross had been Nancy's idea. Refusing to accept that her son was terminally ill, she was willing to try anything to fight the disease once medical technology seemed to have failed. Clearly Mary Elizabeth had gone along only reluctantly. She had seemed reluctant there on the TV screen as well. Of the four adults assembled by the able Marin, she was the least persuaded that a miracle had taken place. But her daughter was wholly persuaded. Even Noah Epstein, once a self-professed atheist, believed.

The two women had laid the late Cardinal's cross over little Brendan's eye. When a change for the better was noticed after about a week, the two persisted in laying the cross over Brendan's face. In ten days, Brendan's improvement was measurable: the cancer's remission was complete. There was absolutely no sign of it. The specialists were baffled, as was Epstein. But he was more grateful than perplexed. Now, weeks after the alleged cure, Brendan was still radiantly healthy. On the television, he looked like any normal youngster, unwilling to sit still for as long a time as the interview mandated.

"It's especially inconvenient that the beneficiary of the alleged miracle is the grandson of a woman who was his intimate friend for most of his life." I continued the Cardinal's original line of thought, hoping that the evasions and circumlocutions would eventually end with an explanation of what he wanted out of me.

"What do you mean by 'intimate,' Laurence?" His brown eyes, bedroom eyes if the truth be told, seemed sad, a fact he used manipulatively to his advantage.

"I don't believe Jumping Johnny ever slept with Mary Elizabeth Reilly Quinlan, if that's what you mean, worse luck for him."

He winced at my candor, which was quite different from his own, though not really candor either. Not by a long shot. Candid I'm not; but I'm better than he at pretending.

"He died in her arms."

"Better hers than a male lover or a little boy."

"Yes, indeed."

"Whispering, according to witnesses, 'God, how I love you!' And the issue is whether he meant her or the deity."

"Arguably both." The Cardinal glanced away from me.

The Cardinal stops the music with comments like that. For a moment I wondered if beneath the mask of a careerist and savvy ecclesiastical politician there lurked a radical heart that could acknowledge human passion as a revelation of divine passion.

"Arguably," I agreed.

"The woman has five, six children, does she not?" The Cardinal watched me intently.

"Yeah." I counted them on my fingers. "Beth was born in 1956. Then, in good Catholic fashion, she had two sons: Peter, who runs the company now, and Anthony Junior, who is a lawyer, then Nancy in 1965. That was it until Caroline came along in 1980."

"Nancy was the one with them when my predecessor died?"

"That's right."

"And her son is the little boy who was allegedly cured by touching him with my pectoral cross?"

"True enough."

"There are those who say that the boy was my predecessor's grandson."

"Bullshit."

"For that to have happened"—the Cardinal spoke carefully—"Monsignor John McGlynn—as he was then—would have had to return to Chicago from his post in Africa some nine months before the birth of the child, would he not?"

"That's the way it usually works . . . did he?"

"Not that we know."

"That settles that, doesn't it?"

"Laurence"—he extended his arms again—"I am under great pressure in this matter."

My real name since the day my mother brought me home from Little Company of Mary hospital is "Lar" (pronounced, despite East Coast distortions, to rhyme not with "bar" but with "hair"). The Cardinal knows I don't like to be called "Larry," and finds "Lar" too familiar. He also has a hard time getting his tongue around our prairie-flat Chicago *a*.

"I understand, Your Eminence. The devotees of your predecessor and the Chicago media on the one hand and the Vatican on the other."

He likes to be called "Steve"—which is why I call him "Your Eminence."

"After all"—he shook his head—"he did die a martyr's death."

"He got in the way of a stray bullet, whether Contra or Sandinista no one knows, in a place where he ought not to have been, as part of a firefight which was none of his business."

"You didn't like him very much, did you, Laurence?"

"Jumping Johnny was one of the great assholes of the western world. He was a rich, spoiled River Forest brat and a Cub fan too."

I overstated my case, though I do believe that salvation, to say nothing of sanctity, is difficult for Cub fans, though with God all things are possible.

"His spiritual writings are deeply moving." The Cardinal was ticking off the arguments in favor of the theory that John Cardinal McGlynn was a saint.

"Conventional piety, then Freudian happy talk."

"The theology of his pastorals was orthodox and yet relevant to the needs of his people."

"Till he discovered Liberation Theology. Too bad he didn't live to see the Berlin Wall come down. But he would have found a new fad to ride on. Might have discovered James Madison."

"He was greatly revered by his people."

"Best media managers in town."

"His loyalty to the Holy See was unquestioned."

"Yet there is always Mary Elizabeth."

"Indeed . . . do you know her, Laurence?"

"Marbeth? Yeah, sure. A knockout, isn't she? No law against a woman in her middle fifties being sexually appealing, is there?"

"I'm not sure"—he smiled faintly—"that the Holy See

would completely agree with you. But you see the problem?"

"Her picture is always next to his in the papers and on the tube, including some early snaps with her in a swimsuit. The Holy See doesn't like cardinals, especially martyred cardinals, to have had companions like that."

"Regrettably," he sighed.

"Marbeth is not a retiring woman either."

"Tell me about it." His smile was almost a grin. Oh, Marbeth was magic all right, even with a cardinal whose affection for women seemed limited at best.

"Then there's the matter of whether he smuggled money from the Vatican Bank to Poland to fund Solidarity, as at least one British author has argued."

"I don't think he did." The Cardinal frowned. "Rome denies it."

"That and a dollar and a quarter will get you a ride on Rich Daley's subway. There are also rumors that he used money from the Catholic Cemeteries Office to bail out his brother at the Board of Trade."

"If he did, the money was paid back. There is no trace of a loss that year. . . . One always hears such rumors, and they are almost always false."

"But they become embarrassing when his admirers demand a canonization process."

"Decidedly."

"The Vatican wants you to put a stop to the cult of your late predecessor and doesn't take your word for it when you tell them you can no more do that than you can stop Chicago Catholics from practicing birth control."

"Do you believe in miracles, Laurence?"

I considered the question. "Not particularly."

"And saints?"

"Sure, I'm Catholic. We believe in saints—stories of God's love and human response. I don't believe in canonization."

"Do you feel John Cardinal McGlynn was a saint?"

"Hell, no."

We both pondered his martyred predecessor, a man who in his own ways was even more magic than Marbeth.

"I knew him, of course." The Cardinal closed his eyes. "Not well. No one knew him well. Perhaps not even Mrs. Quinlan. I served with him on several committees. He was, ah, impressive and, de mortuis nil nisi bonum, often, how should I say it . . ."

"A tough sumbitch?"

He waved his hand delicately. " 'Difficult' is the word I would have chosen."

I continued to wonder what all of this had to do with me. I knew Johnny McGlynn from the Seminary, though he was six years ahead of me. We were not friends. Quite the contrary, after he became my Bishop our relations were uneasy, to put it mildly. Maybe I was too much like him, even if he was a Cub fan and son of a millionaire and I was the son of a cop and naturally a Sox fan. It was no secret that we did not get along, and that we kept peace by ignoring each other's existence.

To give him his due, he never tried to mess with me as other bishops would if they had a contentious and outspoken cleric as one of their subjects.

"You didn't invite me here just to ask me whether I thought Johnny McGlynn should be canonized," I said.

"Only eleven cardinals have ever been canonized." He filled my teacup.

"Occupational hazard."

The Cardinal actually laughed.

"The Holy See"—he lifted his glass of ice water to his lips and sipped it as though he were tasting expensive wine—"wants more saints to canonize."

"There've been more during the last decade than ever before," I said.

"Especially from the third world and from the ranks of the laity, even the married laity."

"So long as the laity didn't have sex too often or enjoy it too much."

"The Holy See does not want to canonize cardinals," he said.

"Especially if they have girlfriends that are good-looking and very much alive."

"Especially," he whispered softly, "if the Roman rumor is that the sick boy was in fact Cardinal McGlynn's grandson."

That was one I had heard, but I was a little surprised it had circulated as far as Rome.

"As you know, in the reform of the canonization procedures of 1983, the local bishop has de facto control of recommendations of the beginning of the process," he continued.

I didn't know that. I didn't care either. My idea of sanctity makes me view the Roman canonization processes as irrelevant and often comic.

"They shot down the efforts of your friend in New York to have his predecessor canonized," I said.

"No claims for miracles there. . . . The Holy See wants me to order an investigation by a prudent and responsible priest who is not initially disposed to credit the belief that my predecessor was a saint."

That one had my name on it.

"No!" I emptied my cup of tea in a single gulp.

"Laurence, please!" He refilled my cup with his most vulnerable of gestures. "I am under enormous pressure."

"Goddamn it, Steve! You know that I'm neither prudent nor responsible! I've never been called prudent in all my life!"

The Cardinal grinned happily, content that he had for once outpointed me. "The Holy See doesn't know that."

"I don't have time."

"Father Keenan, your inestimable curate, can handle the parish while you pursue this quest, which must of course be secret and unofficial, as I'm sure you understand."

Yeah, right. You go around poking into the debris of John Cardinal McGlynn's life and keep it a secret. But he was right about my New Priest. He could run the whole Archdiocese without working up a sweat—and find time for two sets of tennis or a game of one-on-one every afternoon.

"I didn't like him."

"I know. That's why I want you to do the investigation. Admit it"—he was on a roll and he knew it—"Laurence, your curiosity is already piqued."

"I'm no fucking voyeur!"

"Ideally"—he smiled benignly—"you will come back at some point in the future and tell me that you have found reasons that make it impossible to ask that John McGlynn be declared a 'servant of God,' which as you know is the first step in the process."

"And until then you can keep both the media and the Vatican at bay by saying that an investigation is being conducted and at the present time the Archdiocese has no further comment."

"Exactly." He positively beamed.

"Why me?"

He spread his hands. "Isn't it obvious? There are few priests in the Archdiocese who disliked him more than you did . . . it is said because you two were so similar in, ah, temperament."

"Bullshit!"

"And there is no one besides you who disliked him who also has the integrity to tell me that perhaps my complex and opaque predecessor might just be a saint."

"Impossible!"

"That's what I want you to find out. I can provide you with staff help when and if you need it."

"I'm not about to be Johnny McGlynn's Devil's Advocate!"

"As you know, the reform of 1983 abolished that role."

"It's what you want me to be."

"Lar." He spoke very quietly. "It might surprise you—it might surprise many people in fact—but in this matter of my predecessor I really want to know the truth, however palatable or politic it might or might not be."

It did kind of surprise me. A cardinal interested in the truth? This time, however, I did believe him. He rose and extended his hand, knowing that he had me.

Curiosity, huh? Hadn't it killed the cat?

"The truth, the whole truth, or at least as much of the truth as you feel free to tell me at any given time."

"Why do you want to know?" I demanded, still looking for a way out, though not all that vigorously.

"Damn it, Lar. He sat at that desk. He lived in my house. He slept in my bed . . ."

"With or without Marbeth."

"He said Mass in my chapel, he presided over the priests of what I foolishly call my Archdiocese. If he's working miracles, I want to know."

"Why?" I persisted.

"We're the only church that has miracles and saints. If there was a real saint in this office, maybe we still have a future."

"You mean if Jumping Johnny McGlynn is working miracles from heaven, then what the temporal Church prefers may be immaterial."

It struck me then that for all my ostensible pessimism, I probably had more faith in the future than the Cardinal did. But we sat in different offices, didn't we?

"Something like that." He shook my hand again. "But please don't quote me."

He stopped me just as I was walking out the door. "Do you think he really, uh, made love in the Cardinal's bedroom?"

"I doubt that he ever made love with her. If they did screw, I hope they did it there at least once."

The suggestion didn't seem to bother him all that much.

"She is a very devout woman." He sounded judicious, weighing Marbeth's virtues and vices.

"Beware those intensely devout women, Your Eminence; raw passion can come in many guises."

"So I am told. At a younger age in life, she might have been the kind who would, ah, find such a deed amusing."

I only shrugged.

"Now let me make sure I have my mandate clear in my own head. I am to determine whether there are grounds for not considering the canonization potential of Johnny McGlynn. In particular"—I began to tick the charges off on my fingers—"I am to look at rumors that he used Church money to help his brother when the latter was in financial trouble at the commodity exchanges, the possibility that he smuggled stolen money into Poland to help the Solidarity union, and the nature of his relationship with Ms. Quinlan."

"And," the Cardinal added, "the possible use of his mother's money to obtain ecclesiastical promotion. As you know, one cannot buy ecclesiastical offices at the present time . . ."

"Yet gifts can be given in a good cause?"

He shrugged helplessly. "It has been known to happen."

"And I am to be in all these matters most discreet, particularly with Ms. Quinlan?"

He shivered. "You read what she called the Pope because he wouldn't come to my predecessor's funeral?"

"A prig?"

"That was the euphemism the media used." He shivered a second time.

"What if I fall in love with Marbeth during my investigation?" I asked him as he opened the door.

"Is that possible?"

"She's a gorgeous and fascinating woman."

"At your age?"

"Have you ever been in love, Steve?"

He hesitated. "Not really."

"It can happen at any age."

"But"—he smiled happily—"it's not very likely that you'll ever be a candidate for sainthood, is it?"

|| 2 || As I left the Cardinal's office I remembered all too vividly the time Mary Elizabeth Anne Reilly and I met in the ballpark at the little town of Watersmeet, Michigan. Watersmeet was a small summer country town near Clearwater Lake where the seminarians from Mundelein were taken each August for a two-week vacation from the red brick Georgian mansion north of Chicago where they were incarcerated for seven years learning to serve the Catholic laity.

In those almost forgotten days the Church feared for the safety of those who were about to become its priests if they were permitted to be exposed to the dangers of the world in the years before ordination. So, after a brief visit home we were given a holiday at the Church's Clearwater Villa, where we were allegedly protected from contamination by the laity, especially female laity. Given that this was the setting where I met Marbeth, it is evident that the system was not all that effective, even on its own terms.

We were both watching Johnny McGlynn heaving fastballs at the Watersmeet batters.

I had met Johnny McGlynn for the first time eighteen

months previously when I was still at Quigley Seminary. Every Christmas holiday we challenged the students from Mundelein to an annual basketball game at our gym. Johnny and I had heard about one another before the confrontation. I was probably described as the big kid from 79th Street who had a pretty good hook shot. He was described to me as a cinch to be the first Chicago seminarian to be sent to Rome to study since the War, a sure bishop, the possessor of the highest average in the thirty-seven-year history of Quigley, and a rich kid from River Forest who was a helluva good center on the basketball court.

As we practiced before the game, I saw that I was taller than he was but that his broad shoulders and solid body outweighed my skinny physique by a good twenty pounds. Moreover, he was graceful and I was still fairly clumsy.

Johnny stood out among the twenty or so of us who were practicing, not merely because he was tall, with thick and wavy black hair, pale Irish skin, and a dimple in his chin. He also had presence; as I look back on it, he was patently, indeed blatantly, a man who knew who he was and what talents he had and was not ashamed to radiate his personality and gifts. He had the confidence and charisma of a young Jack Kennedy. His smile was irresistible, though I have spent a lifetime practicing resistance.

That day I resolved that I would stop him from scoring, no matter what.

At tipoff we shook hands with the appearance of cordiality.

"Good luck, kid." He smiled at me.

"Fuck you," I replied.

In the first five minutes of the game I realized that I was not likely to score any more than an occasional tip-in. Johnny was too agile and jumped too high for my hook to have a chance. The first two times I tried it, he stole the ball from me and rifled it down the court to one of his forwards for two quick and easy baskets.

All right, I muttered to myself, I don't score, you don't score. But his quickness made that vow difficult to honor. He couldn't shoot over me but he could and did go around me. Twice he left me in my tracks like I was cemented to the gym floor. So the answer was to play him close—the way Charles Barkley plays Michael Jordan—even though we didn't play "physical" NBA defense in the nineteen-fifties. But I did.

"McAuliffe is pushing." The priest who was reffing the game blew his whistle, spun around on his toes, and pulled a chain, opening one of the high windows in the gym—standard practice when a bit of roughness disturbed him.

There was much laughter in the stands.

"Who, me?" I protested.

More laughter.

Even Jumping Johnny, whom I had knocked to the floor, laughed at that.

I fully expected him to fight back. That's what I would have done. That's what most of us would have done. Only Johnny McGlynn was too graceful, too self-possessed, to do that. He let me push him around and didn't push back. What's wrong with this guy? I wondered.

Anyway, he didn't score another basket until I fouled out in the fourth quarter. The ref had caught maybe one out of every eight of my violations, so the final call was long overdue. They cheered moderately for me when I walked out. Johnny shook hands with me. They cheered more loudly for him.

He scored only two more baskets after I had sat on the bench. I guess I wore him out. So Quigley won by five points. And I won. I'd slowed down, if not stopped, the alleged best center in the history of Quigley.

But Jumping Johnny was the real winner. When he was pulled off the floor in the last twenty seconds they gave him a standing ovation. Grace and charm and a smile had triumphed over a thug from Saint Sabina.

He walked up to me in the steamy shower room, handsome and self-assured in his nakedness. "Great game, kid." He offered his hand. "I'm glad I won't have to play against you next year." (By tradition only the first two years of the Mundelein seminarians participated in the game.)

Not at all sure of my own body in a shower room, I turned away.

"Go fuck yourself."

He laughed and walked back to the locker room. But before he did I caught an expression in his eyes that baffled me, then a quick flicker of pain.

So Johnny McGlynn was a vulnerable son of a bitch—but he was a son of a bitch just the same.

My negative opinion stemmed from the same reasons then as it did over a year later at Watersmeet: he was a shallow and superficial person, covering up his lack of seriousness and discipline with charm and wit and wealth.

Sitting in the stands, watching him heaving fastballs with more energy than control, I knew he was and would always be a phony. Although he pretended that day to be pressed into service to save St. Mary's baseball team from rout, in fact he had not played baseball in several years. The game was lost the moment he stepped on the mound. Yet he would emerge, win or lose, as a hero.

"Asshole," I muttered through clenched teeth.

"You're the kid who told him off at practice yesterday at the Villa, aren't you?" a woman's voice said next to me.

She was the most beautiful girl—young woman—I had ever seen, much less sat next to: a tall, lithe, brown-eyed nymph with long brown hair and a flawless complexion, whose aloof beauty could haunt a man's dreams for the rest of his life. She was wearing a white blouse and beige slacks with a matching sweater tied loosely around her shoulders and a matching ribbon keeping her hair in place. I had no idea of the name of her scent, except it seemed to blend with the whiff of pine needles in the air.

Later I would learn that Marbeth's family and Johnny's lived near each other and that she had grown up as best friends with Johnny's younger sister, Kate. Actually, it must have been God's will we were all together that summer, as Johnny was no longer an official seminarian. As a promising young man he had been shipped off to the North American

College in Rome, a boot camp (in those days) for future bishops. He had come home from Europe for the summer—at his
mother's insistence and against the wishes of the North American Rector—and was spending two weeks at the Villa to
"keep in touch" with his classmates from Mundelein. I also
was not living at the Villa. I was a counselor at Camp Saint
George across the lake—once a camp for rich kids and now a
camp for kids from Maryville Academy, a home for young
people from broken families.

It was my Sunday off; I had hitched a ride on one of the open
trucks in which the seminarians were transported to the ball
games—the Villa was not a luxurious place, to put the matter
mildly.

Johnny had been pressed into service as a pitcher for the
Watersmeet game—the biggest of the season—because of his
reputation as the best pitcher at the seminary in the last ten
years. I wanted to watch him because I figured that I was
better than he was and that I'd be the best pitcher in the next
ten years.

Naturally, Johnny did not ride with us in one of the trucks,
but rather drove his mother and his sister and, it turned out,
his sister's "best friend" to the game in one of the family
Cadillacs. Cordelia McGlynn, Johnny's overbearing mother,
had agreed to his slumming with his inferiors—seminarians
not destined for the hierarchy—on the condition that she and
some of the rest of the family would minister to him from the
most expensive lodge in Eagle River, the plush resort area
reserved for the Chicago Irish New Rich. "Doctor," as
Johnny's father was always called, could not join the family
in the North Woods, of course. No doubt the practice of medicine in the Chicago metropolitan area would have ground to
a halt in his absence, or so it would seem from the way the
McGlynns acted.

Legend today has it that the young Johnny McGlynn once
turned down a minor-league contract from a farm team of the
Cubs, but he didn't look like a potential Three I league star
that day in Watersmeet, when Marbeth first spoke to me,
asking why I had told the beloved Johnny McGlynn off.

There was no hostility in her question, only serious interest. "He offered to let you catch warmup for him?"

"Yeah."

"And you refused?"

She didn't seem inclined to smile. What, I wondered, would she look like in a swimsuit? That was about as far as a seminarian's fantasy ventured in those days.

"Yeah."

"What did you say to him?"

I was so dazed by this astonishing young woman that I couldn't think of anything to say but the truth.

"I told him I wasn't his spear bearer and he should go fuck himself."

She smiled faintly. It was this same wry smile I have been treated to many times in the years since, whenever I succeeded in amusing her. "In the car driving up here, he quoted you as using more polite language. He likes you, you know. Said that you could easily make the North American College list if you didn't fight so much with the Jesuit faculty."

"I'm not running for bishop."

"I'm Mary Elizabeth Anne Reilly."

"Hat trick."

"Pardon?"

"Every Irish Catholic woman has to have one of those names. You have all three."

She smiled again, ever so lightly. "And you're Laurence with a 'u' O'Toole McAuliffe. Impressive."

"Martyred Archbishop of Dublin."

"I know."

"What do they call you?"

She hesitated. "Marbeth. My brothers gave me the nickname when I was a baby."

"I like Mary Elizabeth better."

"So do I."

So she has always been Mary Elizabeth when we have spoken to one another—not all that often in four decades. Not often enough.

We exchanged basic information. Her father was a lawyer;

the family lived on Lathrop in River Forest, two houses down from the McGlynn clan. She had graduated from Trinity and would attend Manhattanville in the fall.

River Forest, Trinity, Manhattanville—in 1952 that said aristocracy to me. My face grew warm as we talked. I had never sat next to an aristocratic girl before. She seemed to be a totally different kind of being from the young women with whom I had attended Saint Sabina and who were now planning to study nursing or primary education. She was of Johnny McGlynn's world, not mine.

Looking back on that day, I can see that I didn't know what a real aristocrat was. We Chicago Irish Catholics have produced rich people, a lot more of them since 1952, but few aristocrats like the Kennedys. Thank God I almost added. We are not into aristocracy. In 1952, as the Korean stalemate was winding down and Dwight Eisenhower was preparing to bury Adlai Stevenson, that fact was not obvious to me.

Mary Elizabeth and I had a lot more in common than she would have with many of the East Coast Irish wealthy she'd meet shortly at Manhattanville. While I suspect she knew that then, I didn't. So, despite the cool air of the North Woods, my face was hot and my hands sweaty as I spoke to this dazzling young woman from, as I thought, a world utterly unlike my own.

"You're right about him." She broke off her discussion of her college plans and raised her solid chin.

"Oh?"

"He *is* an asshole."

Not the kind of language I was used to hearing in those days from a young woman, especially a putative aristocrat. I felt my face growing warmer still.

"Oh?"

"He doesn't have a vocation." She nodded at Johnny, who was back on the mound.

"Really?"

"His mother does." Her full lips tightened into an angry line. "I can't stand her. She thinks she's God. Her oldest son must be a doctor like 'Doctor'—and I don't care how much money he has, he's an asshole too—and her second son must be a priest and a bishop if she can buy it for him; and her third son a politician and Governor of Illinois and she thinks she can buy that too, the old bitch!"

That outburst was the first sense of the pit bull who would appear in years to come. It made me like her even more.

"I've never met her," I replied cautiously.

"You're not missing anything. I love poor Kate, but her mother will ruin her life too."

Cordelia McGlynn and her daughter were sitting a couple of rows in front of us, next to the Auxiliary Bishop, who was visiting the Villa, cheering noisily for the St. Mary of the Lake team. The daughter was a pretty if somewhat wistful young woman, and the mother plump, silver-haired and noisy. She had wrapped the Bishop around her little finger, as she had also done with the priests who administered the Villa. Mrs. McGlynn was clearly used to being in charge. What she couldn't win by willpower and exuberant charm she would obtain by hints of financial contributions—hints which, I would later learn, were not always followed up with actual payoff when she had her way.

Now I would say she was vulgar. Then I thought she was rich and powerful and that's the way rich and powerful matrons were supposed to behave.

"You think Johnny's life is ruined?" I asked in surprise. "He's rich, handsome, smart, popular, he's the top student at the North American just like he was at Mundelein. He's certain to be a bishop and probably a cardinal. What more could he want?"

"Come on, Laurence O'Toole McAuliffe, you should know better than that. Would those things make you happy?"

"No," I said promptly.

Her eyes flashed dangerously. "Would they make you happy if you didn't want to be a priest and didn't even believe in God?"

I was astonished. "Johnny doesn't believe in God?"

"Absolutely not." She unwrapped the sweater from her shoulders and slipped it over her head.

"How can you know that?"

"I *know!*" She turned away from me as if our conversation was over.

I rediscovered the baseball game. We were at bat, there was a man on first, and Johnny was at the plate.

He swung at the first pitch, a fastball right over the plate, and drove a hard line drive into the diminutive left center field bleachers of the Watersmeet field. St. Mary's five, Watersmeet three. Our crowd went crazy, all except for Mary Elizabeth Reilly, who sat next to me with the stiff back and stony face of a mourner at a wake.

"Do you want to be a priest, Lar?" she asked, obviously having learned my true name before she sat next to me.

"You bet."

"It is not your father or mother's vocation?"

"Not at all. . . . I didn't think that happened except in the old country."

"You'd be surprised," she said bitterly.

And later, when many of my classmates left the priesthood as soon as they could do so, I realized that she was right and I was wrong.

Why, I wondered, has she sought me out? Why was she telling me these things?

"If Johnny doesn't want to be a priest, he should leave the seminary. He'll never be happy."

"Happiness doesn't enter into it."

As someone who had never wanted to be anything but a priest (and still doesn't) I did not understand her. How could anyone become a priest who didn't want to do so?

"He doesn't even believe in God," she said again. "It's all a terrible act."

"I hope you're wrong."

"That's because you're a sweet boy." She touched my hand, and I thought I'd die from the electric shock which raced through my body.

"Thank you," I murmured, hoping that my blush was not too obvious.

"I'm sorry for bothering you. I had to talk to someone. Promise me you won't tell anyone what I said?"

"Of course," said the knight who was above reproach.

"Thank you." She smiled. Watersmeet, the Upper Peninsula of Michigan, and a substantial segment of the State of Wisconsin disappeared from the face of the earth.

In the last of the seventh (it was a seven-inning game), Watersmeet got Johnny for four runs, beating us seven to five. Despite our defeat we cheered enthusiastically for Johnny as he shook hands with the Watersmeet players. Why the hell were we doing that? I wondered. What's there to cheer about losing?

"We were lucky to come as close as we did," a priest explained to me. "No pitching this year. Johnny did a great job."

Marbeth had slipped away to rejoin the McGlynns.

"He still lost."

The priest looked at me like I was some kind of freak. "Winning isn't everything, Lar."

"I guess."

In my three years of pitching at the Villa we went six and zero against Watersmeet. No one ever cheered so loudly for me as they did for Johnny that day. It is better, I would learn, to lose with charm than to win with ruthless determination.

If you're really clever you can win with charm—which is what Johnny did through the rest of his life.

After the movie that night (*Show Boat* in the Howard Keel/Kathryn Grayson/William Warfield/Ava Gardner version) the McGlynn family provided a "haustus"—an ice cream party—on the porch of the building that served as recreation center for the Villa. It was cold enough to wear sweaters or jackets, but the full moon reflecting on the smooth surface of Clearwater Lake hinted at the possibility of romance—at least to a seminarian who had decided that Mary Elizabeth looked like Ava Gardner. In order to examine that possibility, I kept my eyes on her all evening.

"The Drummer," as we called the Jesuit who was director of the Villa, thanked the McGlynn family for the ice cream and for honoring us with their presence and Johnny for making it a close game in Watersmeet. Loud cheers went up from the crowd. When the Drummer wanted us to cheer, we cheered. Besides, ice cream is ice cream.

The Auxiliary Bishop repeated much the same words, adding that he was proud that the Romans from the Archdiocese could remain part of their seminary classes in Chicago.

More loud cheers; hell, there might be more ice cream tomorrow night.

As you might surmise, despite my antipathy toward the wealthy, I had every intention of eating their ice cream. You ought not to push principle too far, ought you?

The McGlynns and Mary Elizabeth stood at the center of the porch, talking to the Bishop and the Drummer and some of the priests and a few of Johnny's close friends. There seemed to be a special glow about the group, the confidence and radiance that comes from money and power reflecting the soft moonlight, the bright smiles and the hearty laughter of those who knew that they were the beautiful people and entitled, as a matter of right, to the admiration of others.

Did they really feel that way, or looking back, was I reading my own resentment into them?

I guess both are true. They did feel that way, though perhaps not consciously. I did resent them and I did not see that tragedy is as likely in the lives of the bright and beautiful as it is in the lives of people from 79th Street.

"Would you look at that bimbo." Terry Tracey, one of my fellow counselors, had appeared behind me. "Look at the way she eats him up with her eyes."

"Which bimbo?" I demanded, knowing full well who he meant.

"The one in the light-brown sweater with the big fancy tits."

"Mary Elizabeth?"

"Yeah. It's a disgrace that they let someone like her into the Villa."

"She's a friend of Kate McGlynn."

"She's got the hots for Johnny."

"I don't see it."

I did see it. Or what I would describe less crudely as admiration and possibly a teenage crush, an expression like that of a kid yearning for a lemonade on a humid day.

"Yeah. They get away with it because they're rich."

"I don't think so, Terry. They're nice people. Everyone likes them."

"Yeah—and all the cheers after he blew the game today. That's phony. The Drummer and the Bishop have the whole place sucking up to the McGlynns."

"He didn't have any practice"—I defended Jumping Johnny—"and if he hadn't agreed to pitch they would have murdered us. No pitching at all this year."

"I suppose you think you'll be the pitcher we need when you're over here."

"Could be." I drifted away from him.

Terry had not noticed as I had that Johnny returned the expression of admiration and yearning, so quickly indeed and so cautiously that only someone who was watching the two of them as closely as I was would have seen his face when he gazed at her.

They're in love, I thought, hardly able at my age to understand what that meant but at least comprehending that the emotion between Johnny McGlynn and Mary Elizabeth Reilly was not the tawdry desire which Terry had wanted to make it.

I walked back around the lake to Camp Saint George that night with formless fantasies rushing through my head. Looking back, I suppose that I wished that I had grown up in River Forest too—or perhaps Beverly, which was a South Side River Forest. And I also must have been wishing that I might have someone like Mary Elizabeth Anne Reilly as a lifelong friend.

Oddly enough, that latter wish came true—in a strange sort of way.

The next day they were out on the lake water-skiing. The

sport had just come to the United States, and very few of my generation had experimented with it. There were no boats on Clearwater Lake powerful enough for skiing and no ski equipment. Johnny McGlynn had rented a boat with a 75-horsepower motor and somewhere found skis and a towrope. He spent the day giving rides to his classmates and friends, assisted by Kate and Mary Elizabeth.

There was no specific Villa rule that forbade such persons— in the relatively modest strapless swimsuits of that era—from skiing on Clearwater Lake, because there were no rules to cover water-skiing. Hence, Jumping Johnny was in no explicit violation of the rules forbidding womanly occasions of sin from the Villa beach. Some of the future priests with more delicate consciences would surely protest to their confessors or spiritual directors, but there would be no repercussions because, by definition that summer, anything Johnny McGlynn did was behavior approved.

The next summer a new edition of the Villa rule book extended the ban against members of the opposite sex to include their presence in water-ski boats, worse luck for us.

In late afternoon the ski boat floated to a stop just off the Camp Saint George beach where, though off duty at the moment, I was watching a swarm of frolicking kids.

"Want to give it a try, Lar?" Johnny called out.

Did I ever! But I was too stubborn to admit it and too dazzled by Mary Elizabeth in her white suit.

Her presence did, however, constrain me to give a civil answer.

"I'd love to, but I have to keep an eye on these little monsters. Thanks anyway."

Johnny beamed. At last he'd coaxed a pleasant response out of me. Probably he didn't know the reason why.

"Catch you later on," he yelled. "It's great fun." He glanced at her, perhaps to say, you're right—Lar can on occasion be friendly. The glance turned into a fleeting expression of devouring hunger as he quickly consumed her bare shoulders and back.

She waved at me as they pulled away.

Can't blame him, I told myself. But if he feels that way, he should tell his mother off and get out of the Seminary.

I walked over to the Villa that night for the film, a Western whose name I forget. It was a hot and humid night, one of the rare such in the North Woods.

At the haustus, again paid for by the McGlynns, Mary Elizabeth walked up to me, intent and serious as she always seemed to be. She was wearing, I remember it as clearly as if it were yesterday, a pale blue, sleeveless summer dress.

"We're going home tomorrow, Laurence O'Toole McAuliffe." She extended her hand. "It was nice talking to you."

"Likewise, Mary Elizabeth Anne Reilly."

"You'll mellow eventually"—she continued to hold my hand—"and you'll be a wonderful priest."

"Don't bet on it," I gulped.

"Absolute sure thing, Lar. And pray for me now and then, will you please?"

"Sure . . . you do believe in God, then?"

Dumb thing to say. Her eyes flashed dangerously for a moment and then her anger was chased by amusement and she forgave me with her brief smile.

"Oh, yes—I, at any rate, do believe in God."

The words "he doesn't even believe in God" have been branded on my brain ever since. Not much chance that I'd ever forget them.

A fifth question to add to the four that Cardinal Steve had given to me: Did Johnny McGlynn believe in God?

MARY
ELIZABETH

|| 3 || "Mary Elizabeth? Lar McAuliffe."

"I thought I might hear from you." I tried to sound cool yet detached, making no promises.

"You know what I'm up to?"

Hilda, my maid, had called me from the shower. I was preparing to attend a benefit for the Lyric Opera that night. I didn't have time to talk to Lar McAuliffe, as good as it was to hear his voice again.

"I've heard." A brief laugh. "May I say that I appreciate the irony."

"You don't have to cooperate. Indeed, you can tell me to go jump in the lake. But I wonder if I might see you and talk about it."

"I'm always happy to talk to you, Lar."

"I don't want to violate your privacy."

"I'll be happy to help you in any way I can. . . . I'm going back to Lake Geneva this afternoon and will be there till after Labor Day. Would you mind driving up?"

"Not at all."

"We can recall the days at the Villa, can we not?"

That arch comment was designed to unnerve him, a not particularly easy task. He was wondering how much of the truth about me and the late Cardinal I would tell him. He probably felt that I would report a lot of the truth—more truth than he would expect to get out of me—but not the whole truth.

I'd let him go on thinking that.

It would be a painful conversation. All the memories of Cardinal John McGlynn would come flooding back. Over the next few weeks, as I tried to search for times lost, for myself as well as for Lar, and put them down on paper, those times lost haunted my waking moments as well as my dreams. How could I make sense out of my relationship with John McGlynn—which meant how could I make sense out of my own life?

I would never be free of those memories of my life with him. Never.

4

I fell in love with John Arthur McGlynn on a cloudy autumn day, a week before Halloween in 1940. I was five years old. He was ten. I never stopped loving him. Never.

On that pre-Halloween afternoon, Kate and I were playing with the big dollhouse under the stained glass window on the landing in the McGlynn house. There were pumpkins all around us, I remember, and pale misty autumn light which made the vast McGlynn staircase seem like the inside of a cathedral.

Delia was supposed to be in charge of us, but she had vanished somewhere. We were having an exciting time with our imaginary husbands and children. As I remember, "The White Cliffs of Dover" and "The Last Time I Saw Paris" were playing on a phonograph somewhere.

"What are you two up to?" John bounded up the stairs, schoolbooks under his arm.

"Playing," I replied promptly to his question.

"What are you playing?" He smiled broadly.

"With our dolls," Kate answered.

"And Kate's dollhouse," I added.

"What are the dolls doing?" he asked, as if he seriously believed that dolls did things and that he should be interested in what they were doing.

"They're talking about their husbands," I said boldly.

"Where are their husbands?"

"They're away. They're working."

"Where are they working?"

That stopped us. We had not bothered to think what the dolls' husbands did for a living or where they did it. Their employment was not our concern—or the concern of the dolls either.

"We won't tell you," I replied, thinking quickly.

"Why not?"

"Because you're a boy."

"So are they."

That was undoubtedly true. There was a weakness in our stories, a lack of credibility as I would say now. So we had to make up stories quickly.

"This one's husband is in the army," I said.

"And this one," Kate chimed in, "is a doctor."

Naturally.

John curled up on the floor next to the dollhouse. "Where in the army?"

So it went, I thought then, for hours. I suppose he was there for only five minutes at the most. But he was the first big brother who had ever been interested in the world of little sisters. He took us seriously; he seemed even to like us.

And he had such pretty eyes. And such a lovely smile.

"I'm going to marry your brother, Kate," I told her when John left us.

"You can't."

"Why not?"

"He's going to be a priest. Priests don't marry."

"Why is he going to be a priest?"

Even then I felt the world slipping out beneath my feet.

"Because Ma wants him to."

Both Kate and I were the youngest in our families and the

only daughters. I had three brothers: Ignatius Loyola, Francis Borgia, and Aloysius Gonzaga (need I say that my parents, from Holy Family parish down on the Near West Side, were Jesuit fans). Kate also had three older brothers, Michael and Jim, in addition to John. Her brothers and my brothers were about the same age and grew up as great friends, though their paths diverged after mine graduated from St. Ignatius and hers from Fenwick.

Kate's mother, Delia (or, very rarely, Cordelia) was at that time a beautiful woman in her very early thirties; passionate, affectionate, and unpredictable. Doctor McGlynn, her rarely seen father, was, like my parents, much older.

My parents had married late in life, as had Doctor McGlynn—the Irish were still into late marriages in those days. My mother was in her forties when I was born. I must have been a surprise, not unwanted, not neglected, but often not noticed either. My father was a political lawyer and a pillar of the Democratic Party. He was a generous, cheerful, talkative, and loving man—when he was around, which was not all that often, but we saw him more often than the McGlynns saw Doctor.

I saw Doctor only rarely in the McGlynn house. He would wander in, fingers in the watch pockets of his vest, smelling of hospitals and operating rooms. He'd blink in confusion and beam absently at the children, who were scattered around the place, as if he was not sure which of them were his own. Between his long absences and my father's intermittent ones, it's hardly surprising that our dollhouse fantasies included no men. The only real male presence in either of our lives came in the form of rough, dirty, noisy big brothers and the stupid boys our own age on the block. Of such men we wanted no part.

At least that was how I felt until the man of my dreams came into my life, a boy who fit my fantasies perfectly, or so it seemed then and so it seems even today.

The little girl who comes after a bunch of brothers may be admired and petted, but she also spends much of her time trying to catch up. Watch such a family sometime—strolling through a park, walking down a beach, coming out of a theater. First you see the boys in the family, tumbling ahead, heedless of any authority that would curb them. Then, trailing behind, almost as an afterthought, comes little sister, running to catch up.

That's how she spends her childhood: chugging along after her big brothers, breathlessly trying to catch up. No one deliberately ignores her or leaves her behind. On the contrary, they probably brag about how "cute" she is. Nonetheless, her typical mode is that of an "add-on," a person who must rush after her big brothers to keep up.

Occasionally someone, parent or brother, will notice that she is missing and turn and urge her to hurry up, blissfully unaware that little sister is exhausted from hurrying up all the time.

Then suddenly little sister catches up; she becomes a young woman. Her brothers, who had ignored her most of her childhood, now consider themselves her protectors and chaperons. They give her orders on how to dress, how to behave, whom to choose as friends, whom to date, what to do on a date.

Needless to say, such "wisdom" is never welcomely received. I know I came to resent it and to fight it off forcefully.

If you measure achievement by wealth and power, then I have achieved more than any of my siblings. I've certainly achieved more fame. The press may chalk it up to native instincts and a savvy business acumen thriving through the early hothouse days of the women's movement. But, in truth, the woman I am today has more to do with the little girl I was and my consequent rebellion against being relegated to the role of the little sister, a role my brothers would keep me in still, if they had their way.

The one time in my life when my brothers might have warned me to good effect was before my marriage. They might have perceived that Bud Quinlan was an empty man, a harmless and well-meaning locker room loudmouth. They might have warned me that he was quite incapable of standing up to a woman of the sort I had become and that I would be a patient mother to him more often than a passionate spouse.

I do not blame them, at least not in my more serious moments. Bud's emptiness was not easily perceived at that time. Yet I still wonder how it was possible for everyone to be so mistaken.

My early years were not unhappy ones. My family was not torn by conflict. If we were much less demonstrative than our neighbors the McGlynns, we nonetheless were close to one another. We remain close, even geographically. Our homes are at the most only three blocks away from those of the other three siblings. Our children are as thick as thieves. My sisters-in-law have learned to tolerate each other and even to be fond of one another. They look at me as their leader in taming the folly of the male Reillys, a venture at which we are moderately successful. We enjoy one another's company. Most of our friends admire the strength of our family bond.

Anyway, on that memorable, misty October day, John had treated me like a person. It was the first time in my life that anyone treated me like anything more than just a "little sister." I was always an individual with John, always. I understand now that his charm was less than perfect, that he often used it to manipulate people (myself included), that it was part of the same repertoire of tricks which Delia used (with his halfhearted cooperation) to promote his ecclesiastical career.

Yet the raw origins of John's concern for others was real, if not always quite as intense as others perceived it. His interest in me that day was real, not feigned. I knew I amused him. It was all my wild fantasies needed. John was defined forever after as the love of my life.

As fate would have it, I could never truly possess the only man I ever really loved. At first his mother wanted him. At the end God seemed to want him, although I'm not sure about that. However, I have never regretted loving him. If I had to do it again, I would still love him, no matter how frustrating that love was and is.

|| 5 || "Hi, Marbeth—are you coming or going?"

I knew the voice without turning around to see the face. My throat tightened, my stomach turned over, my legs grew weak. John McGlynn always had that effect on me, even when I think about him today, long after his death.

I took a deep breath before I turned around to face him. I couldn't let him know how much power he had over me.

"I'm going home," I said calmly, "from my music lesson."

I was sixteen and he was twenty-one. I was a junior at Trinity and he was at Mundelein. It was two years before he left for the North American College in Rome, though everyone said that he was already marked for the "school for future bishops." It was mid-June and we were on the Desplaines Street El platform on a cool spring evening. I silently cursed myself as I turned to face him for not dressing more elaborately or putting on more makeup. As my mother had always told me, you can never tell whom you're going to meet. Perhaps even the man you'll marry.

I was coming from a music lesson and wearing the uniform of the day: plaid skirt, blouse, sweater, bobby sox, saddle shoes, ribbon in my hair. I felt acutely embarrassed to be talking to my hero dressed in such unromantic garb.

"You're as pretty as spring itself," he said, bathing me with his smile.

"And you're Irish blarney personified," I replied as smoothly as I could. I thought I just might die.

"I've heard that accusation before," he laughed. "Can I give you a ride home?"

"It's only a few blocks' walk," I said, my voice now obviously shaken.

"Not if we stop at Petersen's for ice cream." He cocked an eye. "What's your favorite?"

"Chocolate," I stammered.

"Mine too." He took my arm and guided me off the El platform and down Lake Street to his new Ford. I floated along next to him, unresisting on my cloud of embarrassed bliss.

Not only did I have my first date with John McGlynn—that would have been exciting enough—I also had noted the way he looked at me when I turned to face him. With a quick flick of his eyes he had evaluated me as a woman and found me pleasing. My love, my only true love, thought I was attractive.

I had not yet come to terms with physical attractiveness— does one ever? I wanted to be thought beautiful, was afraid that I wasn't, occasionally suspected that I might be, and feared the effect my body seemed to have on men.

However, I reveled in its effect on John.

"What are you reading these days?" he asked as he opened the car door for me.

The question was as sincere as was his long-ago question before the doll's house. He was not making small talk; he really wanted to know what I was reading and what I thought about books.

I poured out a summary of my book reports on François Mauriac and Georges Bernanos, hoping all the while that my thick and elaborate bra would prevent the hardening of my nipples from showing through my thin blouse and form-fitting sweater.

I prayed that the ride to Petersen's at Chicago Avenue and Harlem would last for all eternity.

"I wish I had read as much as you have," he said. "And could think as deeply as you do."

Paradise was complete. He liked my mind as well as my body.

My love for John was grounded not on the one event by the dollhouse under the stained glass window. The respect for us as persons and not just little sisters had continued through the years Kate and I were in grammar school. Even though he was a Quigley student and a very important person, he would occasionally drop in at our little concerns, our Christmas plays, our volleyball games, our birthday parties. He liked us; he enjoyed being with us. We were not his whole life (as I wanted to be), but we were important to him.

He was almost as happy as we were when, in his final year at Quigley, St. Luke's won the CYO volleyball championship. I was the captain and Kate was the co-captain.

Then we went to Trinity and he went off to Mundelein. I missed him desperately because he was still the only love of my life. Kate missed him less because to her he was only a brother, though, as she herself admitted, the nicest possible brother. Our paths crossed rarely on his vacations because we were going in different directions. When I did see him my heart would stop beating. To my awakening sexuality, he was gorgeous, the ultimate in an attractive man.

I thought I was ready for a romantic affair, even though I had little knowledge about what those words meant. In fact, I was substantially less ready for serious passion than my ten-year-old daughter, Caroline, is today.

John was, as always, friendly to me, gravely interested in my schoolwork, my plans for college, and my deadly serious ideas. Unlike other boys, he did not make fun of my precocious intellectualism. He also noticed that I was no longer a cute little girl who hung around with his sister. I had become an attractive and perhaps disturbing young woman. At least I hoped I was disturbing.

I could tell that John liked my body, in an affectionate and respectful way. That spring afternoon on the Desplaines Street platform, however, I knew that he more than just liked me. He wanted me.

I thought I would die of happiness and vague and as yet unspecific desires.

By that time I had permitted myself to be kissed and pawed and mauled as much as any respectable young Catholic woman of that era. I found such activities mildly diverting but also tiresome. With John, I told myself, it would be different. I hoped that that afternoon I would soon find out.

"You sound like a radical," he said as I finished my comments on the political implications of French Catholic fiction. It was less a criticism than an interested observation.

"Capitalism is a social system," I said piously, "which has respect for only the wealthy."

I was sitting as close to him in the front seat of the car as a decent young woman dared to in those days. Perhaps closer.

"We're wealthy, Marbeth," he said gently. "We're the ones who benefit from capitalism."

"We are *not,*" I insisted, not altogether sure, despite my insistent tone.

"We're the ones that are making all the money from the postwar prosperity." He glanced at me and smiled gently, liking my intense—and oh so naive—social concern.

"The Depression will return," I said irrelevantly, and, as it turned out, inaccurately. Just then, however, I didn't care about economics. I didn't care about anything. Except him.

"What are you going to do with your life, pretty spring maiden," he said, opening the car door for me. "Run for congress and correct all the evil in the world?"

I felt my face flush hotly. "You're making fun of me!" I snapped.

He took my arm gently in his hand. "Not really. Or if I am, I'm sorry. I'm impressed by your intelligence and your enthusiasm. I hope you don't lose it."

"I won't," I said grimly, telling myself that I should pull my arm away from him and knowing that I wouldn't. "But I don't know what I'm going to be when I grow up."

I flushed again at those four final gauche words.

"I hate to be the first to tell you, but you're already grown up," he said, taking possession of my other arm.

Again I thought I would collapse on the spot.

"Sometimes I think I'd like to be a writer," I said hoarsely.

"You'd be a great one . . . did you say chocolate ice cream?"

"Yes," I gulped. "Or maybe a chocolate malt."

"They have the best in the whole world," he observed.

"They really do," I agreed, though I had no experience of other ice cream stores.

He led me into Petersen's. In my fantasy he was leading me into a luxurious bedroom.

My kids went to Petersen's when they were teenagers. My grandchildren go there today. Caroline drags me in there a couple of times a week. I suppose I've sipped their wonderful malts at least a thousand times in forty years. Yet whenever I walk into the store I feel an ever-so-faint afterglow of that conversation with my hero. Even today. Sure enough, the sense of surprise, the feeling that I was nurturing a great secret within me like an unborn child, absorbed me for a few precious seconds.

I'm sure I babbled that afternoon, trying to impress my love with my intelligence and wit and sophistication. I probably made a fool of myself by flaunting my body as shamelessly as I was flaunting my intellect. If there were other people in the ice cream store—and I was in no condition to notice—they must have thought I was a shameless show-off. Which is what I was. But my love, the only one in the world who mattered at that moment, was fascinated, enthralled. He listened, it seemed to me, with open mouth, while all the time his eyes were devouring my breasts.

We both had second malted milks and talked till it was long past suppertime and daylight had turned to dusk. I was happy as I had ever been in my life. I told myself that I would never be happier.

"You're dazzling, Marbeth," he said as we finished the second malt, "absolutely dazzling."

"Thank you, John," I stammered. That was not the way to respond to a compliment at my age and at the time, but I was too emotionally exhausted to say anything else. He adores me, I told myself.

Looking back on it, I probably exaggerated. I don't think Johnny felt about me the way I felt about him. I don't think he ever really did. He was the love of my life and I was a pretty and amusing girl-child. I wonder now how many other women he told that they were dazzling. In his way, I'm sure he meant it every time.

After the malt we drove home leisurely and indeed in a very roundabout way which required a stop at the Thatcher Woods parking lot, the standard lovers' lane of our time and place, without either of us admitting we knew where his Ford was taking us. Then, in mutual, unspoken consent, we threw ourselves into each other's arms.

I'm sure I kissed him before he could kiss me.

He could have done anything he wanted to me as the shades of night wrapped themselves around us. He did a lot, more than I had permitted any other boy. I wondered as we kissed and caressed and as he fondled me whether we would actually make love—an activity about whose precise dimensions I was not all that sure.

In retrospect, actually we did not go very far. My blouse may have been open but it remained on. So did everything else. Yet I was convinced when I finally got home after dark that he would leave the Seminary before the summer was over and marry me when I finished my first two years of college. That was only three years away.

I made up a number of lies I would tell my parents and my brothers to explain my absence from supper. But they were watching a baseball game on our new TV—with a screen four inches square—and said nothing of little sister's absence.

I fell asleep that night dreaming of the fun my love and I would have at Lake Geneva that July and August.

|| 6 || "You'd drive a man out of his mind," John whispered as he held me close. "He'd be caught between your brilliant mind and your glorious body."

I purred contentedly. I was trying to seduce John away from Delia and away from the Seminary and I seemed to be succeeding. And away from God? That I didn't think about.

I wouldn't have called it seduction then, not even with my bare breasts glowing in the moonlight. I would have said that I was trying to show my love how much I loved him. I was too innocent to know how reckless the chances I was taking were.

"I'm glad you like me."

"How could anyone not like you?"

It was the first time in my life that I had been even partially naked outdoors. I was thrilled rather than embarrassed, terribly proud of my body, about whose beauty I finally had no doubt. If John wished, I would pull off the bottom of my two-piece swimming suit too. As it turned out, he didn't wish it.

I threw myself at him on every possible occasion that summer. Our families did not seem to notice. My mother wanted only a wedding from me at that age in her life. As her only daughter, I was her only shot in terms of planning and organizing a large affair. My brothers were not at the lake except on weekends. Delia had consecrated John to God and was confident that God would protect him—only later did she begin to worry about me, when all need for worry was over.

Kate alone was aware of what was happening. She was my confidante, ally, double date, and occasional messenger. She also warned me of the risks, not of my seductive behavior but of trying to circumvent Delia's plans.

"She made up her mind long ago," Kate said when we were laying plans for a Friday night date. "It's all settled as far as she's concerned."

"Not," I insisted, "as far as I'm concerned."

I was only sixteen, going on seventeen, and I was in love. I couldn't help but win, could I?

That night, as I lay half-naked in his arms on the old wooden Higgins boat that Doctor had bought for his family in the middle nineteen-thirties, I was sure I would win. We had gone to see *All the King's Men* in nearby Geneva with Kate and her date—I can't remember who he was, if I noticed him even then. We had cuddled affectionately during the film. We dropped Kate and her date off. Then I proposed we take out the Higgins and swim in the moonlight. It was an offer John couldn't refuse.

I dressed in my new two-piece swimsuit—tantalizing, as I then thought and as extensive as a corset, I now realize. I pulled on a Notre Dame sweatshirt and waited for him on the pier.

Although the bikini had been introduced into America that summer, it would be many years before it came to Lake Geneva, and especially to Irish Catholics at the Lake.

"Gorgeous night, Marbeth," he said as he helped me into the boat. "Perfect for a midnight swim."

"I can hardly wait," I agreed.

He anchored the boat a couple of hundred yards offshore and left on the running lights so no one would run over us. We both pulled off our sweatshirts and dove into the water. We swam and wrestled in the water. He and I were the whole world. No one else inhabited our moonlit planet. I was ecstatic, a permanent condition for me that summer.

"I'm exhausted," he said finally, clinging to the side of the boat.

"I'm not," I said, truthfully enough.

"That's because you're still young," he said, playfully swatting my rear end.

"I'll always be younger," I said.

"I'm going in," he said. "You'd better come in too. I don't want to lose you in the dark."

"It isn't dark," I argued.

"Marbeth," he said firmly.

"All right, all right, you climb in and help me up."

"You're stronger than I am," he said with a smile, but he pulled himself into the boat.

He was always worried that I would be hurt. I might be a brash and forward young woman, but even to him I was also a little sister whom he must protect and care for. Only, unlike my meddling brothers, I loved his protection. I loved everything about that summer.

As he climbed into the boat, I pulled off the top of my swimsuit—as comprehensive and elaborate as the most modest of bras—and tossed it over the side. John didn't see what I had done. So he was surprised and quite overcome when he lifted me out of the water.

"Do you like me, John McGlynn?"

"I sure do." He swept me up in his strong arms and I thought the world would end for joy. I belonged completely to him at that point. I hoped he would remove the rest of my suit, I hoped he would make love to me, whatever that meant (I assumed he knew even if I didn't exactly). I hoped that our ecstasy in the moonlight would go on forever. When he laughed and then kissed my breasts, I thought my heart would burst in agony of happiness.

"We'd better go back to the shore," he said most unromantically. "Our families will start to worry about us, and we both have busy days tomorrow."

He had a busy day ahead: golf with fellow seminarians. I didn't—only lunch with Kate and her mother and my mother.

"All right," I said listlessly.

"You're spectacularly beautiful," he sighed. "But you probably ought to put your clothes back on before we tie up at the pier."

"All right," I agreed.

I reached for my sweatshirt.

"Everything." He laughed, giving me the top of my swimsuit.

"All right!" I joined his laughter. The two of us giggled all the way to the pier. The night of serious passion ends in laughter.

The laughter was more appropriate than I realized then. I was a silly child, quite unprepared for love, who took a terrible risk. Not very many men would have been as gallant as John was.

I look back on that brash kid on the Higgins boat and see her as a little fool who thought she was a passionate heroine. I cannot reject, however, my memories of the joy of that experience. I feel traces of it every time I slip into the waters of the Lake, especially after dark.

He kissed me goodnight on the pier, very gently. "You're wonderful, Marbeth," he whispered.

"I love you, John." I leaned against his chest and then ran up to our house, my face flaming, my heart beating wildly. I was both ashamed and rapturous.

I did not fail to notice, however, that he had not responded to my profession of love. He never did.

The annual lunch of the women in the McGlynn and Reilly families was not only a bore, it became more of a bore every year. Our mothers had little to do at Lake Geneva. Their children were no longer small, and required little or no supervision. They did not have athletic or literary interests. Their husbands were absent during the week (Doctor on most weekends, too). Time hung heavily on their hands. Lunches and gossip were their only amusements—and in Delia's case scotch and soda.

Because we were who and what we were, the lunch was an elaborate affair even if it was staged on the lawn in front of the house—linen, china, silver, crystal, two uniformed maids, one black, one white, to serve it. Kate and I were required to wear dresses appropriate for Sunday Mass, along with nylons, girdles, high heels, no matter how hot it was. That summer, the day of the lunch was particularly hot. Kate and I fretted anxiously. We wanted to put on our comfortable blouses and slacks and rush to the golf course, I to see John, she to gaze from a safe distance at another seminarian on whom she had an adolescent crush. Mind you, Kate had a crush, I was in love!

Our mothers gossiped harmlessly about their neighbors and sipped expensive sweet white wine. Then they turned to bragging about their children. Mom looked forward to weddings, Delia was in no rush to see any of her boys married—poor Kate didn't seem to figure in her calculations.

"Ah, that Johnny of yours," Mom said, "is a fine-looking young man. He'll make a handsome priest."

"He's the joy of my life." Delia drained her wineglass. "I consecrated him to God and Jesus and Mary the day he was born and the day he was baptized. I consecrate him again every year on his birthday and the anniversary of his baptism. He's certainly going to be a priest."

Still dizzy from the romp of the night before, I said, "Doesn't God get a choice in the matter? Doesn't He have a chance to say He wants John to be something else?"

Kate rolled her eyes. Mom favored me with her there-you-go-again look of displeasure.

Delia was untroubled. "I know God wants my Johnny. Otherwise he wouldn't have sent me a second son, would he?"

That was that. Kate made a wry face as she tried to suppress a laugh.

"He's the light of my life," Delia went on. "I don't know what I'd do without him. He'll be more than just a priest, too. Aren't they sending him to Rome to train him to be a bishop?

I only hope I live long enough to see my Johnny wearing the cardinal red."

It was the first time I had heard that hope. I considered Delia. She was a striking woman, old by my standards of course, but still attractive, I figured, to men who were old. Was John really all she had in life? Or had she decided to make him that?

"Aren't those promotions often accidental?" Mom asked.

"Ah, there are ways of seeing they're not, believe you me. And don't I know them all?"

"There are so many pretty girls around Lake Geneva this summer," Mom went on vaguely. "I'm sure some of them have their eye on John."

Secretly Mom had her eye on him as a potential catch for me, "when you're older, dear." She wanted a wedding, but she didn't want her beloved daughter to grow up too soon. So, in her hazy world, I was for all practical purposes a twelve-year-old. She couldn't see me yet as someone who had her eye on Johnny. "In a year or two, dear," she would often say, "you'll see things differently."

She'd been saying that for four years.

Kate, to whom I had given an edited account of the previous night's events, was experiencing a fit of coughing.

"It won't do them any good." Delia looked around for more wine. "The Blessed Mother and the Holy Angels will protect my Johnny from the little hussies."

"What will happen to them?" I asked, still bold enough to embarrass Mom.

"They'll drown in the lake, that's what they'll do. . . . Ah, dear" (this to one of the maids), "would you ever fill this glass with a little scotch and soda?"

I joined the coughing.

After what seemed like several eternities, Kate and I were freed to "run along with your little friends, dears." We dashed to my room to change to more comfortable clothes. "We'll never be that way," I promised.

"Never," Kate agreed solemnly.

It would not have occurred to us that once our mothers had been young girls like us, glowing with the hope and vitality and the eager expectations for life that possessed us that summer.

I suppose my two older daughters have made the same solemn promises about me.

"Just the same"—Kate tugged on her white slacks—twins to mine—"she's determined to make John a priest."

"I'm determined too."

"I don't know about him," Kate said thoughtfully. "He doesn't go to Mass during the week at all during vacations. I don't think he owns a rosary."

"Does he believe in God?" I asked, admiring myself in a mirror as I buttoned my blouse.

"If he does, he never talks about it."

I pondered that information. If he doesn't really believe in God, then he can't be a priest. I filed the fact away for possible future use.

We rushed over to the Country Club and arrived just as John and his friends were teeing off on the 18th. He was not pleased to see me waiting on the veranda overlooking the green.

"The lads from the sem," he frowned slightly, "might get the wrong idea."

I had thought that after our romp the night before, he would have told them that he was not coming back to the Seminary.

"I'm sorry," I said, close to tears.

"Don't be," he laughed. "At least they'll think I have good taste."

We all ate supper that night, not at the club, which John said was too pretentious (he had learned, as had the rest of us, to play down our wealth with our school friends), but at a hamburger stand outside of Geneva town. I remember vividly my happiness that night. Then we huddled around a bonfire on the McGlynn lawn, roasted marshmallows, and sang songs from *South Pacific*. The four seminarians seemed to enjoy the company of two pretty girls and to agree vigorously that there was "nothing like a dame." Well they might with the woman-less year at Mundelein stretching out implacably ahead of them.

I would never forget that night, I insisted mentally. I was with the only two people in the whole world who were important to me: John and Kate.

And I never have forgotten that night, though it means something much different to me now than it did then.

When that summer came to an end, I thought my heart would break. John kissed me goodbye one night at the end of August, wished me well in school the coming year, and said that perhaps we would bump into one another when he came home from the Seminary at the midyear vacation.

I was astonished that I did not have time to rail at him as I did in later letters—which I never sent—that I had been nothing more than a summer interlude for him.

In retrospect it was more than that, though perhaps not much more. He was genuinely fond of me. I was little sister with a fine mind, turned sexually alluring. He could have taken advantage of my naive attempts at seduction. Most men, well, many men his age would have. Even when he was fondling me and kissing me, he was treating me with affection and respect. As I write these words I admire once again his enormous restraint.

So I was not quite a summer fling. But neither was I a serious love, and certainly not one which would lead him to risk Delia's wrath by leaving the Seminary.

I had not, however, given up the fight.

‖ **7** ‖ "I want to talk about us," I informed John McGlynn with all the considerable grim determination of which I was even then capable.

It was the autumn after my summer "fling" with John. I had stopped my Studebaker convertible, motor still running, on the side of the Seminary road, which ran by the lake. The gymnasium loomed on the hill above us, as if it were watching this unusual tryst next to the damp and dank shrine to Our Lady of Lourdes.

"Us?" He was puzzled and uneasy, anxious that none of the Seminary priests would see him talking to a young woman in a white convertible on one of the Seminary back roads.

It was by chance I had found him. I had only the vaguest idea of where the Seminary was, and none at all about how you found a seminarian on the grounds. I was lucky to encounter him alone, as he later told me, because seminarians were not supposed to walk alone. However, he had been sent to bring medicine from the infirmary to the residence hall in which he lived.

As I drove around the grounds, staring intently at each

group of seminarians I passed (and thus creating a sensation), I decided that the red brick buildings reminded me of a mental institution—though I had never been in one. The hazy autumn light and the brilliant red and gold of the changing foliage did not soften the impression of a place of deliberately and cruelly forced isolation.

It was, I thought even then, a terrible way to prepare men for the priesthood. I gather that the Church came to agree with that position, though I see no evidence that the priests they are ordaining today are any better than the ones ordained in the nineteen-fifties.

It was time that John Arthur McGlynn and I had a confrontation. Did not his own sister admit that he was not sure about the existence of God, and that the question didn't bother him much one way or another? Was not this obviously the time for him to end his unrealistic vocation and take me as a much more solid and flesh and blood substitute for the God of which he was uncertain?

I knew there was a God, and I flattered myself that, while He might not approve of what I then called heavy petting, God was on my side.

My body ached, or so I thought, for his demanding caresses, my lips for his bruising lips. I would drive out to Mundelein and settle our future once and for all.

"Do you believe in God?" I asked him, firing my first broadside.

"That's a pretty blunt question, Marbeth." He looked away from me.

"I'm a pretty direct person."

He looked back at me and grinned, ruefully and charmingly. "I've noticed."

"Answer my question," I demanded.

"It's a complicated one."

"No, it's not."

"It is, Marbeth; at least it's a complicated answer. I don't not believe in Him. I'm not an agnostic or an atheist or anything like that."

"Either you do believe in God or you don't. If you don't, then you don't belong in the Seminary."

"I wish life was that simple." He lowered his eyes as if in prayer. "Unfortunately it's not."

"It is too."

"Do you always act like you believe in God, Marbeth?" There was a plaintive, pleading tone to his voice.

"No . . . of course not."

"Then you're not that much different from me. I believe in God sometimes, but other times I act as if I don't."

"You're being sophistic, John Arthur McGlynn. Even when I don't act like I should, I know there's a God who's watching me."

"Sophistic is a big word for a high school kid."

"Don't patronize me!" I screamed.

"Sorry."

"Well?" I must have sounded like the Lord High Inquisitor himself. Marbeth as Torquemada.

"I'm not always sure, Marbeth."

"That's a weak answer . . . what about us?" I repeated my question.

"Us?"

"I love you, John. You know that. After this summer, how can you not know it?"

"I'm very fond of you, Marbeth. I always have been," he said uneasily. "But I'm going to be a priest. We can always be friends, very good friends, but not lovers."

"Damn you, how can you be a priest if you don't believe in God?"

"I believe in God enough to be a priest."

"You have to be a priest"—I was now beside myself with rage—"because your mother consecrated you to God the day you were born."

He swallowed and looked very forlorn. John never was very good with women he could not charm out of their anger.

"That's not altogether true, Marbeth. I know she wants me to be a priest, but God does too."

"You're full of shit!" I screamed. Then I jammed my car into first and roared away.

We were seen by two priests, I later learned. They denounced him; but John was able to calm everyone down as usual. It may be that I am a prisoner of my own fantasies. In the real world—and when the subject of John McGlynn is concerned, it is hard for me to distinguish between the real and the fantastic—I might have turned away from his imagined proposition I described with disgust.

Suppose that night in Rome, for example, when I had just turned forty, he did whisper that he wanted me. Would I have in truth left my husband in the bar of the Cavalieri Hilton and run to John, stripping off my clothes (literally and figuratively) as I ran? Or would I have been the sensible person I was by that time in my life and said, "Come on, John, let's act like grown-ups"? Who knows?

The agony of my love for John is that I did not know and do not know whether it was ever returned. Perhaps he loved me, but I doubt that he loved me the way I loved him. He always found me an attractive woman; he enjoyed my company; he looked forward, I think, to seeing me; he may have fantasized, as men do, about taking off my clothes (I find myself, perhaps perversely, hoping that he did); in later years he leaned deeply on me for advice—and without any pretensions to protect his masculine ego. But love me, especially the way I loved him? I will never know.

When I returned to River Forest after my disastrous trip to the Seminary, I parked the car, dashed over to Kate's house, and threw myself into her arms, sobbing.

She cried with me.

"Oh, Marbeth," she said, "I'd so love to have you as a sister-in-law some day! Wouldn't it be wonderful if our children were cousins! But Delia will never let you have Johnny. She consecrated him to God the day he was born. He *has* to be a priest."

"We'll see about that," I wailed furiously.

We did and I lost.

In my moments of inexcusable self-pity, I occasionally permit myself to think that Kate and John were the two most important people in my life. And I lost both of them.

8

There was some excuse for my follies in Thatcher Woods and at Lake Geneva and on the road at Mundelein. My behavior at Eagle River, two years later, however, was intolerably tasteless, foolish, and even self-destructive. It was also, God help me, funny—though I was not much amused then.

I pushed my way into John's room in the lodge and began to undress—provocatively and dramatically, as it seemed to me then. I was almost completely naked before he grabbed my hands and prevented a continuation of my striptease.

Dear God, how I blush every time I recall that absurd dance. But even now, God forgive me for it, I feel a certain sense of satisfaction—and excitement.

I was not quite as innocent as I had been at Lake Geneva. I knew by then quite explicitly that my behavior was seduction. I didn't care. I wanted to seduce him. I was eighteen, wasn't I? Wasn't this the way you captured a man?

John was two years from ordination and home for the summer from Rome. He and his family had come to the Villa, the reasons for which trip still escape me. Kate had remained a co-conspirator, so my invitation to join the family was easily accomplished. The first afternoon, John and I were left alone for an hour or two in the Lodge, where we were staying. I seized the opportunity to launch my attack.

"Marbeth?" he shouted in alarm as he held my arms. "What are you doing?"

"I want to make love with you!" I shouted, already enraged that he was not responding the way I had intended.

"No," he said, but, I thought, without much conviction.

I broke free from his grip, threw my arms around him, and began to kiss him. While rain pounded on the windows, thunder rocked the wooden building, and lightning gashed the skies, our hands frantically explored each other's bodies. I tore at his clothes. Now he seemed as hungry for me as I knew I was for him. I virtually gave myself to him.

He enjoyed the romp but didn't quite take me. I was furious at this rejection.

"What the hell's wrong with you?" I screamed with deplorable lack of imagination. "Don't you want me?"

"Sure I want you, Marbeth," he groaned, "but I can't do it to you. I care about you too much to take you and then leave you." So began our second confrontation.

"You should leave the Seminary and marry me, John Arthur McGlynn."

"I have to become a priest!"

"Why?"

I must have been a fierce sight, hands on hips, breasts jutting at him, clad only in a diaphanous black lace panty (chosen for the occasion, of course).

"It is expected of me."

"By whom?"

"By my mom and Doctor and God."

"You don't believe in God!" I shot back, kicking off my panty.

"You are so beautiful, Marbeth," he murmured. "So very beautiful. But if there is a God, He wants me."

"How can you become a priest when you enjoy a woman as much as you enjoy me at this minute?"

I was now experiencing genuine, full-fledged sexual arousal for the first time in my life. I was astonished and a little frightened by what my body was doing to me. I was also feeling even more reckless. I walked up to John and pulled his lips to my breast.

He twisted away.

"I am giving up women for the service of God."

"When are you going to start giving them up?"

"Next year, when I take the subdiaconate and make my promise of celibacy. You're wonderful Marbeth—a perfect woman. But I just can't."

I was beaten. I had been from the beginning. Now I knew it. I turned my back on him and put my clothes on; my arousal vanished, to be replaced by acute shame.

What a perfect little fool I had made out of myself.

Now I am astonished again at John's restraint. And grateful. As I would find out later, in the first weeks of my marriage, I was, naked or not, quite unready for sex.

He slumped in the chair next to his bed, dejected and beaten. "Do you understand?" he asked wretchedly.

"No!" I shouted, not yet appeased. "I wouldn't mind losing you to God, but you don't believe in God. So what am I losing you to? Your mother's vocation? I'm sorry, I think I'm better than that."

"Don't say it that way, Marbeth," he pleaded. "It's not her vocation, it's mine."

"How can it be your vocation if you don't want to be a priest?"

"It's more complicated than that."

We had been through this before, but I persisted anyway. "I'm listening and I'm supposed to be intelligent. I can understand almost anything."

"I don't understand it myself. I just know I have to be a priest whether I want to or not."

"Because your mother says you have to be a priest, because it will make Doctor happy, and because you will be Archbishop of Chicago some day."

"It's nothing like that."

"I don't believe you and I never will."

"I care for you a lot, Marbeth. Believe me. It can never be."

"OK. You win. It can never be. But you're a fool."

I stormed out of the room, slamming the door behind me.

It was also the last time I approached Johnny in a manner that could be considered erotic. I knew I had lost. I did not know exactly to whom I had lost, though I assumed it was his mother. Yet I had enough sense and enough willpower to accept my defeat, even though I thought my heart was broken.

It was, in fact, broken, though it did heal before the summer was over.

I told no one about what had happened, though Kate guessed pretty quickly.

"Another turndown?" she asked sympathetically.

"Yes." I fought to hold back my tears.

"Goddamn Delia," she said.

I thought John would be furious at me. I had embarrassed him, having virtually assaulted him. I'd insulted him. Yet that night at the Villa party he was as charming and friendly as ever. My clumsy and cruel attack had already been forgiven.

I am well aware of his faults. For all his intelligence, he was weak on ideas; he left his intellect undeveloped because he was afraid of complicated questions and problems; he was shallow in his judgments and decisions and inconstant in his reluctance to carry out decisions once they had been made. He drifted through life, till the last couple of years anyway, without any overarching goals or aims, but rather floated from project to project and from person to person, happy if even a single interview with a troubled priest worked out reasonably well.

He was a pushover for a pretty woman, myself most definitely included; I often thought the days I was helping him to run the Archdiocese of Chicago—on occasion actually running it myself—that if my legs and thighs and breasts were not in the proper alignment, he would not have followed my advice, no matter how wise it was.

He was Delia's son, her favorite son, because in so many

respects he was a perfect foil for her. He was the kind of man Delia might have married if she had not stumbled on Doctor, indeed the kind of man with whom she would have been blissfully happy.

If you tell me that he was a shallow, unpredictable, unreliable, inconsistent, and easily manipulable man, I will not deny the charge, though I will add that the extent of those characteristics were and are often exaggerated. As he showed in the last years of his life, he was capable of mysterious depth and a will of steel, though such characteristics required effort and discipline and did not come easy.

He was astonishingly reckless. He seemed to love danger as other men might love women, or perhaps I should say to pursue it the way some of them pursue extramarital affairs. I was able to moderate his risk-taking, though patently not enough. I don't have a very good record at protecting the men in my life from self-destruction.

So I know his faults, but after I list them I must add that, regardless of his faults, I still loved him because he continued to care about me as a person. He was and is special to me, because I was special to him, in a way I was never special to anyone else.

At Eagle River, after he rejected me, I cried the rest of the afternoon and all the night, tears of rage and humiliation and frustration.

The next day I dried my tears and dismissed my humiliation (though it would not leave for a while). But I still felt profoundly sad.

What was the point, I asked myself, in going on with life?

|| 9 || Afterwards, I needed someone to talk to. Or perhaps someone on whom to spill my anger.

Since then I have been able to cope with most of the problems of my life. I solved the problem of my husband without consulting anyone. I made my own decision on birth control. I have never absolutely needed to talk to a priest—outside the confessional—about anything. But that summer, when I was eighteen, I needed a priest.

I did not trust any of the priests at the Villa, so I decided to talk to a seminarian, one who, John had informed me on our ride to the game at Watersmeet, had told him off.

I figured the young man, just my age, must be someone special if he was able to resist John's charm. You could tell he was special by just looking at him—a tall, slender giant with the most tender green eyes and the sweetest smile one could imagine. He was all the more appealing because he hid his gentleness and sweetness under a transparent veneer of a slum kid from 79th Street. Unlike John, he had "priest" written all over him, so there was no danger I would fall in love with him, though it was hard not to like him a lot.

John liked him too, despite the fact that he told John off on every possible occasion.

"He's a great kid, Marbeth. A lot of fun. He'll make a wonderful priest." We were still in the Cadillac, driving to the ballgame in Watersmeet. From John's demeanor it was impossible to tell our quarrel the day before had ever happened.

"Does he believe in God?" I snapped.

John chuckled. "I'm sure he does. Probably fights with Him a lot, or pretends to. With Lar that's a sign of affection."

I suspected that as different as Lar might be from John, this attractive giant from the South Side might share the most appealing of John's traits—he might like people the same way John did.

So I sat next to him in the stands at Watersmeet and dumped a lot of my anger on him, leaving out, needless to say, the specific details of my erotic assault and subsequent humiliation.

Although he was astonished by my fury, he actually was very sympathetic and sweet. My guess was accurate: He did have something of the same liking for people and concern about their problems that John had; in his case it was hidden under the predicted South Side Irish churlishness, which in its own way was not unattractive.

"Mary Elizabeth," he began as the crowd cheered for John's grace in defeat.

"Yes?"

"You're an important person. You're bright and you're pretty and you have big dreams."

"So?"

"So you shouldn't let John interfere with those dreams."

"I should stop loving him?"

"Did I say that?"

"No."

"All right. He may need a lot of help as his life goes on. I don't think you'll be the one to give it to him."

He was wrong about that, in the long run, but at the time he was right.

I sighed. "I suppose that's true."

"Suppose?"

"All right. I know you're right, damn you."

He was silent.

"So?"

"So?" he replied.

"I should cut my losses and get on with my life?"

"I said you were smart."

He made me give myself his advice. Clever man, even then.

"I hope to see you around, Laurence O'Toole McAuliffe."

"So do I, Mary Elizabeth Anne Reilly."

Through the years I've often thought it would be nice to have a priest to whom I could talk occasionally as a kind of confidant. It would have to be someone like him.

Anyway, I went off to Manhattanville and was romanced by several East Coast boys who, as far as I could see, were no different from Fenwick High School boys. I fell in love, as I thought of it, with Bud the next summer and managed to collect my diamond before I was nineteen. He was big and handsome and gregarious and lots of fun. What more could a girl want?

John was what I wanted. I had one more shot at him.

LAURENCE

10

My associate pastor, Father James Stephen Michael Finbar ("Jamie") Keenan, thinks he knows everything. Unfortunately for what little dignity is left to my role as pastor, he does in fact know everything.

"Tell me about the canonization of saints," I said to him.

We were sitting in the parlor of my suite in the creepy old Gothic Rectory which serves The People of God in Forest Springs, as a parish is called these days. I had spent the evening in the office working on marriage cases—preparation for, counseling about, and annulment of.

Mozart was on the CD; the windows were open to admit the fresh summer night air; Jamie was sipping Bushmill's Single Malt, I was sipping decaffeinated ice tea; Nora, the parish pooch (a loping Irish wolfhound), had joined us because she deems it essential to attend all meetings between pastor and associate.

"You gotta realize," Jamie began his lecture, "that there are more than ten thousand saints in the Catholic tradition and only about five hundred of these have been canonized by Rome. The Vatican began to take over the process effectively in the time of Urban VIII in the early sixteen hundreds, at the time when the Curia was centralizing the Church—or grabbing power away from the local bishops, if you want. Partially in response to the Reformation, the Vatican shifted the emphasis from miracles to virtuous life. A canon lawyer named Prospero Lambertini—what a marvelous name—wrote a five-volume work on the subject, and when he became Benedict XIV in 1740 his reform became official. It lasted till the new decree in 1983."

Jamie is a tall, good-looking blond kid with enormous energy and great talent. Something like Johnny McGlynn except without the ambition and the neurotic need to be loved by everyone. Small wonder he's so emotionally secure; he's the final child of a Federal judge turned novelist and a sometime president of the American Psychological Association, the ever empathetic (some would say clairvoyant) Maggie Ward Keenan. Jamie is nothing if not well adjusted.

"That decree is the one that eliminated the Devil's Advocate, isn't it?"

Jamie's eye's flickered. That was something I was not supposed to know.

"Correct, as always, boss, so Morris West's wonderful novel couldn't be written today." He grinned at me, as always finding me amusing rather than threatening. "Until 1983 the process was essentially adversary, like a law trial. The Promoter of the Faith, Devil's Advocate, was the prosecutor who tried to prove that the person was not a saint, and the Advocate of the Cause was the defense attorney. The Cardinals of the Congregation were the jury, and the Pope was the supreme court. The trials could go on for years and everyone had a good time."

"No wonder it took so long."

"Rome moves slowly, like they say"—he raised his eyebrows skeptically—"except that John Paul II now makes them move fast. It is said that every time he visits a new country, he wants someone to beatify—the step before canonization, as I don't have to tell you."

"Never assume anything with the ancient Pastor, Jamie."

"Boss, you'll never be ancient. Those teenage girls still adore you . . . anyway, all the other Popes of this century have beatified seventy-nine people. His count already is eighty-five."

"Eighty-five and running."

"Exactly. Someone has said that we are canonizing more and more people who are less and less important. The 1983 reform was supposed to have been an effort at modernization, but it doesn't seem to have worked. Instead of an adversary process, what they have now is a historiographic process. Someone under the supervision of one of the relators of the Congregation draws up a positio, an allegedly scholarly biography of the servant of God, which is what they call them after the local bishop submits the results of his investigation. The relator adds an introduction, which they call an informatio, a medical committee checks on the miracles, though this is not needed if the person is a martyr. Then they open the grave to see if the body is intact. If it is, so much the better. But even if it isn't, that doesn't stop the process. At that point some theological 'consulters' go over the record and make their own judgments, the Cardinals of the Congregation consider the positio and the consulters' judgments and the medical reports and vote. Then it all goes up to the Big Fella."

"They open the grave?"

"Sure. The devotion to the saints arose from the cult of the martyrs in the early Church, probably with the custom of saying Mass on the tombs of martyrs. So the body and its relics are important."

"Relics!"

"That's what all the reliquaries are for all over Europe. They're used for miracles. Cures which medical science can't explain. The cure of little Brenny Epstein would make it past the Consulta Medica easily. Before-and-after pictures. Tissue samples. Doctors' testimony, including a self-described agnostic Jew. No known case of spontaneous remission of that kind of cancer. Lead-pipe cinch, boss."

"Medical science can't explain it now," I said stubbornly. "That's all anyone can say. And in any case, Johnny only seems to have performed one miracle—one with the cure of Brendan Epstein. One more is required for beatification."

"Wrong, boss. They require only one for beatification these days and then one more for canonization. The late Cardinal has already got a leg up. Anyway, they could decide that he was a martyr and he wouldn't need the miracles."

"No one was asking him to offer incense to the gods or deny his faith." I took a deep drink of my apple cinnamon ice tea. You can actually get to like it after a while.

"All that is required these days is that you die in the name of a Christian virtue. Thus Maria Goretti is a martyr because she died defending her chastity."

"She would have been chaste even if the guy had raped her."

My new priest shrugged, as if he were not responsible for the oddities of the Vatican mind.

"Now you're beginning to see the way the game is played," he said, sipping at his Bushmill's. "They make up the rules as they go along—not all the rules, but some of them. You can do that in the Vatican, especially if you're Pope."

It was a matter-of-fact statement; Jamie rarely bothered to get angry at ecclesiastical authority, perhaps because he didn't take it all that seriously.

I shook my head. "Jamie, it's all weird. Like trying to put grace in a measuring cup."

"They gotta do something, boss. They can't let the ordinary people and the local bishops decide who is a saint and who isn't, can they? Like they did for a millennium and a half?"

"I guess. It leaves the people out, doesn't it?"

"Who are they?"

"They've canonized ten thousand saints, the Vatican five hundred."

"Right!" My associate laughed. "Mind you, they've canonized lots of odd ones. The two most popular nonbiblical saints, St. Catherine of Alexandria and St. Nicholas—Santa Claus—probably never existed. But, unlike the Vatican, people think it's better to have stories instead of texts that have been made out of stories."

"Nice phrase."

"Not mine. Ken Woodward's. Religion editor of *Newsweek*. Just a minute—I'll get his book."

The New Priest bounced out of the room. Nora, whom New Priest and Cook had foisted upon me, sat up from her prone position. Her ally wasn't supposed to leave that quickly.

"Quiet, pooch." I petted her massive head. "He'll be back."

"It's a good book, boss." The Michael Jordan of New Priests rushed back in and handed me *Making Saints*. "The process is curious and fascinating. And probably a phase. A hundred years from now we'll have a very different method for making saints."

"In the long run we'll all be dead."

"Keynes . . . but, look—the people have the final word anyway. All Rome can do is propose saints for veneration. The people make up their mind whether they will venerate them. JP II's canonizations will make some religious orders happy because their Founder can be hailed as a saint, and maybe some Catholics in some countries will be happy because now they have their own martyrs. But his saints will never compete with Nicholas or Catherine."

"Right."

I sat silently for a minute, pondering the dust jacket of Woodward's book. Nora glanced up uneasily. I was not supposed to be quiet that long.

"The Vatican won't let them begin a process for Oscar Romero, the Salvadoran Bishop who was shot while saying Mass. They can hardly be enthusiastic about the late Cardinal. Politically inopportune."

"Jumping Johnny was a son of a bitch."

"You've always said that."

"How can a son of a bitch be a saint?"

"Boss, you know as well as I do that God makes saints. All He requires is human receptivity. Even if the Archdiocese of Chicago and the Vatican decide that the late Cardinal isn't a saint, the people might decide that he is, and there's nothing Church authorities can do about it, no matter how much they might forbid a public cult."

We were silent again.

"I never liked the guy."

"You have always been ambivalent about him," my New Priest said, correcting me.

"Whatever."

"If it's any consolation to you, boss, Peter never would have made it."

"Peter who?"

"Peter the fisherman." He shook his head in dismay. "You know—the first Pope. Consider his cause as it would appear to the Congregation in Rome after the relator submitted the positio: he was an ambitious, loudmouth, cowardly braggart who ran out on Jesus and tried to compromise on letting gentiles into the Church. I'm sure there were times when Paul spoke of him the way you do about Cardinal McGlynn, even if he didn't have such expressive Anglo-Saxon words in his vocabulary. Besides, he was a married man, and we have no evidence that he stopped sleeping with his wife after Jesus made him the boss of his crowd. Think about it: the first Pope fondling and engaging in intercourse with a woman. No way would they get a positive vote on him."

"Sounds a lot like Jumping Johnny," I admitted. "Except for the married part."

"There's always the fabled Ms. Quinlan." He shrugged.

"Don't I know it. She's from River Forest, your neighborhood, isn't she?"

He nodded appreciatively. "Some dish."

"You're too young to admire a woman of her age."

That really made my New Priest laugh.

"Great breasts," he observed.

"You shouldn't notice that," I said, trying to sound severe.

"No, what you mean is that priests of your generation think it's not right to admit they notice." We'd had that argument often. He always won it.

AN OCCASION OF SIN || 81

"But you'd think that his relationship with Marbeth," I argued, "would make it impossible for them to canonize him."

"Many saints had women friends with whom they had very intense relationships. St. Francis and St. Clare, St. Francis de Sales and St. Jane de Chantal, St. Benedict and St. Scholastica."

"Erotic friendships?"

"They were men and women weren't they? How could there not have been an erotic component in their relationships?"

"They didn't sleep together," I insisted.

"Probably not," he admitted. "We don't know that the Cardinal and Ms. Quinlan did sleep together, do we?"

"No, we don't," I agreed.

"Yet, I suppose"—he weighed the matter carefully, not as troubled as I was about the prospect—"the possibility that they did would be a big factor in any decision about beginning the process of canonization if it wasn't for the way he died."

"And the miracles, Jamie Keenan. Don't forget the fucking miracles."

Jamie made a face at my language. He could talk about breasts but he never said "fuck." What kind of priest was he?

"Inconvenient miracles."

"The Cardinal's very words."

My New Priest pondered the issue. "My mother says that she learned early in life that God has a sense of humor."

"You think God would make Jumping Johnny McGlynn a saint for laughs? You think it's all a comedy?"

He grinned at me. "Admit it, boss, it's pretty funny that you, of all people, are supposed to investigate him and his miracles."

"Listen to these questions." I flipped open *Making Saints,* through which I had been glancing as Jamie and I talked.

First, Does the candidate have a reputation for having died a martyr's death or for having practiced the Christian Virtues to a heroic degree? Second, What particular message or example would canonization of the candidate bring to the church? Third, Is the candidate's reputation for martyrdom or heroic virtue founded in fact? Fourth, Is there anything in the candidate's life or writings which presents an obstacle to his or her canonization? Fifth, Are there any pastoral or political reasons why the candidate should not be canonized at this time?

"Precisely." Jamie smiled benignly at my agitation.

"First, Jumping Johnny was shot by mistake—an accident according to the woman who loved him; moreover, his life was hardly marked by any more heroic virtue than that of any ambitious bishop and probably less than most. Second, the message would be that ambition and careerism are OK so long as you manage to get yourself shot in a grandstand play. Third, while some people think he is a martyr and a saint, there are no facts to suggest that he is. Fourth, in addition to his careerism and ambition, in addition to the fact that a lot of us thought he was an SOB, he had a lifelong relationship with a woman. Fifth, towards the end of his life, Jumping Johnny turned to the left. Because of that, and because of Marbeth, there are excellent pastoral and political reasons for not canonizing him."

"There's always the case of Pius XII."

"Oh?"

"Consider the facts, boss." He began ticking them off on his fingers. "However valid his reasons, he was basically silent during the Holocaust. He was an arrogant aristocrat, often unkind and even cruel to his staff. He had an intimate relationship with a nun, Madre Pasquilina, from the time she was his young and very pretty housekeeper when he was Nuncio in Berlin. In the last years of his papacy, she had so much influence on Vatican decisions that she was called the Papessa and was the second-most important person in the whole Church. Thousands of people are still alive who know about her. Yet they are thinking about canonizing him—and not Pope John, who they currently blame for all that's wrong with the Church."

"Is all of that true?"

"Sure. No one denies it."

"Were they lovers?"

My Associate Pastor raised his eyebrows and looked very wise, like he was maybe ninety years old.

"Did they love one another? Sure they did. Did she humanize him? Undoubtedly. Did they sleep together? I doubt it very much. But in a matter like that it's always impossible to prove what didn't happen, isn't it?"

"Jumping Johnny almost looks good by comparison."

"The norms are flexible. The alleged fact that you were a great pope covers a lot of other things. Pio Nono is widely believed to have had a mistress before he became a priest—most of the clerics in the civil service during the time of Papal States did."

Where did this kid get so much scandalous information, and why was he so nonchalant about it? I guess because he realized that if Jesus wanted a Church free of human frailties, he would have turned it over to angels.

"What kind of people are these relators and consulters?"

"Most of them have been or are professors at the Roman seminaries. Not the most intelligent men in the world maybe, but not stupid either. They're ready to accept a papal decision even if it overrules their own investigations—either way—but they're competent and honest. They'd only lie for the good of the Church."

"And the doctors?"

"By all accounts totally beyond corruption, not even for the good of the Church."

"So we come back to the miracles." I sighed. "The miracles which are so embarrassing, in all candor, as the present Cardinal is fond of saying."

"And you don't believe in miracles?"

"Even Marbeth said she doesn't know how to explain it. Putting the pectoral cross on the little kid's eye was Nancy's idea, not hers."

"Like you, she's an agnostic on the subject of miracles. But face it, boss, there are many, many cures which medical science can't explain."

"A miracle"—I dug in my heels—"is something that God does when She wants to."

Jamie shook his head. "I prefer the theologically more appropriate meaning, a sign that cannot be explained by medical science and seems to have been accomplished by the intercession of the given venerable servant of God."

"Jumping Johnny McGlynn."

"It's hard to deny him his pectoral cross, especially when it was the one he was wearing when he was martyred."

"Shot."

"Whatever."

"The trouble is, Jamie Keenan"—I pounded the coffee table, upsetting my Waterford glass of decaffeinated iced tea—"working miracles from the other side is precisely what that son of a bitch would love to do. It's exactly the kind of trick Jumping Johnny would pull."

The late-evening discussion about sanctity between Pastor and Associate was over. Jamie went to his room. I turned off Mozart, prayed for guidance, to which I thought I had a right in strict justice, and went to bed.

Nora curled up at the foot of my bed and promptly slept. It took me a lot longer to find oblivion.

It wasn't exactly oblivion. I dreamed about Marbeth.

My talk with Jamie Keenan had been interesting and, as usual, illuminating. But so far no one had assigned me the task of opening Johnny McGlynn's casket with a crowbar. My job was more like a background check—a preliminary before the new Cardinal recommended something as drastic and dramatic as an exhumation.

For the moment, I was trying to piece together Johnny's life, paying special attention to the five questionable areas as established by the new Cardinal and through my own experience of the man. I had already spoken to Mary Elizabeth

Quinlan, probably the likeliest of suspects. No doubt I would need to speak to her again. But for the moment, I decided it was time to check out another source, one who might corroborate much of what I'd learned from Mary Elizabeth. Then again, she might not. So, with a mix of curiosity and some reservation—I still resented this job—I got in touch with Jumping Johnny's little sister, Mary Elizabeth's childhood best friend: Kate McGlynn Crowley.

‖ **11** ‖ Two days later I drove down to see Kate at her elaborate apartment on the North Shore. She ushered me into her vast and impeccably decorated (Empire style) drawing room, whose blue curtains matched the peaceful blue of Lake Michigan outside. Floor-to-ceiling windows lined three of the room's walls. The predicted rain had not yet appeared.

"Do you mind if I smoke, Father?" Kate McGlynn Crowley reached fretfully for a silver cigarette tray on the table in front of her. "I know I must give it up, but I have so many more problems."

Yeah, I minded, because on that subject I have a convert's zeal. But, "Not at all," is what I said.

She lit the cigarette with a gold-plated cigarette lighter. It was the first step in compulsive chain-smoking which continued through the rest of the conversation.

"I have forgiven my brother John for many things. I'm trying to love him as I did when we were children. That said, I feel I must reveal to you evidence that makes his canonization impossible."

"I would be very interested in such information, Kate."

She was a slim and well-maintained woman, whose good looks were no doubt cultivated by all the services money can buy. There remained, however, none of the seemingly wholesome natural beauty of her youth that I remembered from the time at the Villa.

Moreover, her blond hair was patently the result of too much rinse, and her strained voice and tense eyes contradicted the image of elite suburban matron which her pale blue suit was supposed to convey.

"Do you have time to listen, Father?" she asked with almost maternal gentleness. "I don't want to take up too much of your time."

"Of course, Kate. That's what priests are for."

Before I had driven up to the North Shore, I dug out the souvenir book which the Archdiocese had published when he was elevated to the Sacred Crimson, a day of considerably less than ecstatic joy in Chicago.

There were three pictures of Cordelia Meehan McGlynn. The first was a wedding picture, a close-up of her and Doctor excised and blown up from a group portrait: She was a strikingly lovely and very young woman, black Irish like Johnny— who obviously inherited his good looks from his mother—with an exuberant, carefree smile, also just like his. Next to her, Doctor, behind thick rimless glasses, already looked dull and bemused.

How could this pretty girl turn into such a mean and domineering woman? What twisted her away from the promise which lurked behind her pretty smile?

The second picture had been taken a few years later, late nineteen-twenties, to judge her hairstyle and dress. She was holding the newly baptized John Arthur McGlynn in her arms. Jimmy was lurking behind them, a boy approaching two and already looking resentful.

The young mother in that picture was even more beautiful than the bride of a few years earlier, proud of her sons, proud of her family, proud of her fertility. Was the demon already loose inside her, the demon of passion for power and respectability, the latter the result of the former? Against whom was she competing? Money she had more than enough of. According to the brief bio in the souvenir book, she was already an officer in the Daughters of Isabella (woman Knights of Columbus) and a member of the board of Catholic Charities, no mean accomplishment for a girl still in her middle twenties.

The biography said that she and Doctor had met at the Knights of Columbus "Country Club" at Twin Lakes, Wisconsin, where many West Side marriages originated in the nineteen-twenties. Her father, John Arthur "Jack" Meehan, the bio reported, was an investment broker on La Salle Street.

The third picture, which I had never noticed before (because I had never opened the book), was from the Villa in 1952— taken on the porch during a haustus: John, Mick, Delia, Kate, and another young woman whose name was not mentioned. I grabbed for a magnifying glass. Sure enough, Mary Elizabeth, looking even younger than the teenagers who answer the doorbell at St. Finian's Rectory today.

The scene was much as I had remembered it. They did indeed look rich, self-assured, powerful—confident in their beauty and their prospects for the future.

The picture must have been taken the day of the Watersmeet game. Marbeth was wearing the clothes she had worn when she had sat next to me at the game. I thought the pine scent had drifted into my room. My hands were sweating.

I moved the glass to Delia. She was a handsome woman who could have afforded to shed ten pounds. That observation, I sternly reminded myself, was a reflection by a man who now was a good ten years older than she was then, and not of a boy who saw no beauty in anyone over thirty.

In a year she would be a widow and in two years her great dreams would be temporarily shattered when the Cardinal turned down the recommendations that her son be assigned to either the Chancery or to further study in Rome.

She could have easily remarried and found happiness, perhaps more than in her first marriage. Instead she devoted the rest of her life to pushing her son ahead in the Church, only to succumb to Alzheimer's disease and never savor his final triumph.

As I looked back at the smiling young bride, Kate interrupted my thoughts: "You'll let me tell it my way without any questions or interruptions?" She fiddled with notes and a stack of letters on the table in front of her.

"Certainly."

"I miss them both terribly, Father."

"Your parents?"

"Oh no—John and Marbeth."

KATE

|| 12 || My childhood memories are happy ones. There was a distant cloud in my life even then, but it didn't take away my happiness.

The two most important people in my life were my brother John and my friend Marbeth Reilly. I've lost them both and I miss them terribly.

"We must be friends always," I said to Marbeth the day we graduated from St. Luke's grammar school.

"Of course we'll always be friends," she said with that commonsense tone of voice that she used all the time when I became frightened or teary. The difference between me and Marbeth at that age was that there wasn't a cloud floating in the distance over her childhood joy and there was for mine.

I can't recall a time when Marbeth wasn't in my life. We were playmates from before I can remember. She was always in our house, too, because she loved Ma and the singing and dancing and storytelling—her mother was a much quieter woman, though heaven knows her brothers made a lot of noise.

"Do I have to go home, Auntie Deal?" she'd say.

"Get along with you now, you little dickens—won't your mother think we've kidnapped you?"

So she'd go home, and I'd be sad because I would miss her.

"Ah, don't worry, child," Ma would say. "Sure, she isn't going to Timbuktoo, you know, but only two doors down Lathrop. Unless I miss my guess, she'll be on our front porch the first thing tomorrow morning."

Marbeth was the more adventurous of the two of us. She'd climb the tree and then persuade me to. She'd sneak a cigarette and then give it to me. She'd throw snowballs at the boys and urge me to do the same. She'd make out with a boy and tell me how wonderful it was. She'd wear a two-piece swimsuit and egg me to do the same thing.

"You have a wonderful figure, Kate," she would say when I tried on her suit in my bedroom—we wore exactly the same size. "They'll drool over you."

"I don't want them drooling over me," I'd say dubiously, but of course I'd do what she said and the boys would drool over me and I'd be very proud of myself.

I loved Johnny too. He was not like Jimmy or Mick, who thought a little sister was a nuisance or just someone to tease. He was kind to me and talked to me just like I was a grown-up his age. Later, when he went to the Seminary, he drifted away, but I still loved him, even though I never told him that before he died.

When I appeared on the pier at Lake Geneva in my two-piece, no one in the family seemed to be aware of my existence.

There I was, feeling like I was parading in my bra and girdle and wanting to be noticed but not wanting to be noticed. The only thing worse than their making fun of me would be their ignoring me. I was almost ready to slink away when Johnny whistled, just the right kind of whistle of approval and appreciation.

"Marbeth put you up to that?" he asked.

"Yes." I was terribly embarrassed and also flattered.

"Very good idea." He grinned. "The two of you are the most beautiful young women in all of Lake Geneva."

Doctor was too busy with his work to visit in the summers, but he was nice to me the few times he was around. He brought me candy and ice cream and called me his little princess. I adored him because he seemed to adore me. He had such a wonderful smile and such a smooth, pleasant voice.

So I had everything as a girl: a mother who was fun, a father who was nice to me, a brother who treated me like an equal, and an inseparable friend. I had all the money I needed, servants to take care of me, any dress I wanted to buy at Field's in the Oak Park shopping district, a gorgeous summer home, and a Chevy convertible on my sixteenth birthday.

But beneath the surface, things were never quite as good as they seemed. Once, when I was quite little, I found Ma upstairs crying.

I hugged her, begging her to tell me what was wrong.

"No matter how hard we try, darling one, we're never good enough," she sobbed. "Try, try, try, and it doesn't make a bit of difference."

That story sums it up. We were richer than almost anyone else in the neighborhood, including the Reillys down the street, yet we were not good enough. At least in Ma's eyes we weren't.

Doctor was the only son of a wealthy couple who married late in life. His father was in his late forties and his mother in her late thirties, both of them older than Doctor was when he married my mother. The Irish married late in those days.

They were both what my husband, such a wonderful loving man, would call lace curtain Irish, very quiet and respectable and refined. Grandfather was a doctor too. He had served in the Civil War. His father was a doctor too, a military surgeon who was killed in the war. So on my father's side of the family there was a long history of respectability.

One of the few times Ma got really angry at Doctor, she shouted, "You think you're a superior kind of human being just because your family had money all your life."

"Not really superior, my dear." Doctor typically sounded slightly befuddled and confused. "Just better breeding."

Doctor usually smelled of a hospital, an antiseptic smell, like Lysol, over the more comforting smell of good scotch.

"So you can do anything you want?" she screamed. "Buy your way out of all your scrapes?"

"There was at least one out of which I didn't buy, wasn't there?"

"You're an arrogant snob."

"I rather think not, my dear. It is hardly my fault that I was not raised in the back room of a saloon."

I don't remember any other fights between them. They were very polite to one another. Ma respected his abilities and his position, and he treated her like she was some sort of countess, and I think he was mostly sincere.

There was money in the family even before Doctor, though he made lots of it and invested it wisely, my husband tells me, and got out before the market collapsed in 1929, just like old Joe Kennedy. But Ma could never forget her own background or relax and simply enjoy the good things in her life. She was obsessed with the way things looked to other people. She'd fire a servant if she found a speck of dust, scream at any of her kids who weren't perfectly dressed, or weep inconsolably if a dinner party didn't come off exactly as she had intended.

She claimed that her dad was a La Salle Street broker. That was a laugh. He was a messenger in the old Rookery building, a job some of his friends got for him when Prohibition put his saloon out of business. I have an old photo in front of me which Ma forgot to burn: JACK MEEHAN'S SALOON, the sign says in big bold letters. On 31st and Wentworth, right in the middle of Bridgeport. Well, Armour Square Park to call it by its most proper name.

He was an immigrant and worked hard for the money to buy his saloon. He and his wife worked even harder to run it, she behind the bar. Prohibition destroyed his life's work.

He died before I came along, but he was a fine-looking man with wonderful white teeth and a big black mustache and a lovely smile. Sometimes I think that whatever vitality there is in my family must come from him.

Ma used to tell me, when she was getting sick but not completely insane yet, that neither her mother nor her father ever once ate at Ma's house in River Forest after she married Doctor. Ma was ashamed of them. And her mother-in-law wouldn't let her get over that shame.

In the end, the problem wasn't Ma's background. It was the fact that she could never put it behind her. That and the fact that Doctor had obviously been forced to marry her because she was pregnant with Jimmy.

The other problem in the family was that Doctor fooled around a lot. When we were up at the Villa back in 1952, Ma and Johnny and Marbeth and me, the story was that Doctor had too many sick patients to be able to stay at the Lake for more than a couple of days, and that then he had to attend an AMA meeting.

I was the only one home the afternoon before we left. The phone rang. I answered it.

"Doctor James McGlynn, please." The woman's voice was elegant and aloof.

"Doctor isn't in just now."

"Oh my . . . how inconvenient. Would you ask him to call San Francisco, please."

"Yes, ma'am."

"You're his nurse?"

"His daughter."

"How interesting."

She didn't sound like a bimbo. But then I didn't know what a bimbo sounded like.

That night I gave him the message at supper with Ma and the others around the table. It didn't faze him.

"Doubtless about my reservation at the St. Francis for the AMA convention," he said easily.

Ma never batted an eye.

I called the AMA the next morning. The meeting was in Washington, D.C., that year. He must have been away in California with one of his women. Probably Carmel or someplace like that.

I knew, though just on the edges of consciousness, that he was fooling around, perhaps even before I had a clear idea of what fooling around was.

How else could I explain the times he was away from the house when we were growing up? There were other physicians in the neighborhood when we were kids, but none of them were away as often or as long as Doctor was. Nothing was ever said about it. After a while, however, you knew there was something terribly wrong in the marriage.

Ma kept pretending everything was fine, but she began drinking wine at lunch and taking long naps in the afternoon. Worse, the ambitions she had for her sons shifted from gentle hope to belief to obsession.

At first it was just a joke that Ma played favorites: "Well," she would say, "Jimmy is Doctor's favorite because he's going to be a doctor too. But Johnny is my favorite because he's going to be a priest."

Even when I was a little girl I heard that awful statement time and time again. It left out Mick, who was destined to be a politician and, of course, it left me out because I was nothing but a girl.

Dan Crowley, my husband, says that some of the old Irish played favorites because there wasn't enough money to go around. The favorite child would stay in Ireland. The others would have to emigrate to America. But we had loads of money, and there was no good reason for doling love out in such limited amounts.

"So why did Ma play favorites?" I asked my husband.

"Habit." He shrugged his shoulders. "It's what her ma did. I bet she was her ma's favorite too."

"It doesn't do me any good to know that."

"Well, you're my favorite." He put his arm around me. "Always will be."

I suppose my husband was right. Ma was just afraid if she let up, we would stop trying to prove that we were better than anyone else. We spent our lives striving to win Ma's love by showing we were the best, but only Johnny ever succeeded. I tried until I lost Bud Quinlan, then I gave up. Jimmy and Mick stopped trying when they were in their teens.

Jimmy was never very good in school. Ma would say that he was lazy.

"You're not dumb, Jimmy," she would say with a scowl. "Not at all. But you won't work. You think you can get by on your name and Doctor's influence. Let me tell you a thing or two: if you don't apply yourself, you'll end up a failure."

"At least I'll be able to spend some time with my children," he fired back at her once.

She slapped him hard across the face and ran from the room crying.

He wasn't much of an athlete either. He tried hard but he was pretty clumsy. He went out for everything at Fenwick—football, basketball, track, swimming—and never made the first cut.

I don't see Jimmy much anymore. When we do, we fight about Ma's estate. He's drunk a lot of the time and a total failure at the Board of Trade. But he is a good husband and father, like he said he would be. I don't know how Lorett puts up with him some of the time, but they actually seem kind of happy. Isn't that strange?

Poor Mick would have been a good athlete if he hadn't imitated Jimmy instead of Johnny. He was drinking every night when he was in eighth grade. And he wasn't smart at covering up his drinking, like Jimmy was. He was thrown off the football team at Fenwick in first year for fighting in the locker room when he was drunk. The coach said he was good enough to be all-conference, even all-state if he had worked at it.

"Why don't you apply yourself more?" Ma demanded after she had talked to the coach. "If you'd apply yourself, you'd be a great athlete and a great scholar."

I think she was probably right. Mick had loads of talent. Unlike poor Jimmy, he was really lazy. The only thing he ever wanted to be was what he is now: a political hanger-on who makes a decent living without having to do a lick of work.

You know what he said to Ma that day? He said, "We have one hero in the family, we don't need another."

The boys resented Johnny too. Yet he charmed them. They didn't want to like him but they couldn't help it. What Johnny thought of it all, we'll never know. By the time Ma's ambition got really out of hand, he was busy confronting his own fears about his vocation and his attraction to Marbeth. Did he really have a calling from God or was he just terrified of disappointing Delia?

"I don't care what your ma says," Marbeth insisted since the day she was five. "I'm going to marry him."

"He's studying to be a priest."

"That's only because she wants him to be a priest."

It would have been nothing more than a schoolgirl crush if Johnny hadn't paid so much attention to her. He half adored her because she was so cute and so smart. Then, the summer after we were juniors in high school, she threw herself at Johnny and they did a lot of making out in Thatcher Woods and up at Lake Geneva, really heavy necking and petting.

"I'll take him away from her, you just wait and see," she said to me, her lips drawn in a tight line.

"And from God too?"

That took the wind out of her sails.

"If God wants him, I can't fight God," she said. "But I'm not convinced that God wants him."

What did I think about their fooling around? I was her confidante and I didn't discourage her. In fact, our lives might have worked out better if Marbeth had married John. I think they would have been a good match for one another. And I'd still have both of them as friends.

I said to him that summer, "Johnny, are you sure you don't want to marry Marbeth?"

We were eating lunch, prepared by the servants, on the pier—Coke, sandwiches, and ice cream. It was a cloudy, humid day, the kind of weather which always depresses me.

He seemed surprised by the question. "Marry her, Katie?"

"Yeah. Don't you think she'd make a good wife?"

He pondered that idea as though it were the first time he ever thought of it.

"I suppose she would."

"You suppose?"

"She's bright and attractive and lots of fun," he said dubiously.

"But?"

"It would take a special man to stand up to all that strength, wouldn't it?"

"You don't think you could?"

He scooped up a spoonful of ice cream. "It might be a lot of fun." He grinned at me. "Never a dull moment, that's for sure. . . . She put you up to asking me?"

"Certainly not!" I said haughtily.

"It's an interesting possibility," he admitted. "But not for me. I'm going to be a priest—as you well know."

"Are you sure?"

"I'm sure."

He didn't sound so sure. The rest of the day he looked very thoughtful, as though he were thinking about Marbeth as a wife.

But Marbeth lost and Ma won, Johnny became a priest and that was that. Did God win too? I doubt it. I don't think Johnny every had a calling. It was Ma's vocation from beginning to end.

Am I sure Johnny and Marbeth were lovers?

Not before he went to Rome. Maybe that summer we went up to Eagle River when we were eighteen and had just graduated from Trinity. She really went after him then. She did just about everything a woman can do to pull a man into bed with her. She told me that he rejected her. Maybe he did. I wasn't sure.

I know they were lovers after he came back to Chicago. How can a man and a woman be that close and not be lovers?

I'm getting ahead of myself again, however. The summer when we were both sixteen—1951, and we were singing the songs from *South Pacific*—and she was throwing herself at Johnny all over Lake Geneva, that was the summer that Doctor molested me.

13

I loved Doctor. He was kind and generous to me. I would hug him and kiss him whenever he showed up, and he would smile and pat me gently. I didn't think there was anything wrong with it. After . . . after it happened, I did my best not to think about it, to put a huge wall around it as though it were not part of my life. But when I did think about it, I blamed myself for, well, seducing him.

It was the day after a bunch of Johnny's Seminary friends had come up to the Lake to play golf. Marbeth and I were stuck with one of those awful lunches that Ma and Mrs. Reilly used to have. We finally got away and met Johnny and his friends at the golf course and had a fine time eating dinner and singing together. I was very happy, as I usually was in those days when I was with my two best friends.

Doctor came up on the train unexpectedly that weekend and called his chauffeur to meet him at the station. It was kind of a surprise, but we were happy he would be joining us—or we pretended to be happy anyway.

It was late in the afternoon. Ma was taking a nap, as she often did after lunch. The boys were away someplace, playing softball. I think Marbeth was watching the game—she would have been anywhere Johnny would have been that summer. I was sitting out in the pagoda by the lake, a shirt over my two-piece swimsuit, reading Faulkner's *Requiem for a Nun,* nice irony, that. Marbeth had read it and given it to me; I couldn't make any sense out of it. It was a lovely day in late August, not too hot, no clouds in the sky, a light wind rippling the waters of the lake. I guess I must have drifted off to sleep.

Then, suddenly, Doctor was there. His face was very flushed and I could smell the whiskey on his breath even before he bent to kiss me. When I opened my eyes I realized he was very drunk. His words were slurred and his eyes were very red. As I looked up at him it struck me that his eyes were red more from just drinking. It was possible he had been crying too.

He sat next to me, taking the book from my hand as if he was actually interested in what I was reading. Then he let the book drop to the floor. He buried his face in his hands.

"I thought it was an easy case," he muttered. "Just a routine appendicitis. But then there was blood everywhere and I couldn't stop it. I must have nicked the aorta. He was just a baby. Younger than our Johnny. He died and I had to tell his parents."

I put my arms around him and hugged him tight, trying to ease his pain. I had never seen my father this way. Even when he'd been drinking, he was usually still in control.

"One of the interns said that I'd been drinking, but I hadn't been. Christ, it was before lunch."

"Of course you hadn't been," I said, hugging him tighter still. But even at sixteen I knew that the amount he drank at night didn't lead to very steady hands the next morning, but I just kept holding him, trying to reassure him the way Ma used to when we were sick as little kids.

His shoulders rose convulsively. I gently kissed his cheek. He looked up, but his eyes seemed blank and empty, as if he was considering a past that no longer existed. He sighed and gathered me up in his arms. We sat quietly for a while. Then his grip tightened and another look crossed his face. "Delia, Delia," he cried. "Why did it all have to be destroyed?"

Suddenly he was kissing me on my mouth, his tongue parting my lips. I struggled desperately, trying to get away, but it was as if I was in a dream, a nightmare. I couldn't get him off me, couldn't push him away. It was as if he had mistaken me for one of his whores, or, worse yet, the bride he once loved— my mother.

His hands loosened the top of my bathing suit; his fingers probed my breasts. I could feel the hard fence of the pagoda against my back. I tried to scream, but wet lips covered my mouth and he ripped the pants of my bathing suit down to my knees.

The fear was suffocating. I could feel him hard against me. Then he was inside. The pain was awful. I finally screamed. I screamed and screamed and with three short thrusts it was over.

I looked up at his face and saw that my father was suddenly aware that it was me, his Kate. A terrible look of agony crossed his face. I've never seen a human being in such pain.

"I never meant . . . I never realized . . ." He fumbled with his pants and zipped them. A moment later he was gone.

He must have gone back to the car and driven to Chicago, because we never saw him again that weekend.

Afterwards I lay on the pavilion floor for what seemed like hours. It was only when I was afraid someone would come looking for me for dinner that I struggled back into my suit and robe. But it was still a long time after that before I slunk back to the house and up to my room.

I showered for over an hour. How could this have happened? What had I done to cause it? Terrified that if anyone ever looked at me they would suspect, I called the maid and said I had an upset stomach; I wouldn't be coming down to the dinner table.

Later that night Ma came up with a tray of tea and toast. She asked me if I'd seen Doctor and I began to tremble. She said it was odd that the chauffeur had gone all the way back to Chicago if Doctor hadn't been on the train.

I began to weep uncontrollably, growing more and more hysterical. I couldn't speak. To this day I'm not sure how much

I told her, but she suddenly drew herself up and slapped me across the face hard. "You must have been dreaming," she said. "Nasty, dirty dreams because you're a nasty, dirty girl."

With that she got up off my bed and left the room. No one ever spoke of the incident again. The next day I refused to go to Communion. Johnny noticed and asked me what was wrong. I tried to tell him, but I couldn't find the words. Johnny looked embarrassed, then distressed. He pretended not to understand what I was trying to say. After a few minutes he said he had to go, using the excuse that he had to see Marbeth. So he offered no comfort at all. I wondered bitterly if he hadn't been so involved with her whether he'd have been more willing to face my reality.

So I didn't tell anyone until two years ago, when there was so much publicity about the subject. Then I told Dan one night, almost on impulse. He found me this wonderful therapist. I feel that I've grown more in the last two years than I had in all my life before then.

At the time I'd tried to tell a priest in Confession, but he got terribly angry, insisting it was all my fault. But he did give me absolution. So much for the Church's enlightened view on child abuse.

But Johnny should have helped me. He shouldn't have spent the rest of the summer enjoying Marbeth. It was then I began to resent them both. And after that awful afternoon at the pagoda, I was always scared to be around Doctor. Even though he never touched me again, I was always afraid.

I knew I couldn't talk to Ma, but Johnny might have helped. After all, wasn't he the future priest? Wasn't he the sensitive one?

At the end of the summer I tried to talk to him about the family. Not about what Doctor had done to me, but about his women, Ma's increasing craziness, the fact that Johnny was always her favorite.

"Honestly, Kate," Johnny said, "I never noticed. Of course it's not fair. I'd do anything to make it up to you."

"Well, it's too late now! You're her favorite. You always

have been and you always will be. And the rest of us will always suffer for it."

"It isn't that easy being her favorite, if that's what it is I am," he said with a sigh. "A lot of expectations go with it."

"You'll have it both ways!" I shouted at him. "You're her favorite and you're going to be a priest just the way she wants you to, but you'll still screw Marbeth whenever you feel like it."

"That's not true, Kate," he said, his face turning red with anger. "I've never done that and I don't intend to."

"You have too!" I kept on shouting. "Believe me, I know."

He asked again that I forgive him for not noticing. Suddenly I wasn't sure if he was referring to the favoritism or to that fateful episode with Doctor. Something in his eyes made me think it was the latter. I couldn't control myself anymore. "I'll never forgive you! What kind of monster are you not to notice?"

He seemed genuinely bewildered, but then Johnny was always good at seeming bewildered when he didn't want to deal with something.

"Kate, I'm sorry," he muttered. "I had no idea you felt so strongly . . ."

"I'll never forgive you. Never."

He seemed utterly dejected. He hated it when people didn't melt all over him, particularly the few times women didn't. Once more he told me he was sorry. And then he walked away.

Ever since, I've wondered if I was really trying to tell him about that afternoon with Doctor. In my heart of hearts, I still think he already knew.

14

Back at school I pretended that it never happened. The humiliation and anger and resentment must have boiled inside of me, but I acted like I was fine. Junior year of high school was supposed to be fun. I even developed a crush on Bud Quinlan. I was absolutely delighted when I thought he was looking at me like he was imagining me with my clothes off. I flaunted myself at him, though so cautiously that no one, not even Marbeth noticed. Certainly Bud had no idea about my crush.

"Hey, Kate," he said to me after Mass at St. Luke's one Sunday that autumn. "You're really looking great."

It was the first time he had shown any awareness that I existed. My heart jumped into my throat.

"How is Notre Dame, Bud?"

"Oh, it's all right," he said. "They're pretty arrogant down there about their football team. That's why I quit."

"I heard you had a fight with the freshman coach."

"He made fun of me."

"How unfair."

"Can I take you to the movies tonight, at the Lamar maybe?"

He would want to make out, of that I was sure. The idea appealed to me. So did the film, *A Streetcar Named Desire.*

"I have homework."

So it went all through my junior year. I wanted to throw myself at Bud but didn't. He pursued me and I enjoyed it but ignored him.

That dance, as Marbeth called it, went on for the rest of my junior year.

"You like him, Kate," she would say. "Admit it. You like him a lot."

"I can't stand him."

She'd look puzzled and shake her head as though she didn't know whether to believe me or not.

"He's kind of spoiled," she'd say. "All he wants from a woman is adoration, but he's cute and he's got a great personality."

"I will never just adore a man," I said firmly.

"I won't either," she agreed.

She heard on the grapevine that Bud wanted me to invite him to the junior prom at Trinity. I was overwhelmed with happiness but told Marbeth to send word back that I absolutely would not go with him.

I was scared silly.

"He's a nice boy," Marbeth argued with me. "He's good-looking and popular and lots of fun."

"He didn't invite me to his prom when he was a senior at Fenwick."

We were sitting in my Impala convertible in front of her house.

"That was years ago."

"So what?"

"You were only a sophomore."

"That doesn't make any difference. A lot of seniors took sophomores."

"You need a prom date."

"I don't want to go to the prom anyway. They're a drag."

"But who will I double with?"

"I don't care!"

So it went for two days. Finally I gave in.

Did Marbeth know that I wanted in the worst way to ask him to the prom? Sure she did! I didn't tell her because I knew that she knew. Later she would lie and deny that she knew that I thought I was in love with Bud.

"You look wonderful, Kate," he said when he came to pick me up.

I thanked him and told him he looked great too. Then we went to get Marbeth.

The prom was at the Oak Park Arms Hotel, and I had a really dreamy time at first. Then Marbeth, who was wearing a white chiffon off-the-shoulder gown which most of the girls thought was too daring, ruined it for me.

"Can I have a dance with Marbeth?" Bud asked me politely. "Would you mind?"

I was sure she'd refuse. Instead she danced with Bud almost as much as I did and flirted with him. He leered at her every time she was in his arms. There was plenty to leer at.

"He's such a nice boy, Kate," she said to me. "Why don't you show him a good time?"

"I don't like him that much," I said. For the first time in my life I was jealous of her. She was so uninhibited. Why couldn't I laugh and flirt like that? In any case I thought she was in love with Johnny, so why was she going out of her way to attract every boy at the dance? But it wasn't until she went over to Doctor that I really began to hate her.

He and Ma were chaperons, the first and last time he ever came to anything. Marbeth asked him to dance with her.

"Would you like to dance, Doctor McGlynn?"

"Yes, of course, my dear," he said in that bemused, polite voice of his.

He danced very close to her, and seemed even more interested in her cleavage than Bud was.

Meanwhile Bud was trying to get me back on the dance floor. "No, no," I gasped, almost unable to breathe. "I need to rest a minute."

||

I met Dan Crowley in a bar on Rush Street where some of my friends from Rosary College and I had stopped for a drink after seeing *From Here to Eternity.*

He was a third-year law student and at least an inch shorter than I. He had burning brown eyes and a dangerous smile.

He took me home that night—in my car.

"I want you, young woman," he said to me as he kissed me goodnight, more passionately than was permitted on a first date in those days.

"What do you mean by that?" I asked nervously.

"A thousand years ago I would have carried you off to my castle on a mountain and made love to you all day, every day. Now I guess I'll have to marry you."

"You're crazy," I told him, not altogether displeased at his impetuosity.

I was glad to be able to go out with him because it kept me from having any regrets. The next summer, when Marbeth and Bud Quinlan got engaged, six months before Johnny was ordained, I was totally astonished. Marbeth had never told me that she was dating him.

"We did a lot of writing while I was away at school," she explained.

"Is he your kind of man?" I asked dubiously.

"He wants to marry me." She shrugged. "It might just as well be him as anyone else."

"He's not at all like Johnny."

"I don't want someone like Johnny."

If I was not still so angry at her, I would have warned her that Bud was empty. Instead I concentrated on my own relationship with Dan. A few months later he asked me to marry him. I figured that if Marbeth had a ring, I might as well have one too—everyone in our crowd was getting engaged that summer. So I said yes, the luckiest word I've said in all my life.

Ma was furious. "Mark my words, Kate, he'll never amount to a hill of beans. He's too short to be a good lawyer, too short altogether."

Then, to my astonishment, she invited Marbeth to come to Rome for Johnny's ordination and first Mass. I hardly said a word to Marbeth on the trip. On the way back I told her that I would not be at her wedding.

"But why not, Kate?" She started to cry. "You've been my best friend since I was a little girl."

"You know why not."

"No, I don't. Honestly."

I knew I was being unreasonable. Even if she hadn't been chasing Johnny, he wouldn't have been able to help me that day at the pagoda, and she certainly hadn't been anything more than polite in asking Doctor to dance. So, unable to tell the truth, I blurted out the first thing I could think of: "You took Bud away from me."

"You never told me that you were interested in him."

"You knew just the same."

"As God is my witness, Kate, I didn't know. You never said anything."

"I don't want to talk about it."

I wasn't going to attend her wedding, but at the last minute I slipped into the back of St. Luke's to watch. She was a radiant bride, I'll give her that. I wondered that day whether the color of her skin and her smile and the elegant way she walked were for her groom or for Johnny, who was officiating. They were very tender with one another up there on the altar. I wondered whether anyone else could see that she loved Johnny more than she loved Bud Quinlan.

She must have seen me when she was coming down the aisle. Before I knew it, she leaned over and embraced me.

"I love you, Kate. I'll always love you. Thanks for coming. Please come to the reception for just a minute."

I didn't say anything back to her. I couldn't; I was crying too hard.

She was so beautiful that I almost loved her again, but even after that I wouldn't ask her to be my maid of honor, and I refused to let Johnny officiate.

Ma was furious. As she was fixing my veil, she said, "Well, you don't look half bad, Kate dear, but your groom is shorter than you are. Mark my words, he'll never amount to a hill of beans."

I was horribly scared that day. All the memories of what Doctor had done to me came flooding back. I was in mortal terror of the wedding night. I tried to think of ways of getting out of the marriage. But I was trapped.

As it turned out, the wedding night was fine. Dan was sweet as well as determined.

Ma was wrong about him. Dan, God bless him, was a huge success, although Mother never admitted it, not even when we bought the house in Kenilworth.

"It will be pretty drafty in the winter," was all she would say.

Still, I had the last laugh on them. Marbeth's Bud turned out to be a creep and then a suicide who is damned to hell for all eternity. Ma is senile; Johnny is dead. Mick and Jim are failures. And I have a fine husband and a beautiful family and we own more than Ma and Doctor ever did.

And I'm a better Catholic than any of them.

But I still remember fondly the times so long ago when Marbeth and Johnny and I were such good friends.

15

These letters show what Johnny was really like—a weakling who could never stand up to Ma.

Ma keeps them in a box on the table next to her bed. She made copies of all her letters to him and clipped his responses. She doesn't know whom they're from anymore, but she knows they're important. I could take only a few or she'd suspect that something was wrong. I'll slip them back in when I visit her tomorrow.

This is one she wrote after Doctor died in 1953. I was at Rosary; Jimmy had flunked out of medical school, Mick had been expelled from Notre Dame for drinking. Johnny was in his second-to-last year at the North American, and expected to be assigned immediately after ordination to graduate work in Rome. The letter shows what our family was like at that time.

Well, I hope you're all happy now. I've been left alone by myself, except for Kate, and she's worthless as we all know. Jimmy and Micky refused to live at home with me. You're off in Rome and Doctor is dead. If I said once I said a thou-

sand times to those two young scoundrels, you'll be the death
of Doctor if you don't apply yourselves in school.

Well I was right, wasn't I?

As for you, young man, you don't seem ready to take advantage of the opportunities that God has given you. Even
if the Cardinal didn't find time to come to Doctor's funeral
(after all the money we have given him to help you get
ahead) you should have visited him when you were here for
the funeral. You're the only one I have left, Johnny, please
don't let me down.

Johnny did not reply to tell her that Church offices are not
for sale. He never told her that. Not once. His replies are pious
and sweet, like he's going along with it. If it will make Ma
happy, it's all right with him. His ordination and first Mass
were just an excuse for Ma to try to buy him favors. Ma wrote
this letter in January of 1955, after he was ordained. He was
still in Rome, finishing up his theological studies.

I was happy I had brought along those thousand dollar
bills as Father Ed at the shrine suggested I do. I was able to
give away all of them to your friends as a stipend to say a
low Mass for the repose of Doctor's soul. I'm sure those little
gifts will be a big help when decisions are made about who
is going to study Canon law.

Never stop thinking and planning for the future, my darling boy. As I've told you, you have to fish or cut bait.

The Cardinal was furious at her for meddling, so Johnny
was assigned to a difficult parish on the South Side. Somehow
Ma managed to get him out of there eventually. Just listen to
this letter she wrote in 1961, after he went back to Rome and
got his degree in Canon law:

Well, at long last we've finally got you into that College of
Noble Ecclesiastics place where you should have been long
ago. It cost me a pretty penny, let me tell you, to get you into
that school.

Father Ed says that most of the students aren't noble, but
are smart and poor peasant kids on the make. Well, you're

smart, my darling, and you're not poor. So make good use of the money I keep sending you and turn as many of your teachers and fellow students into friends as you can. Remember, we're both doing it for Doctor's memory.

Now here's a typical reply from Johnny, written that same year. It shows that he went along with her plots and schemes.

Money, as you've often said, is a way to buy trust. But only if you can be sure that you are giving the money to someone whose trust can be bought. That isn't everyone, not here.
I'll keep trying.

Then they sent Johnny to Africa in 1962 and she pulled every string she could to get him a better assignment.

Well, at last, I've got you out of that stink hole in Africa and into a decent city. I don't want you settling in. Vienna is a station on the way to Rome and Chicago. Don't you ever forget that. I want to live to see the day when you come back home as the boss. That will show those people who made fun of me when I married Doctor and who celebrated when my other two sons failed me.
Don't spend too much time working with them Pollacks either. Nothing good ever came out of trying to deal with them.

She was still trying to prove herself to Doctor and his mother. Johnny was her only hope of proof. By this time I suspect that she was a little crazy on the subject. She actually thought she could buy Johnny an archdiocese.

I took one more letter out of her file along with Johnny's reply. It's not dated, but it must have been written in the early seventies, when he was working in Rome for Archbishop Benelli. She took credit for getting him out of Vienna and obtaining him the job in the Secretariat of State in Rome.

Now I tell you what I want you to do. Apply yourself, like I say, to your own career. Fish or cut bait. Do a good job for

this Benelli, but don't get too attached to him. I say never
trust Italians, especially the short ones with greasy smiles.
Your Benelli looks to me just like a barber who lived down
the street when I was growing up. My father thought he was
a killer for the mafia and my father was always right about
those things.

You say that this little Dago with the sneaky smile might
be the next Pope. Fine, but answer me one question: what
happens to you if he isn't the next Pope?

Where are you then?

In a shit hole, that's where you are.

See what you do is this: you wait till an American city
comes open, not too big, not too small, and you find out how
much it costs. Don't worry about how much. We can afford
whatever they want.

Did Johnny reply? Oh, sure he did, Father. Same old stuff.

Sorry not to have written for such a long time and to have
to be so brief. Don't worry about Archbishop Benelli. He's
not a mafioso.

Can the Church canonize a man like that? Especially when
these letters exist?

LAURENCE

16

I drove over to the Seminary to visit Johnny's grave with a heavy heart after listening to poor Kate.

I felt some sympathy for Johnny. He had survived by ignoring what he could. But I had enough notes to destroy his memory forever. The question was whether the letters ought to be taken seriously. Might one not contend that he was merely keeping a beloved, if partially demented mother at bay?

Before proceeding any further with my investigation, I knew I had to speak to a more objective observer of Johnny's life. Kate's accusations of a continuing illicit affair might only be figments resulting from her own deeply disturbed past. They could not be taken at face value.

Breathing deeply the nicotine-free air of north Cook County, I turned into the Seminary grounds, trying to imagine Marbeth leaning out of her Studie convertible and reading the riot act to Johnny. Some scene. Then I found in the Sacred Orders building the elderly priest to whom I wanted to talk. I hoped he would be the unbiased witness who could accompany me on my visit to Johnny McGlynn's grave.

"He wasn't an intellectual," the old priest said, huddling under my umbrella. "He was smart and quick and had an incredible memory. He learned quickly how to play the academic game here and played it brilliantly. But I'd say he was devoid of curiosity and of any inclination to probe beneath the memorized answers his teachers wanted."

"Uh-huh."

"Unlike you, Lar"—the old priest chuckled—"he never asked an embarrassing question; he never really seemed interested in anything but good grades, and he achieved those with ease and grace."

We were standing in the St. Mary of the Lake cemetery, a secluded, tree-ringed meadow across the road from the Seminary's Sacred Orders building. There were twelve tombstones in front of us, six seminarians, four faculty members, and two cardinals. A renaissance Gabriel, trumpet in hand, presided over the peaceful scene, just now soaked in an Ireland-like late-summer drizzle.

"Not much depth, huh?"

"I wouldn't quite put it that way, Lar." The old man shook his head. "He was a conventional seminarian of his time, conventional in his ideas, conventional in his piety, and conventional in his behavior."

The elderly priest, short with thin white hair, a baby face, and rimless glasses, was one of the great characters of Seminary history, a splendid teacher and a loyal friend to several generations of seminarians.

"Everyone liked him, Lar, everyone except some of the Jesuit faculty. He was so good in his studies that even they couldn't stop him, though heaven knows they tried. There was a situation when he was in Third Philosophy when a girl he knew stopped in a car on one of the roads to talk to him for a half hour. He promptly reported it to the Philosophy Prefect of Discipline, which was a good thing, because two of the Jesuits saw him and they went running to the Rector."

"He kept the rules, then?"

"Always did, though the Jesuit said that he reported himself only to beat them to the punch." He chuckled again. "They were fighting a losing battle against Johnny."

"Did anyone really know him?" I tilted the umbrella over the old man's head because the drizzle was turning into a steady rain.

"Funny thing." He spoke slowly and carefully. "I was just thinking that too. Despite his charm and energy, I don't think he was really close to anyone. The inner recesses of Johnny McGlynn's soul were mystery. All his life, as far as that goes. Except maybe at the end, and even that's hard to tell."

The Cardinal's grave was covered by fresh flowers; new bouquets every day, the elderly priest had told me. Despite the rain, a dozen or so people were kneeling or standing around it in deep prayer. At least fifty every day, the priest said. None of them looked like the slightly demented miracle worshipers who followed Father Ralph. Johnny McGlynn's cult had breadth as well as depth.

"Too bad his intellectual talents weren't challenged."

"You won't find me disagreeing, Lar." The old priest shook his head sadly. "But we weren't into intellectual challenge in those days, as you surely remember. Indeed, we were just a little bit suspicious of those who worried about deep issues and problems. I don't suppose they challenged him much in the Canon Law program in Rome, or later at the College of Noble Ecclesiastics, where they taught him how to be a diplomat—not that Johnny needed lessons from anyone on that."

"It's still a shame," I persisted, "that a cardinal as smart as he surely was didn't develop more intellectually. His pastorals were pretty much strings of clichés, weren't they?"

"Sometimes." The old priest sighed. "Johnny was just a bit of a hollow man—till the end."

"Till the end? That's the second time you've said that."

"Go back and look at his pastorals, Lar. The last couple of them seem to have been written by a different man. Some people say he went through a big change—conversion is the fashionable word these days—in the last couple of years of his life. No one knows what caused it, or exactly when it happened, and it seems to have been so gradual that no one noticed it, but those who were close to him said he was a different man."

"How was he different?"

" 'Intense' is the word everyone used. Prayed a lot more, talked a lot more about God, seemed much more concerned, genuinely concerned about people, gave away all his money, if you can believe what they say."

"That I very much doubt. . . . Did you notice the change, Tom?"

"He certainly seemed different the last couple of times he came out here to see us. Excitable, very excitable, like he wanted to catch up on the last twenty years of theological history in a couple of conversations."

One group of supplicants left the grave and another group drifted in. They paid no attention to the two clerics watching on the edge of the lawn.

"I've heard about the so-called change," I admitted, "but to tell the truth, I never noticed it myself."

"You wouldn't have, would you, Lar?" the old priest asked mildly. "You of all people?"

"I suppose not."

The priest and I drifted over to the grave. The crowd around it was bigger than when we had walked into the cemetery, maybe thirty people. I was losing my focus on Jumping Johnny. He was becoming elusive, a will-o'-the-wisp flitting ahead of my outstretched fingers.

I made the sign of the cross and began to pray.

Look, you SOB, I don't believe that you're a saint. I think these poor people are being taken in. But maybe God has made you a saint. If He did, I don't want to get in His way. But if you're really working wonders, you're going to have to pull off something pretty spectacular to convince me. Understand?

If Johnny really was monitoring the prayers of those of us around his grave, he would surely find that outburst pretty funny.

So I drove back to St. Finian's, Kate's hatred and the old priest's gentle moderation contending in my mind.

I read the two pastorals he had given me as soon as I entered the Rectory.

The old priest was right, they did represent a dramatic change from the early letters in which he praised "Our Most Holy Father" in every other paragraph and quoted from the Vatican document in the intervening paragraphs.

In a Saint Valentine's Day pastoral he wrote, "For us humans, love is cyclic. It has its ups and downs, its highs and its lows. That's why the festival of this good saint is in our calendar, to offer to human lovers the possibility of breaking out of the routine and the monotony of winter and anticipating the glories of spring."

What the hell, I thought. That doesn't sound like the same guy who went along with Delia's crazy ideas. Now he sounds like a liberal or even a radical. How come none of us noticed the change from his early pastoral letters?

Well, maybe some people did, but I sure didn't.

His Labor Day letter was even more astonishing. "Many men and women in other countries and even some in our own are not able to earn by the sweat of their brow the kind of lifestyle which we Americans take for granted. I do not say this to make you feel guilty, because I do not believe that your good fortune is the result of other people's bad fortune.

"Nor do I think there are any easy solutions to the problems of world poverty. But it is appropriate to ask that you at least be aware of the problems of poverty, be concerned about such problems and do whatever you can to alleviate them. This autumn I will visit Central America on a fact-finding trip. I will report to you when I come back. I hope you will pray for me and my associates that our journey is a safe and productive one."

OK—he had changed. He was not the Johnny McGlynn of the letters Kate had shown me or of his early pastorals. Something had happened to Jumping Johnny, something had twisted loose. The ice floes in him were cracking up.

The most important part of my job might be to chart the course of that change and find its cause. Maybe that would prove the key to all five suspicions against him—the affair with Marbeth, misappropriation of diocesan funds, transfer of stolen money to Poland, purchase of Church offices, and, my own special one, absence of faith in God. Meanwhile I wasn't making much progress. The first thing in the morning I'd have to call the Chancery and demand more cooperation from the Cardinal.

17

"The Cardinal regrets," Don Price said smoothly, "that at the present time he cannot permit you to have access to the McGlynn files."

"How am I supposed to do my job," I snapped at him, "if I can't read his letters?"

"Ah . . . the Cardinal feels that there is no material in the files that would be pertinent to your study at the present time."

"Put the Cardinal on the phone, Don, or he'll have to find a new Devil's Advocate at the present time."

There was a brief pause.

"Hello, Laurence." The Boss sounded nervous, as he always does when he must face conflict.

"I can't do this job if I can't have all the facts."

"I understand that. But you have all his pastoral letters, don't you? They're on the public record. I believe they are in the file Don arranged for you."

"Drivel."

"I don't think you'd find his personal correspondence more revealing. And certainly not his letters to the Holy See. He was in this regard a very cautious and proper ecclesiastic."

"Look, Cardinal, I write up a report that says *A* about Johnny McGlynn. Then, a few years from now, someone does get access to his private correspondence and discovers that *A* is not true and *B* is. I look bad, but that doesn't matter. The Church looks bad because it looks like it's covering up. And that does matter."

"I understand."

"Do you?"

Long pause. "We could arrange for you to see the files of his official correspondence," the Cardinal said slowly. "You may be able to find more in it than I have."

"Fine, but I suspect I won't find more than you. It's the private correspondence which is essential if I want to find out about his virtue and his holiness."

"I understand."

"Well?"

Another long pause.

"This is embarrassing"—the Cardinal's voice trembled—"but, ah . . . we don't have those files."

"Don't have them? Why the hell not?"

"They seem to have disappeared immediately after his death. Monsignor Carey has not been, ah, cooperative in explaining what happened to them."

"Does he have them?" I demanded, now very angry at ecclesiastical incompetence.

"We don't think so."

"Then who does?"

Silence.

"Do you have any idea who has the private correspondence?" I repeated the question.

"We have reason to believe"—he hesitated—"that, er, Mrs. Quinlan has much, if not all of it."

"Marbeth! Have you asked her?"

"You are acquainted with her, are you not, Lar? Then I leave it to your imagination how she replied to our discreet inquiries about Cardinal McGlynn's missing archives."

"I see."

"Perhaps she will permit you to examine them."

"Yeah. I understand. I'll see what I can do."

"I'd appreciate that very much, Laurence."

"Yeah. And, Cardinal, there are two other people I need to get to cooperate. Len Carey, Johnny's right-hand man, and 'Killer' Kane, Bishop of Alton, his classmate, questioned the purity of Johnny's motives. Would you lean on them to send their memos about Johnny to me? They absolutely refuse to cooperate."

"I'd be reluctant to bring pressure on them."

"Do you want this job done? How am I supposed to gather my materials if those who knew him well won't cooperate?"

"I understand that."

"Good. Lean on them. I need those memos soon."

"Does Mrs. Quinlan intend to cooperate?"

"Who knows? Probably. She's smart enough to want to put her spin on the story."

"How interesting."

Isn't it? There was no reason to think Marbeth would cooperate with me any more than she would with those who wanted to borrow Jumping Johnny's pectoral cross to work miracles.

What a typical Marbeth move!

The answers to my still vague questions were almost certainly in those archives. Would she let me look at them? Probably not. Had she burned them, as Archbishop Feehan's housekeeper had burned all his files the day Chicago's second Archbishop died? Somehow I thought that she had not. Marbeth had always loved him. She would not destroy the intimate remnants of the man she loved.

Could I get them away from her?

It would be easier to get the gold, such as may be left, from Fort Knox.

18 While waiting to see what pressure the Cardinal could bring to bear on Len and "Killer" Kane, I decided to have another try at setting up a meeting with Johnny's brothers. Certainly they should have some insight into Johnny's relationship with Marbeth, and Jimmy was obviously privy to the arrangements made to bail him out of his trading scandal.

I had been unsuccessful in my efforts to gain cooperation from Michael or James McGlynn. Michael was always "unavailable" when I called his office in the County Building. I then used some of my political clout. My friend, who talked to a friend of his, came back with the message that Mick would not "even as a personal favor" discuss his brother, the late Cardinal, with me or anyone else.

If you can't get something from a Chicago pol as a "personal favor," you might as well forget about it.

So I turned back to Jimmy. Before trying to corner him, however, I met with a trader from St. Finian's who always knew the CBOT gossip. I wanted to know what the word was on the street about the Cardinal saving Jimmy with Church money. We met on the Michigan Avenue bridge.

Jerry was one of the gnomes of La Salle Street, a short bald man with a puckish face, darting blue eyes, and a rasping tenor voice.

"Did the Cardinal cover Jimmy's losses when they called his margins?" I asked the question bluntly.

Jerry Crawford glanced nervously up and down the Chicago River. "Don't ask a thing like that, Father. Not even here on the bridge. You can never tell who will hear us."

I had whispered the question.

The Michigan Avenue bridge, now almost seventy years old, badly needs repairs. The city hesitates to close it down because of the monumental traffic problems which will occur when the Magnificent Mile is cut off from downtown Chicago. Every time a bus crosses the bridge, it shakes and rumbles like a minor California earthquake. Despite guarantees from the city that the bridge is still perfectly safe, I have fantasies every time I cross it that it will fall away beneath me and deposit me unceremoniously in the Chicago River.

"OK, Jerry," I replied to my parishioner. "You tell me what happened in your own words."

It was a humid day, with the temperature hovering near ninety. Jerry was in his shirtsleeves. I removed my Roman collar and put it in my shirt pocket and took off my coat and draped it over my shoulder.

"Well." Jerry glanced up and down the bridge again and fixed his eyes on the upriver skyline. "Let's say that our mutual friend was really in over his head. He's a bear, he tends to sell short to make a profit when prices fall. Nothing wrong with that. You know what they say: bulls win, bears win. Pigs lose. Our mutual friend was a pig. He always got out too late. Sometimes he still made a lot of money. Sometimes he didn't make anything and sometimes he lost his shirt. He was living off the income from his trust fund, so he could afford to take chances, but he took too many."

"Pigs do that."

"Yeah, they do. Anyway, this one time he is more a pig than usual. He had sold on a downswing, and then the yen market, which he was playing then, shoots up and keeps going. He hangs on. Why, I don't know. They keep calling in his margins. He has run out of capital. The 'outfit' is involved in some loans that he couldn't pay back. Our friend is up the creek. Without a paddle and without a boat. You even heard that the outfit was whispering in his ear what they'd do to his wife and daughters if he didn't pay them off."

A Wendella tour boat, filled with yelling kids, pulled out from its berth next to the bridge and chugged its way toward the lake. I wished I was on the boat instead of listening to his sad, sordid story.

"We call him before the ethical practices committee. We give him an ultimatum and he leaves our room trembling. It doesn't have any windows, Father, and it's one scary place. Every trader is terrified at the thought that someday he'll be dragged into it."

"Inquisition."

"You said a mouthful. Anyway, Jim . . . our mutual friend is going to have to come up with a couple hundred thousand dollars overnight or he's kaput with us. . . . And he comes up with it. Would you believe that? This guy finds that kind of money overnight."

"So people think that the Catholic Cemetery Office is picking up the tab."

"Who else? Doctor McGlynn left trust funds for his kids and the rest of the money to his missus. They can't touch her money while she's alive—and she's still alive, I guess—and the money the Cardinal is getting from the trust fund is a nice little nest egg, but not enough to cover our mutual friend's position."

"And no records of any of this?"

"You got it, Father. Who would keep records?"

"Who indeed."

There would be no records of the deals in which Johnny apparently engaged. I'd talk to the Catholic Cemeteries director, but he was the successor to the man from whom Johnny might have received the money. He might or might not know about the "loan." If he did, why should he tell me? Why admit to someone who was working for the Cardinal that he had remained silent during an illegal transfer of funds?

I walked over to La Salle Street and down its canyon to the Board of Trade, a solid mountain defying anyone to assault it.

I cornered Jimmy McGlynn at Traders' Inn, the bar near the Board of Trade where he hung out for most of the day. From him I heard only invective.

"He was a spoiled brat, padre."

Jimmy McGlynn—now about sixty years old and looking shriveled and at least ten years older—murmured into his vodka martini, "A selfish, miserable, rotten, spoiled brat."

That was an interesting reaction from a man whom, it was said, Johnny had bailed out when margin calls on him put him in jeopardy with the "outfit."

"Ah?"

"I hear you talked to Kate, padre? Waste of time. She's always been crazy. Dumb Dan Crowley goes along with all her nutty ideas. I can't figure out how such a dumb guy makes so much money drawing up wills."

"I shouldn't believe Kate?"

"She's on an incest kick now, isn't she, padre? As soon as something shows up in the papers or the women's magazines, it's happened to her. Doctor was a cocksman all right, no doubt about that. May be that he felt her up a little once or twice, but nothing more. Doctor wasn't crazy or anything like that."

"I'm glad to hear it."

"She's really angry at Johnny. Always has been. Like me and the Mick. Only she can't admit it, know what I mean?"

"I think so."

"Johnny was the problem in our family. Always was. He was the only one who mattered." Jim McGlynn's face, already crimson from drink, turned almost purple. "He got all the attention, all the money. What you priests saw was his god-damn charm. We had to live with his selfishness. He was the only one our mother gave a fuck about."

"He wasn't all that popular with priests, Jim."

"Yeah?" He flicked the long ash off his malodorous cigar.

132 || ANDREW M. GREELEY

"Well, you guys didn't have to live with him. Let me tell you, I got down on my knees and offered prayers of gratitude the day he died, and I don't want to talk about him now."

Nonetheless, Jim McGlynn did talk about him for another hour of increasingly incoherent mumbling, punctuated by efforts to relight the cigar. He did not progress much beyond his initial statements about Johnny being a "spoiled brat."

I finally made my escape, convinced that I would never get any useful information out of Jimmy McGlynn.

I was wrong. The next morning he called me at the Rectory.

"Lorett—my wife—says I should tell you all I can." He sounded cold sober. "You want to know about the money he lent me, don't you?"

"That's an important issue, Jimmy."

"OK. I'll tell you all I know. You'll have to figure out what to make of it. I got nothing to gain or lose either way, know what I mean?"

JAMES

19

"It is not necessary that everyone be a medical doctor." Doctor seemed embarrassed like he always was when he talked to one of us. "Perhaps, young man, you don't have the aptitude for it. That's hardly a disgrace."

He called each of us boys "young man" because he had a hard time remembering our names.

"Yes, Doctor."

"One must pursue one's own destiny."

He looked like a tired old leprechaun, withered and worn out, but always genial and courteous.

Ma had set up this private heart-to-heart talk so that Doctor might express his anger and disappointment at my flunking out of Loyola Medical School. The anger and disappointment were all hers. Doctor didn't give a shit one way or another.

"Perhaps you will be much happier in another profession," he continued tentatively, "in the commodities trade, for example."

"I think that's true, Doctor," I said respectfully.

I no more wanted to be a doctor than Johnny wanted to be a priest. He made it, so the old lady approved of him. I didn't make it, so she never approved of me.

It was the old lady's idea that having failed at medicine, I should go on the Board of Trade. "There's nothing else left for him to do, Doctor. Maybe he'll make a success of that. To tell the truth, I doubt it. He won't amount to a hill of beans."

"Well, we'll buy him a seat, that's simple enough."

"He'll pay it back, every last cent of it."

"Well, that's neither here nor there. . . ."

Doctor was a gentleman. He did his best never to hurt anyone. Yeah, he screwed around a little. Maybe even a lot. But Ma drove him to it, that's for sure. She made us idolize him, and then manipulated us with the excuse that we had to please him, and manipulated him to take responsibility for us. Ma was a real ball-breaker, just like that bitch Marbeth Reilly. No wonder Ma liked her more than any of us.

Med school was the perfect example. I had let Doctor down and so now Doctor was responsible for me. She deballed both of us.

I didn't have the brains for med school. I was lucky to graduate from college, much less get into Loyola Med. Ma couldn't permit herself to believe that I had inherited her brains instead of Doctor's. I guess Johnny got all the family intelligence.

So I hated college and I hated medical school and was really happy when they finally threw me out. No more studying, no more reading, no more pretending. I haven't read a single book since that day. I let Lorett, my wife, do all the reading. She's got nothing else to do these days.

"You'll break Doctor's heart," Ma said to me as soon as the bastard who was dean of Loyola Medical called her and told her.

"Not so you'd notice it."

Then she says to Doctor, "I wash my hands of him. He's your problem now."

How about that for getting two sets of balls with the same swish of your carving knife.

Both of us went along with it. With Ma you didn't have much choice.

The Board of Trade was her idea, and it was a good idea too, though I don't think she realized it. I was a damn good poker player. Maybe I inherited shrewdness from the old lady too. She certainly manipulated Doctor brilliantly from day one. And I knew how to cheat when I had to.

So I figured I'd do all right on the Floor; and, goddamn it, I have done all right, ups and down like everyone else, but more ups than downs. I made a few fortunes and lost a few too. Made more than I lost on balance. I showed the old lady a thing or two, let me tell you. She never acknowledged my successes and said "I told you so" every time I stumbled a bit.

Anyway, I said to Doctor that afternoon when we had our heart-to-heart, "I do think I could do very well in the commodity business."

And he kind of grins, a little crooked grin like we understand each other perfectly. "I'm sure, young man, that you will do very well indeed."

Five weeks later he was dead. The old lady goes all to pieces, like she had loved him, which as far as I could see she never did. She began to act crazy then and never got better. All the Johnnie Walker didn't help.

Yeah, Ma was an alcoholic. As far as I can remember. It became obvious only after Doctor died.

And Johnny isn't there when Doctor died, the big white hope in the Roman collar is still off in Rome rubbing shoulders with all the faggots in black shirts. So who has to take charge?

Yeah, and did I ever get any credit for it?

I don't have to answer that one, do I?

Shit! Didn't we have great times, in the old days before Doctor died? Thing was we had the money then and we could do anything we wanted with it. Lake Geneva was the greatest. Lots of girls there, if you had the dough, and we had it. Lots of good softball too—and that bastard Johnny wasn't around to lord it over us because he was better at the game than we were. Give him credit, he was one hell of a good athlete.

Yeah, we had a lot of fun, more than my kids did when they were that age. Even Kate.

Then it all ended. Funny thing. I guess we all knew that it had ended, except Johnny maybe. But it happened kind of gradually so we barely realized it was happening. Real funny thing.

Then one summer it was all over. The old lady was hanging around a priest named Father Ed at some Sorrowful Mother Shrine or something like that. I always claimed that he started to push her over the deep end. Doctor's death was just the final shove.

The games Ma used to play about what we were going to be all became serious. Well, Johnny was already in the Seminary, but I never thought until then that it made one fucking bit of difference whether I wanted to be a doctor or not. Then all of a sudden it did.

The dough seemed to dry up, no new cars or boats, not even enough for booze. Girls got kind of scarce without dough.

The Reillys were our buddies in both Forest River and Lake Geneva. We had a helluva lot of fun with them. They didn't have as much dough as we did, but they had enough. They weren't so much interested in girls as we were, but they drank like fish. Really heavy drinkers and lotta laughs, drunk or sober—Iggy, Ally, and Franny. Good guys.

I never liked that little brat of a sister of theirs. Cute all right, great jugs, but a real bossy bitch. I told them that she'd end up running their family and she sure does. I never thought, though, that she'd do me in too. If it wasn't for her I'd be on the Floor today making millions on oil contracts. They're way too high. Gotta come down.

They're all big successes now, Iggy a Federal judge no less. I suppose they think they're better than we are. Well, I could tell some stories about their drinking bouts which would take them down a peg or two.

I don't see much of the family. Kate is married to a stuffed-shirt Republican lawyer. Mick is so busy pretending that Rich Daley calls him every day for advice that I can't stand to be with him. And the old lady's money is still tied up so I can't go back on the Floor until she dies.

Anyway, to get back to Doctor's death, because this shows
what sort of a bastard Johnny really was, I come in from the
Board, oh, about three in the afternoon, I've stopped for a few
quick ones at the Traders' Inn with some of the guys who are
showing me the ropes. The phone is ringing. No one is around
the house. I yell for one of the servants to answer it, but
they're gone. Ma has fired them again. So I pick it up.

"This is Doctor Maurice Kelly calling."

"Yeah, sure, Doc." I already have a bad feeling in the pit of
my stomach. "This is Jim McGlynn."

"Oh, yes, Jimmy. I'm calling from West Suburban hospital.
Doctor McGlynn has had a mild heart attack. We're treating
him and he's responding well. But we want your mother to
know."

First thing I do is to fire off a cable to Rome: DOCTOR HAS HAD
A MILD HEART ATTACK. SUGGEST YOU COME HOME. JIM.

Then I hunt down Mick, who's somewhere with his broad,
and get Kate over at Rosary. Then Ma comes in and I tell her
as gently as I can. She goes to pieces completely.

"He's going to die, I know it, he's going to die. You've killed
him. All of you. You've taken my Doctor away from me!"

So she stays hysterical till Johnny shows up. She's absolutely useless. Kate tries to calm her down, but she's wasting
her time. Now this baffles me. Ma and Doctor have slept in
separate bedrooms for as long as I can remember. Doctor is
screwing around and she knows it. I figure that the hysteria
is a big act, but no one can act that way for ten days.

We all go over to the hospital. They say that Doctor is "resting comfortably." We go in to see him. They have him in
oxygen, but he's conscious and smiles at us. "Sorry, my dear,"
he says to Ma. "Minor incident. Everything is under control."

Ma throws a real fit of wailing and shouting. Doctor closes
his eyes like he wants to go to sleep. An intern and a couple
of nurses have to drag her out. Doctor Kelly says we should
keep her out of the room until she calms down.

"I don't think she's going to calm down, Doc," I says.

"In that case," he says, "I'll prescribe a sedative."

So Ma goes back and forth from hysteria to drugs for the next ten days. I'm running ragged, trying to put in some time at the Board, keep Ma quiet, calm Kate down, and prevent the Mick from leaving town.

"I don't give a shit whether Doctor dies," he says.

I can't argue with him because he's really been pushed around. But still he stays around because I ask him to do it as a "personal favor."

"You'll owe me one," he grumbles.

Can you imagine that? He stays around while his father is dying as a favor for which he's going to call in his marker some day? He does call it in a few years later when he hears I have a sweet deal going and I make him a bundle of money. He never even says thanks.

Anyway, the next day I get a cable back from Johnny: CAN'T LEAVE NOW. TWO CARDINALS AT THE COLLEGE. KEEP ME INFORMED DOCTOR'S PROGRESS. JOHN.

See what kind of an ambitious bastard he was? Two Cardinals are more important than his dying father.

Anyway Doctor seems out of danger. Then one morning—the priest has just given him Communion and left the room—his eyes open wide and he kind of smiles and stops breathing.

I'm not ashamed to admit it. I throw my arms around him and sob. Then I drive home to tell the family.

Mick first. "It's about time," he says and laughs.

Kate breaks down and sobs, but she's not hysterical like the old lady. She's sobbing because she thinks she ought to sob.

Ma goes completely off the deep end—smashes her head against the dining room wall like she wants to kill herself—and shouts all kinds of obscenities at us. It's pretty terrible. Like I say, she never really acts sane again. Kate and I keep feeding her the sedatives, so she's walking around like she's a zombie at the wake.

I send another cable to Rome: DOCTOR DEAD. HOPE YOU CAN MAKE THE FUNERAL. JIM.

I get no reply.

Guess who has to do all the funeral arrangements—choose

the undertaker, buy the casket, schedule the Mass, invite the Cardinal to say Mass (instant refusal), purchase the cemetery lot out at Mount Carmel.

Then, just as the funeral Mass is about to begin, Johnny, dressed up in his cassock and surplice, strides out into the sanctuary as if he's the Pope himself, breathless, like he'd run all the way from the airport.

Everybody in the church cheers. I do all the work and he's the big hero. That's the way it always was. I can make loads of money on the market and I'm a failed doctor. He knocks around the world in a bunch of crummy assignments and he's the big success.

"Nice of you to come home," I sneer at him at the cemetery.

"I left as soon as I got your cable. Asked someone else to tell the Rector."

He talks like I think he is a fucking hero too.

Marbeth Reilly hugs him at the cemetery in the pouring rain. She always had the hots for him. I mark it down just in case I might need it some day.

After that Ma lives only for two things. Her Johnnie Walker and her son the priest. "You took Doctor away from me," she screams at me every time she sees me, "but you're not going to take my priest away from me."

Shit, why would I want to try? But I'm glad Johnny is dead, the self-righteous prick. The way he treated me when I needed a little extra was a disgrace.

All right, I needed cash at the time. I knew the market was going to tumble so I sold short. Only it didn't tumble fast enough. So there are some margin calls and I have to float a few loans. Then the market continues to rise, so I'm kind of in the soup. I ask him for a little bit of extra to tide me over.

He shows up at my home with that goddamn bitch in tow. She's the spike in his spine, with her ice cold eyes and her thin lips and her tight ass. I know I'm in real shit.

"I'm not used to being lectured by anyone, Johnny, least of all by a hypocritical priest."

"We are not here to discuss my hypocrisy, Jimmy, we're

here to figure out a way to extricate you from the appalling mess you've created for yourself."

"Extricate" and "appalling"—I guess that's the way cardinals talk.

"All I need is a little spare, nothing more."

"A little?" says the bitch.

"Hell," I says, "I've been here before. Maybe I'll be here again. The dollar is going to take a beating against the yen in a few more days. I'll make it all back and then some."

"You don't seem to understand," she says, "that your brother is the Archbishop of Chicago . . ."

"Shit, I know that all too well."

"If you end up in the trunk of a car with a bullet between your eyes, or in Federal jail, it will hurt his public image."

"It might hurt me a little too."

"We're not interested in you," she snarls. "We're interested in John. He can't afford to have you making a fool out of yourself and him on the Floor of the Board."

"Your family isn't exactly innocent," I say, figuring she'll lose her temper or break down.

"I'm not the Archbishop of Chicago," she says, composed as you please.

"Now let's not get into personalities," John says, as afraid to stand up to her as he was to stand up to Ma.

"Personalities are irrelevant, John. We have to get him out of the mess he's created for himself. And we have to make sure he never embarrasses you again."

"What do you mean by that?" I get a very uneasy feeling.

"Tell him what we mean," she orders John.

"You're going to have to agree to stay off the Floor for ten years," he says, kind of hesitating. "It's for your own good, and the good of your family."

"Fuck my family!" I shout at him. "You're not going to cut off my balls."

"Yes, we are," she says coldly. "That's exactly what we're going to do."

"Johnny, don't let her do this to me," I told him.

He wants to back down.

"Jimmy . . ." he begins.

She flashes him a deadly look.

"We're doing it for your own good," he finishes up lamely.

Well, I had to take it from them because they had the spare and I didn't. I even had to agree that I'd stay off the Floor for ten years. With that bitch backing him up, he was as much a dictator as the old lady. Course, he's dead now, so I could go back to the Board anytime I want, anytime I get the capital. Which means whenever the old witch dies.

Where did the money come from to meet my calls and pay off my friends on the West Side?

Shit, I don't know. They gave one of the "super traders" a big hunk of cash to back up my positions. He took them over and made a fortune, like I would have if they had given me a chance. So they got their money back and the trade made a bundle. They put the rest in a trust fund for me. Along with what I get from Doctor's estate, we live real good. Lorett says they've done me a big favor.

But if I'm off the Floor, the only thing left in life is my vodka martini. It's not as much fun as trading.

Did they use Church money to bail me out, like they were all saying?

Maybe. Maybe not. Maybe it was her money. I bet she made a bundle selling short then too. If it was her money she got it back. If it was the Church's money, the Church got it back. Everyone made money. Including me. Except I can't do anything with it. They saved my ass, goddamn them, and they ruined my life.

I don't give a fuck whose money it was. You ask me to guess, I'll say it was her money because she wouldn't let him take a risk on something that would endanger his fucking reputation. On the other hand, maybe she knows that he can cover his tracks so well in the Church that it doesn't matter whether he uses Catholic Charities money.

Who cares anymore?

So they're thinking of making Johnny a saint? Fuck him. If

he'd left the Seminary the pressure would have been off Mick and me. The old lady might not have persuaded Doctor to tie up all the money, except for our "allowance," which isn't worth shit for trading capital.

Saint, huh? He was as randy as Doctor. He screwed Marbeth as soon as there was enough of her for him to get into and he did it all through his life. She's a big deal now, development in four countries, on all the boards, gets her picture in the paper, one of the fifteen most beautiful women in Chicago. They don't say her goddamn husband blew his head off.

I bet Johnny screwed her the night before he died.

I don't know what's wrong with the fucking Catholic Church these days anyway.

Yeah, I'll have one more. Why not? Vodka martini on the rocks!

LAURENCE

20

"I am disturbed by the pressures put on me, Father," Bishop Louis Kilmartin "Killer" Kane protested solemnly.

I had been pondering Jimmy McGlynn's story when a peremptory call summoned me to the Four Seasons hotel for a meeting with Louis Kilmartin Kane. While I was driving downtown, I realized that even if the money was Marbeth's, the "scandal" of using a woman's money to save his brother would have almost as negative an effect on Johnny McGlynn's reputation as using Archdiocesan money. Jimmy's testimony hadn't helped Johnny much, and it hadn't helped me at all. The mystery of John McGlynn was still mysterious.

The Bishop of Alton tugged at his enormous French cuffs, a gesture in which he engaged at least once every five minutes. Louis Kane was prim, prissy, proper, and pompous, an aging kewpie doll with thin silver hair, petulant eyes, and a face shaped by permanent self-pity.

He had taken it for granted that he would succeed John McGlynn as Archbishop of Chicago. From that slight, as he perceived it, he would never recover.

We were sitting in his elaborate suite in the new Four Seasons hotel across from the John Hancock Center at the north end of Chicago's Magnificent Mile.

"I'm glad you were able to find time to meet with me, Bishop."

"I came to Chicago only to meet with you. At the Cardinal's request, you may be sure."

He was sitting at a desk in the middle of the parlor of his suite, a desk arranged to give the illusion he was in his office in Alton and that I was a suppliant priest. He arranged a manuscript on the desk so that the four corners were in their proper position. Fussy, stupid little man.

"We want to clear up this matter of the alleged virtue of the Cardinal's predecessor."

"I will do that for you," he snapped. "When you have my testimony, you will need nothing else."

"I'm glad to hear that."

"I have"—he fussed with his papers—"compiled a narrative. I will read from it. You may take notes if you wish. After I read from it I will destroy the narrative in your presence. I assure you that there are no copies of it. You may use only one direct quote from me and that is as follows: I know it to be a fact that John Arthur McGlynn was not a celibate in his days at the North American College . . . would you write that quote down please, Father?"

"Oh, yes, certainly."

What I wrote down was, *Thank God we got Steve instead of this little jerk.*

"You understand that this is all deep background?"

"Yes, Bishop."

"You do know what deep background means, Father?"

"It's the superlative of 'off the record,' the comparative of being 'on background.'"

"Very well. Now I will begin."

21

Initially I was greatly attracted to John McGlynn when we both arrived at the NAC in 1950. He was a personable and attractive man. His good spirits helped us all through the difficult transition from America to Europe and the attendant homesickness. Since we were both from Illinois, it was natural that he and I became relatively close friends.

He also found almost instant favor with the Seminary authorities, who it seemed to me are always and everywhere attracted to handsome athletes. Yet to give him due credit, he did not lord his position as a favorite over the rest of us.

"They certainly like you, John," I remember saying to him during our first year in Rome.

"It doesn't mean a thing, Killer, not a thing. The only payoff is that I get out of here a little bit more often to show the Rector's friends around Rome. To tell the truth, they're dull. Except sometimes"—he winked at me—"the women."

"What do you mean by that?" I asked, more puzzled than disturbed.

"What do you think I mean?"

The plain implication was that he was engaging in sexual

activities with the women. I could not believe that implication at first because the risks were too great and John was too smart to take such risks. Nonetheless, I resolved that for the good of the Church and the good of the College I would monitor his behavior closely.

I must emphasize that he did not frequent Roman prostitutes of a lower class, as did a few of our fellow students at the North American and many students from other seminaries. John's conquests, if I may use the word, were American women visitors in Rome, often women to whom he was assigned to act as a guide at papal audiences. His good looks and his charm made him in the mind of our unperceptive Rector the ideal person for such a role.

One day, again I am quite clear that it was during our first year, I saw him leave the college with a small party of Americans, one of whom was an attractive woman perhaps in her late twenties or early thirties. John was walking next to her and talking to her with more familiarity than I thought proper.

As they passed me, John turned and winked again. Do I have to say that I was horrified?

The next day, while John and I were taking our passeggiata, our little walk, after lunch, he told me in rich clinical detail what he had done to the woman. I cannot even now overcome my modesty to recount those details. One must be satisfied with the notion that there had been a great deal of sexual activity.

"John," I finally exclaimed, "that was a terrible mortal sin."

"Was it?" He seemed unimpressed. "Several theologians back in the Middle Ages thought that fornication was not really a serious sin. I agree with them. What harm did I do? I didn't hurt her. I'd never hurt a woman. It made both of us happy for a couple of hours. Why not do it?"

"But you might have been caught!"

He shrugged indifferently. "Not much chance. I'm careful about the ones I pick. They send me the message that they're ready, and they won't tell before I begin the seduction. And let me tell you, Killer, the process is as much fun as the event itself."

"You've done this before?"

"Now and again, Killer. Now and again."

To this day I do not understand why he insisted on telling me about them. The only reason I listened to his reports of his romps in the rooms of the Hassler or the Flora or the Grand was a hope, vain in the event, that I might be able to dissuade him from such a sinful and dangerous practice.

I must say that his natural shrewdness and skill in the manipulation of people served him well. He was never denounced by one of his victims to the seminary authorities. I must conclude that they were willing victims and that he was most perceptive in separating the willing from the unwilling.

"Older women," he told me with his usual wide-eyed boyish enthusiasm, "are much better than younger ones, but a lot harder to seduce. It's easy enough once they let you begin to undress them, but that first button or zipper is a tough barrier to break through."

"John, I'm appalled that you are doing these things. You are breaking God's law, you are risking disease, you are putting your vocation in jeopardy."

"Don't worry, Killer, the ones I love aren't likely to have any diseases. And it's not really wrong. We've been misled by the monkish morality of our teachers and spiritual directors. They don't understand the real world. Besides, the Church was a lot better off when even the popes had mistresses."

I tried not to listen to such blasphemies, but John insisted on telling me about his escapades and I had no choice but to listen.

He continued to prosper in his Seminary life. He maintained the highest averages at the Gregorian, was top athlete in all the sports, and charmed both his teachers and the Seminary leadership. I told him he was risking it all by his affairs with women.

"Everything is under control, Killer. They'll never find out."

In the end he was correct, but nonetheless the risks were great.

"My problem," he said to me one evening when we were taking our passeggiata around the college grounds, "is that I want them all to love me."

"Isn't it the other way 'round?" I replied. "Don't you want to love all of them?"

He seemed surprised. "That's not what sex is about, Killer. It's about being loved, not about loving."

Once he showed me a picture of his family: his two brothers and his sister and another girl.

"Who is the other young woman?

"This one? Oh, that's Marbeth Reilly, she lives down the street from us."

"Is she one of your conquests?"

"Marbeth?" He seemed shocked, astonished. "Gosh, no. She's a wonderful person. One of the best."

"You don't want to be loved by her."

"Not that way," he said firmly.

I have no doubt that later he overcame those scruples.

"Do you intend to continue these affairs after you become a priest?" I demanded of him on a spring evening in Rome towards the end of our second year.

"I'll stop after I take the subdiaconate." He waved his hand vaguely. "This is just"—he smiled disarmingly—"a bit of wild oats, no harm done to anyone."

"Why will you stop then?" I demanded.

He seemed genuinely surprised. "After I make the promise of celibacy, it would be a sacrilege. I wouldn't do that."

"That's a strange kind of morality, John."

"It's the traditional morality of the real world, Killer. We'd be a lot better off here at this place if there were more of us learning about women first hand."

"You're not serious!"

"Half fun and full earnest as my mother would say."

I often pondered my obligation to report his escapades to the Seminary authorities, but held back. I did not want to be blamed for soiling his record, especially since the influence of his family with the Rector was enormous.

I now regret, deeply and profoundly regret, my lack of courage. John was the kind of person who felt honor-bound to tell the truth. If the charges were brought against him, however anonymously, he would not have denied them. Nonetheless, the Rector would have known who made the charges and it would, I am sure even today, be held against me.

His life, then, at the NAC was a sham. He pretended to be the model seminarian and was believed to be such by everyone—myself alone excepted. Some were wagering that he would be a bishop before he was thirty and certainly the first in our class to be raised to the purple. Both predictions were wrong, incidentally. In fact, I was the first member of the class to be appointed to the hierarchy. Next year I will celebrate my silver jubilee in Alton.

Nonetheless, the real John McGlynn, the man beneath the veneer of perfect seminarian, consumed, I might even say devoured, women with little regard for taste or morality. I estimate that in the first three years at the College, he made love to at least twenty women—and that's assuming that he told me about all of them, which is not necessarily the case.

After we were ordained to the subdiaconate in the spring of 1954, I heard no more from John about his conquests. But I have no doubt that he continued his old practices despite his commitment to permanent and perpetual celibacy. I had learned to recognize the signs of a conquest. John would return to the College, radiating physical well-being with a dreamy smile and a warm glow on his face—the way he would appear after a victory on the basketball court. Neither the smile nor the glow ceased during the months before his early ordination in December.

I found it ironic and just a little shameful that a man with a disgraceful secret life should be honored with early ordination while those of us who were blameless were forced to wait till the following June.

"Does your conversion to celibacy create difficulties for

you?" I asked him a week before his ordination to the priesthood.

He favored me with his most charming smile, one that had
during the three and half years at the College won over his
teachers, his superiors, and most of his fellow students.

"Not particularly, Killer. You make a commitment, you
keep it. Regardless."

"Yet it cannot be easy."

He shrugged indifferently. "My ma always says that everything is hard until you make up your mind to do it."

I have heard rumors of subsequent affairs in Africa and
Vienna and in Chicago. I cannot speak of them with any first-
hand knowledge. The only ones I know of with certainty are
the ones I have heard from John McGlynn himself.

22 As I rode down the elevator I remembered the ancient clerical joke. Why are there more horses than horses' asses in the Catholic Church? Because the horses' asses are in the saddle.

A good defense attorney could have torn Killer apart. It was all hearsay evidence. Johnny might have been pulling his leg all along. He hated Johnny because Johnny had come to Chicago instead of himself. His testimony was biased and dubious.

But not necessarily inaccurate, damn it all. John might well have screwed around in the seminary. He wouldn't be the first or the last. That possibility did not completely preclude sanctity, not unless I found stronger evidence.

Marbeth was still the issue. Tomorrow I would visit her at Lake Geneva.

In my room I checked the file of clippings that Don Price had prepared for me. I glanced (again) through the fluff that Chicago had produced when they named Mary Elizabeth one of the fifteen most beautiful women in Chicago—relentless hater, ball-breaker, tough little bitch, first-rate mind, brilliant planner and administrator, afraid of no one, not even the Pope.

That's my Mary Elizabeth!

Her brothers all live within two blocks of her: Iggy (Ignatius Loyola), two doors away on Lathrop; Franny (Francis Borgia) and Ally (Aloysius Gonzaga) on Franklin. Called the matriarch of the clan, half fun and full earnest. Four homes— River Forest, Lake Geneva, County Galway, and San Diego. Drove a Mercedes and a Porsche—sold her Testarossa. On the board of everything, including Notre Dame, where her kids all went despite the Jesuit names in the family.

I put the article aside. The picture was proof that she deserved the title of one of the fifteen most beautiful. It gave a hint, if you looked at it long enough with the right predisposition, that the real Marbeth was a sensitive and fragile woman, not so much hiding behind the top financial administrator as coexisting with her.

My favorite Marbeth article was one that I had clipped and saved myself. The column described the less than enthusiastic farewell at John's burial—only a few bishops showed up, and Killer Kane in the eulogy never once mentioned the manner of his death.

> I approach his lifelong friend Mary Elizabeth Quinlan, who stands at the graveside with her children, the women all in deep black mourning.
>
> "What," I ask her, "do you say about the Pope's refusal to attend the funeral?"
>
> Her brown eyes dry and implacable, Quinlan replies calmly, "You can quote me as saying that I think the Pope is a prig."
>
> What of the future? A silver-haired priest responded to that question: Nodding his head in the direction of the open grave, he said, "Even the Pope will have a hard time keeping Jumping Johnny in the ground!"

Yeah, I was the silver-haired priest. I spoke to them all. They were cordial. Caroline hugged me. Marbeth smiled at me.

"He loved you, Lar."

"I wasn't the only one."

She smiled again.

I didn't hear the quote, but I don't doubt it for a moment. Vintage Marbeth.

On the way out to Marbeth's I made one more stop, almost on an impulse, to see Jamie's mother, Maggie Ward Keenan. Before probing further into the issue of Johnny's celibacy, I felt it important to get her reading on this aspect of his character. After all, Mama Maggie had, in addition to her well-deserved reputation as an eminent psychologist, an uncanny intuitive feel for people. Between that and her psychoanalytic training, she was quite a formidable judge of character and personality. And, unlike anyone else I'd spoken to about the late John Cardinal McGlynn, she had no ax to grind.

When I arrived at their large Cape Cod cottage on the North Shore of Lake Geneva, less than half a mile from the Quinlan home, Maggie took me out to sit on the pier behind her house. It was not as large or as elaborate as Marbeth's, but still in the top five percent of Lake Geneva homes. A gentle layer of clouds protected us from the sun, and the water was calm. Already many of the kids were back in school, and families were deserting the resort regions, far ahead of time.

Maggie was a pretty woman, rather short and slender, with large, expressive eyes and a quite determined chin. The lines on her face made her seem wise and dignified but not old, an impression that her carefully arranged gray hair confirmed.

As usual, when I told her my quest she was direct and to the point. "With that powerful and dominating mother, I would not want to rule out the possibility of latent homosexuality."

"Oh," I said, gulping. "But what about his so-called relationship with Marbeth?"

"I know Mary Elizabeth somewhat better than I knew him," Maggie went on to say. "Remarkable woman, only I wish she would smile more."

"It's an astonishing smile once you do see it."

"Ah, so you have seen it?" She eyed me carefully, adding a new fact to the rapidly spinning hard disk which was her brain. "They live in St. Luke's, as we do, and some of my children were in school at the same time as hers. Your associate and the young woman who married that adorable Jewish doctor, for example—the mother of the child who was healed by the miracle."

"Do you think it was a miracle, Maggie?"

She just smiled and returned to the issue of latent homosexuality.

"You must not think, Lar, that I'm suggesting the late Cardinal was gay or much less that he had gay lovers, save perhaps in a passing adolescent phase. Nor that he lacked tendencies to womanize. The latent homosexual, as I'm sure you understand, is a man who is in doubt about his masculinity, often because of the presence of a dominating and, indeed, overwhelming mother. He pursues success with women—success of whatever kind and, mind you, I suggest no necessary violations of the celibacy requirement—to reassure himself of his masculinity. However, without sustained psychoanalysis or some kindred therapy, such success does not dispel his doubts and, indeed, often aggravates them."

"Oh."

She poured me a cup of tea from the pot in front of us.

"The Don Juan of myth and legend is a classic case of latent homosexuality. Thousands of conquests and no satisfaction."

"Oh."

"By definition, the latent homosexual is latent. When he comes painfully to terms with this trait through lengthy treatment, he is often liberated enough from his unconscious fears about his own sexual identity to discover that he is, in fact, a heterosexual, albeit perhaps not so compulsive a womanizer as he once was."

"Somebody like that could hardly be a saint, could they?"

I was hoping she would say no, because that would pretty much solve my problem.

"Why not, Lar?" She lifted a hand as if to dismiss my question. "Obviously, homosexuals of either sex have become priests, bishops, popes. Why not saints? Celibacy may be a requirement of canonization, but hardly sexual orientation. Presumably sanctity is what we do with the deck that we are dealt."

"The Sacred Congregation for the Causes of Saints would probably not agree with that assumption."

"Poor dear men. . . . In any event, such a person in mature years often chooses as a companion a substitute mother figure who will nurture and support him and reassure him of his heterosexuality without making too many overt sexual demands on him."

"I see."

"Enter the excellent Marbeth. She fits the pattern perfectly, Lar," she said soothingly. "Fortunately for her and for your late friend, she is the kind of nurturing mother who manages weak men instead of dominating them. Thus the man is permitted to maintain his male illusions and perhaps even develop some authentic masculine selfhood. This is delightful for him, of course, but arduous and often unrewarding for her."

"Were they lovers?"

"Does it matter?"

"So I should address myself not to the question of whether John McGlynn and Mary Elizabeth Quinlan slept in the same bed on one occasion or another, but rather the question of whether the quality of the relationship between the two of them might have changed the direction of his life?"

She shrugged. "Only if you accept my admittedly wild and almost irresponsible speculation as valid. In any case I worry more about Mary Elizabeth, whose behavior it seems to me has been truly saintly. What happens to her now? Must she wait around for another man to manage? Are not two times more than enough?"

"She might marry again?"

"She has what she is pleased to call a suitor."

"An acceptable one?"

"Oh, my, yes; and I have that on the word of the ineffable Caroline, who is an expert on her mother's dates. However, most such women would be afraid to risk themselves on a man they need not and could not manage. The odds are that she will turn away from this suitor. More tea?"

"No, thanks." I stood up and prepared to leave. "Thanks a lot. I may just come back."

"As I understand the way you Irish politicians play the game, one favor deserves another. . . . If you should find the opportunity, would you encourage Mary Elizabeth to accept her suitor—and as quickly as possible?"

That request stopped me cold. "You want me to instruct her to marry this man?" I said in amazement.

"Instruct." Maggie Ward shrugged a shoulder. "Suggest, advise, order—choose your own label. It all comes to the same."

We were walking up the pier toward the house.

"She's not the kind of woman who would marry a man just because a priest told her to do so."

"That depends," Margaret Mary Ward Keenan observed, "on who is the priest, doesn't it?"

23 Fifteen minutes later I was walking up the path to Mary Elizabeth's door.

"Lar." She grabbed my hand and with the same fluid movement planted a kiss on my lips, a kiss which seemed to me to linger a little longer than it had to. "You even look more mellow. See, my prediction was right, wasn't it?"

"Not at all." I stumbled over the words. "I'm as much a boor as I ever was."

"Not true." My hand still a captive, she led me up the walk to the front porch of her vast summer home. "Maggie Ward says she thinks you are a wonderfully sweet man."

"Calumny," I protested, "though it would be worth my life to be caught disagreeing with the magnificent Maggie."

"Carie, you remember Father Lar, don't you?"

That worthy child had come bursting out of the door of the house.

"Sure I do, Mommy, he came to the hospital the night I did that silly thing, didn't he?"

I was properly hugged and kissed again. "All better," I said, repeating words from the night in the hospital.

"All *better,*" Caroline agreed.

The little girl was no longer so little, and the first hints of womanhood were beginning to appear. Another dark-haired Irish lass with creamy skin and quick blue eyes. As smart as her mother? Probably. As pretty? Certainly. And more sunny and affectionate? No doubt about it.

Some things do get better.

The Quinlan summer home was on the north side of the twelve-mile-long, crystal-blue melted glacier, near the town of Lake Geneva, at the east end of the lake. In fact, the proper names were Geneva Lake for the lake and Lake Geneva for the town, a distinction that never escaped the old WASP aristocrats but with which the offspring of the Catholic immigrants could not be bothered.

The big brick Victorian homes on the north side of the lake near the town dated to that era or before—vast lawns, elaborate gardens, long piers, "summer houses" and guest lodges, elaborate wrought-iron tables and chairs arranged at strategic spots, croquet courses—an appropriate setting perhaps for a film of *The Great Gatsby*. It was not quite Long Island's North Shore perhaps, but more livable.

The WASPs had slowly yielded these gorgeous—and expensive—homes to Irish and then Italian commodity traders, real estate developers, and personal injury lawyers, with perhaps an occasional person from the "West Side" who was "connected" but not "made"—which is translated as someone on the fringes of the "outfit" but not really part of it.

It had occurred to me as I parked my car in front of the Quinlan home that Mary Elizabeth must be fabulously wealthy now to afford such a summer home. She'd inherited enough "to live on for the rest of her life, my dear" from her father. Presumably she had managed brilliantly that money as well as her late husband's development company. She had advanced far beyond the Reillys of her childhood.

"Is that the offending pool?" I gestured toward a not-quite-Olympic-size pool at the side of the house.

"Yup," Caroline agreed, "and, do you know what, Father Lar, I'm a junior lifeguard now, for when kids use the pool because the lake is too cold, and, you know what, my mommy says that when I'm a teenager I can be a lifeguard over in the beach by the town."

"I bet you'd be a strict lifeguard, Caroline."

"I hope so, Father. 'Bye, Mommy! Have a nice picnic!"

She bounded off to the smiling black woman in a white dress who had opened the front door of the house.

"Picnic?" I asked.

"Now that the sun has burned away the clouds, I thought we might take out the boat, park it somewhere in the middle of the lake, and talk there. The kids are all back in school, so there won't be any boats buzzing us. And little pitchers have big ears."

"And quick minds."

"You'd better believe. Moreover, Caroline adored John. In some ways he was like a father to her. Then there was the . . . I'll call it miracle for want of a better word. Too much talk about him upsets her, especially the slightest hint that he was less than perfect. She's normally the healthy little girl—well, not so little anymore—but on the subject of Johnny she can become quite tense."

"Understandable."

We walked around to the lake side of the house, collected a picnic basket that was awaiting us at one of the wrought-iron tables, and strolled down to the pier.

"Twenty-four-foot, two-hundred-and-fifty-horse, eight-cylinder Chrysler marine, 1935," I said. "Red leather cushions, same as the original color."

The name "Caroline" was painted on the cruiser's stern.

"Brand-new engine," she replied. "You didn't learn that on 79th Street or in St. Martha's."

"I'm glad I still amuse you."

"Always, Lar. Always . . . Bud bought this twenty years ago and let it deteriorate. I thought it deserved better. It's great for the kids when they want to tube or water-ski."

She jumped into the boat and held it against the pier so I could follow her.

"You still water-ski, Mary Elizabeth?"

"I've been known to. But the teenagers seem younger every year."

Marbeth had not changed much. Her legs were still smooth, her white shorts could still fit tightly without embarrassment, her breasts were still firm against her white tank top, the lines on her face were a gracious concession to age, as was her salt and pepper hair. At Clearwater Lake she had worn no makeup; what she wore now had been applied with a nice blend of economy and skill.

The woman had taken very good care of herself.

She turned over the ignition and the engine started promptly, almost a violation of the natural laws of marine engines.

"Remember the time we skied at Clearwater?"

"I remember you in a white swimsuit. You could probably still wear it."

"Not quite, but thank you." She pushed the boat away from the pier and inched it forward. "There are caps and sunglasses in the compartment in front of you. I don't want either of us to fry. Or get skin cancer."

"Spoken like a mother."

The caps said, "Quinlan Company."

The *Caroline* roared into life and darted at full throttle out into the middle of the lake. Nothing gentle about our start.

How many times in almost four decades had I spoken with this lovely woman? Twice at Clearwater, one night at my brother's cottage across the lake, her husband's wake, a couple of days in Ireland, a hospital in Elkhorn, an occasional chance encounter in the Loop—nothing more than that. Yet she occupied a permanent place in the fantasy region of my brain.

There was something between us that had always been there. It was nice, good, pleasant. It was also just a little risky, which made it even nicer.

She turned off the motor near a place called Black Point and opened the white wicker picnic basket.

"I have ham and cheese, roast beef, corn beef, and egg salad."

"Yes."

"All of the above? All right, I have diet Coke, white wine, and ice tea and also, just maybe, some chocolate chip ice cream, probably much better than that which you so shamefully devoured at the Villa."

"Ice tea."

She leaned against the cushioned side of the boat and trailed a hand momentarily in the crystal blue water. "Ready when you are."

"I hardly know where to begin, Mary Elizabeth."

"Then let me begin for you. We were not lovers in the ordinary sense of that word." She bit into a roast beef sandwich. "No great virtue for either of us. When one of us was ready the other was not. Some petting, particularly when we were kids. The nuns said it was a mortal sin. Johnny said that was silly and I believed him. He said it was a way of expressing love and it helped men and women prepare for marriage. I take it that he was right and that's standard teaching these days."

"Unofficial. No one has told the Vatican yet."

"Poor dears." She continued to work on the roast beef, her eyes, already excluded by her businesslike shades, bent on the sandwich. "I don't mean that we didn't love one another, I more than he. Obviously we did. For as long as I can remember. I miss him terribly. I always will. Nor do I mean that erotic emotions were completely absent from our love. I'm not that dumb. But you saw us together, did you think you were observing a love affair?"

"No . . . . Johnny became very intense about everything towards the end, didn't he?"

She pondered that thoughtfully as she refilled my iced tea glass. "I guess he did. I noticed it especially in his relationship with me, but I suppose it affected everything. I thought of it as the emergence of the real Johnny, the one that his terrible mother had not been able to destroy."

"Can you recall when that change began or what caused it?"

She picked up the second half of her sandwich. "It just seemed to happen. So slowly that I didn't notice it. Then there it was. . . . You have one more sandwich to go, Lar. Should I bring up the reserves?"

"Can't hurt."

"All right." She removed a second sandwich for herself, hesitated, and then unwrapped the wax paper. "I don't have his missing archives like that awful man hinted when he spoke with me."

"Who?"

"Your new Cardinal." She dug her teeth fiercely into the ham and Swiss on rye. "I called Len after that terrible man stumbled and bumbled and stuttered all over himself. Len didn't know either. He said that your friend had been bugging him too. Slimy ecclesiastical politician." She shuddered.

Obviously the Boss had not won her over. No new Cardinal could have.

"Sorry," she said, exhaling strongly. "It's one of the many subjects on which I get irrational. . . . I suppose," she went on, "that someone who was trying to cover up got to the files before we came back from Nicaragua. We were stuck down there for a couple of days, you remember, while the Sandinista Government and the State Department tried to score points against each other. Len said the cabinet was empty when he went into the office as soon as he got in from O'Hare. He also said that there was never much in it. Johnny was not really into privacy, not careful enough if you asked me."

"Probably."

She nodded solemnly. "Ready for the ice cream now?"

"Always."

She dished far too many scoops of chocolate chocolate chip into a paper dish. "Your next question is about the miracle, isn't it?"

I laughed and gobbled ice cream.

"You saw the tape?"

"I did."

"And?"

"And you seemed the most skeptical person on it."

"I was. And am. Nancy is head over heels into the cult. She

was always close to him, and is now absolutely convinced that Johnny is a saint. I can't blame her, poor thing. Noah is trying to figure out if he can be a Catholic and a Jew at the same time. Can he?"

"Yes, if he finds the right priest."

"That's what I told him."

"And you?"

She shrugged and refilled her wineglass. "Still agnostic—not about God, but about the miracle. Any miracle. I love Brenny something awful. But why should we be singled out for special favors? All I know is that he is a fine, healthy little boy and I'm happy about that every day."

"Noah said in the interview that there are no cases on record of spontaneous remission of retinoblastoma."

"There are in fact three such cases, one of them confirmed. That doesn't diminish Noah's faith, if that is the word. In any case, the next question you want to ask is whether I think he's a martyr and a saint—St. John of Chicago, bishop and martyr, correct?" She began to tidy up the remnants of our picnic with quick, efficient movements. No mess tolerated on her 1935 Chris-Craft.

"What's your answer to that?"

"I'm not sure what a saint is—I suppose everyone says that, don't they? But whatever a saint might be, I have a hard time applying the word to him. That might be true of everyone who knew someone who turned out to be a saint. He was a kind and good man who did his best in a job that he did not want but could not refuse. I find that admirable certainly, but not saintly."

"He did a good job with your help," I said.

"Mine among others, for what mine was worth. The point is that there was practically no one to whom he could turn for help when he came. But I didn't mean Chicago. I meant the priesthood. As I told you that lovely afternoon at Watersmeet—when you were so sympathetic to a silly adolescent—Johnny did not want to be a priest. He was supremely qualified for it by personality and intelligence, and everyone thought that was enough. But he did not want to be a priest and did not like being a priest. A priest, especially a diocesan priest like you and Johnny, has to relish parish work. Johnny liked people and was great with them, but he hated that parish in Putnam Park he was in for five years, every single moment of it."

"The Pastor was nuts," I said.

"That only made it worse. Johnny just didn't fit the job. He tried hard to make himself fit and succeeded so well that everyone thought he liked being a priest. Actually he hated it. He hated everything he ever did in the priesthood, but by sheer intelligence and willpower made himself good, or good enough at his work, so good that everyone thought he was happy."

Later it would occur to me that one of the reasons for the ride on the lake was that it provided her with a pretext for wearing glasses which masked her eyes—and the possible but unlikely appearance of tears.

"I just wish that Delia had arranged her priorities a little differently," she continued. "John would have made a wonderful lawyer or doctor, wouldn't he? And he'd have been perfectly happy in either profession. And either Jim or Mick would have been a good priest. She cast them in the wrong roles, poor dumb bitch."

Leaning back against the cushions, she trailed her hand in the water again, a movement which outlined her breasts against her top.

We sat quietly, our faces touched by the lightest of late summer breezes. After what seemed like years I decided that I must say something.

"Why would John be happy as a lawyer or a doctor and not as a priest? Celibacy?"

"Certainly no. Most of the time that was not a great problem for him, once he made up his mind."

"What, then?"

"I can't believe how stupid I was that day in Watersmeet when I said he didn't believe in God. But he did tell me that he was 'religiously insensitive,' not tuned in on religious things. He'd heard some sociologist say that there were people like that and he thought he fit perfectly."

"It was different in the end, wasn't it?"

"Oh my gosh, yes. He became almost a religious fanatic. The doubts, if you can call them that—they were always kind of vague and formless—would come back but they didn't affect his life."

"I understand."

"No, you don't. I was closer to him than anyone else on earth and I don't understand. I don't think anyone knew the real Johnny McGlynn, including Johnny himself."

She fiddled with the ignition key, drained by our dialogue and eager to be done with it, though no more eager than I was.

"Better man or worse?"

"Different. More serious, more anxious, more worried about people. Less worried about the Pope or the other bishops, more—the word sounds strange after what I've been saying— spiritual. I asked him if he had noticed that he was different. He denied that anything had happened, but I was sure he knew better. It was like . . . But"—she shook the ignition key impatiently—"that would have been so unlike him. Still, he was living on a high wire just before we went to Central America, stressed out to the limit, no sleep, restless. He would have driven himself into the ground eventually. Probably ruined his health and killed himself. Yet . . ."

"I've had enough, Mary Elizabeth."

"Me too. More than enough. I'm writing a memoir. It will all be there anyway. Less contentious maybe."

"I don't think you've been contentious."

She patted my hand. "I think I also said in 1952 that you were a sweet boy. You're still sweet."

"Thank you, Mary Elizabeth."

"Understand"—she put the key into the ignition—"that I always loved him. I still love him. I always will love him." She started the engine.

"You do still water-ski, Lar? Haven't I seen you out on the lake with nieces and nephews?"

"Long in the tooth for it, but I still do. You?"

"Not quite so long in the tooth, but I do indeed. I tell you what, let's go back, collect the Princess Caroline, and undo the mistake you made at Camp Saint George in 1952."

Before I could disagree, the 250 horses inside of *Caroline* came alive. I had no chance to decline the suggestion that we ski.

So we did.

Mary Elizabeth wore a white swimsuit which somehow seemed the same as the one from almost four decades before. To my longing eyes she looked at least as beautiful as she did then. Both of us were still capable of slaloming with some degree of proficiency, which was more than the upstart Caroline could do quite yet.

"By the time I'm a teenager, I'll be better than either of you."

"No argument there," I admitted as I pulled in the ski rope.

Marbeth laughed often during the afternoon and smiled almost always. I had never seen her happy, even transiently happy. It was quite an improvement, one that made her utterly irresistible.

Later, she and Caroline served me swissburgers cooked on the outdoor grill. Then she kissed me again and I drove back to Forest Springs, leaving Mary Elizabeth drifting back into memories of the past, reliving again her youthful crush on Johnny.

MARY
ELIZABETH

|| 24 || "Do you believe in God now?" I demanded outside the Grand Hotel across from the Stazione Termini in Rome.

John shifted from one foot to the other. His eyes danced nervously.

He was, I had noted as soon as I had seen him, more handsome than ever. And, in his new priestly robes, even more gracious and charming. The priesthood fit him, I had to admit, like a tailor-made glove fits a hand.

"Some of the time, Marbeth."

It was a cold winter evening in Rome just before Christmas. Red lights decorated the front of the terminal and the buildings around. Our breath turned to mist in the frosty air. John had been ordained that day. We are about to celebrate with a vast banquet in the hotel. The two of us, by unspoken mutual agreement, had trailed behind the other guests, to write finis to our romance. Or rather to my romance. The piazza in front of the terminal was crowded with cars and noisy, though not as noisy as it would become in later years when Italy caught up with the prosperity that was sweeping Western Europe in the early fifties. We had to shout to make ourselves heard. Not exactly the right atmosphere for a nostalgic farewell.

"That's what you said before."

"Twice." He wouldn't look at me.

"How can you be a priest?"

My crush returned in full force when we went to Rome for his Ordination and First Mass. I kept it under control because he was now a priest and I was engaged. But at the slightest hint from him, I would have thrown my pretty new ring in the Tiber.

"Are you sure?" I demanded.

"More or less," he replied.

He hesitated and then tried again. "I can't explain it, Marbeth. I like women, as I don't have to tell you. I'm not sure what it is about being a priest that I will like. I don't think that I'll be a very good priest—I have too many faults. Maybe what happened here this morning is a big risk for me. Yet I am absolutely certain, as certain as I am that you're wonderfully beautiful and that the sun will rise in the morning, that I should be a priest. I . . ." He hesitated. "There's something I must do, but I don't know yet what it is."

"If I have to lose you, John," I said, tears welling up in my eyes, "I don't mind losing you to God, so long as I'm sure that it's God."

"You're not losing me, Marbeth. We'll always be friends."

"I'm not sure about that, John. I wonder if we can ever be just friends. Not your fault. Mine . . . for throwing myself at you so often."

I was able by then to hold back the tears, but not the self-pity, of which I would always be thoroughly ashamed.

He laughed easily. "You didn't throw yourself at me, Marbeth, furthest thing in the world from it."

"Well, what did I do then?"

"You made me an offer, a sweet and beautiful offer." He touched my shoulder gently. "The memory of which I'll always treasure."

"I felt cheap afterwards." I looked away from him.

He laughed again, this time more vigorously, and tightened his grip on my shoulder. "It wasn't a cheap offer, Marbeth. Don't ever think that. It was a glorious one, filled with laughter and love and promise and goodness. Anyone would have been enormously flattered by the offer." He took possession of my other shoulder. "I sure was."

"But you didn't want me," I said stubbornly, refusing to accept his absolution.

"Sure I wanted you. I said it to you then and I meant it. I'll never forget your fragile gift of your whole self. It will always be etched on my brain. If I had been chosen to marry, it would have been to you or someone very like you." Even as he was talking I felt a certain sneaky skepticism. The words came to him a little too easily. Still, he was being very kind. Some of my shame was being wiped away.

"I see."

I didn't see. But I admit that I was intrigued by the sense of mystery in what he had said. Also I wanted to part friends.

"Do you really see, Marbeth?"

"Well, not really. But you see, and that's what counts. May God make you a good priest."

"He'll have His work cut out for Him." John laughed at himself again. "Come on—let's go in and get something to eat!"

He kissed me on the forehead and released my shoulders. The image was perfect: a handsome and vigorous young man who was giving up a young woman he found attractive for someone more important. It struck me then that maybe it was ninety-percent true. Or maybe only sixty-five-percent true.

That was that. I was a smart young woman. I was engaged. I had a life ahead. I would follow the advice that Lar McAuliffe had forced me to give myself—cut my losses and get on with life.

|| 25 || "What's he doing?" Bud said, unable to conceal his astonishment.

"He's unrolling toilet paper," I replied, equally astonished, "and spreading it out on the lawn of the schoolyard."

My fiancé and I were standing hand in hand in front of St. Egbert's Rectory in the Far South Side of Chicago. It was ten months later, and Johnny had been brought back to serve as a priest in a local parish in poorer sections of the Archdiocese. The Rectory was an old wooden house on a side street. The big parochial school stretched out behind it, a white brick building filled with kids. They would soon come out at two-thirty, in neat, orderly ranks, and see poor Johnny, in cassock mind you, unrolling toilet paper.

I had heard that his pastor was a cruel psychotic, but this was too much.

"John, can we help?" I ran up to him, Bud trailing behind me.

"Marbeth." He embraced me and shook hands with Bud. "Wonderful to see you!"

"Uh, what are you doing?" Bud asked.

"What does it look like?" He laughed. "Unrolling toilet paper."

"Why?" I demanded.

"The Pastor bought a huge shipment for the school year and stored it in the Rectory basement." He shrugged. "It was soaked in a backup of the sewers during a rainstorm—you can kind of smell the sewers—and he wants it to dry out."

"The miserable bastard!" I shouted.

"Calm down," he said softly. "It doesn't bother me."

"Well, it bothers me!"

"You're marrying a beautiful, fierce wife, Bud," he said to my intended.

"Don't I know it."

"Who are these people?" A little old priest in a dirty cassock, with long white hair and pitiless eyes sunk in a withered face, appeared next to us.

"Friends of mine from my old neighborhood, Father," John said with, I thought, a touch of weariness.

"You don't have my permission to talk to them. Finish your task."

"We want him to officiate at our marriage." I was spoiling for a fight.

"Are you from this parish? I do all the marriages here."

"No, we're not."

"He will not receive my permission to officiate at a marriage in another parish."

His diabolic face glowed with happiness.

I jabbed my finger in his face. "Look, you miserable bastard—he will too officiate at my marriage. If you try to stop him, I'll go to the Cardinal himself."

"He will not," the old man screamed, now a little frightened by the banshee he had encountered.

"You're a vicious, evil, sick old man," I shouted. "Don't you dare get in my way or I'll send you to hell, where you belong."

"Get off my property!" he shouted back.

"Come on, Bud, let's help Johnny clean up this mess."

"You do not have my permission to touch that material," the old man snarled.

Then I had an idea. Not for nothing was I a lawyer's daughter.

"Do you want me to file a complaint with the Board of Health about your using contaminated toilet paper? What will the Cardinal think of that?"

The old man turned on his heel and stormed away.

"Will we cause you more trouble if we help?" Bud asked.

"Things couldn't be worse than they are," he said grimly, "but I don't want you—"

"Let's get to work," I said.

When the kids poured out of school, they spontaneously rushed over to help.

So they liked John.

"I think you scared him off." John was his cheerful self again. "Normally he'd be out here chasing the kids away from me."

"You will do our wedding, no matter what he says."

"I'd be afraid not to!"

As we drove back to River Forest I thought to myself that John might have done better with me—an inappropriate idea, I suppose, for a maiden on the verge of her wedding—than with God.

At our rehearsal dinner, with Bud and his half of the wedding party already pretty well drunk—a condition in which he took refuge from a week before our wedding until well into our so-called honeymoon, I asked Johnny about parish work.

"I don't mind Father so much." He shrugged. "He's crazy, but the people are good."

"And they like you?"

"I guess so. They seem to."

"So you must be doing good work with them."

"It's easy, Marbeth. All you have to do is smile and be nice to them and friendly with their kids and say the right things at the right times."

"What right times?"

"Baptisms, wakes, weddings, funerals . . . you know, the times when people need or want a priest."

"Is that hard?"

"I felt awkward at first. My words seemed kind of empty. I felt like I was mouthing clichés in response to terrible tragedy or great joy. They don't think so. It's what they expect a priest to say."

"It's important to them that you say those things?"

"Terribly."

"You like saying them?"

He frowned as he tried to think through an answer. "I wish I believed them more strongly than I do. Somehow, if I had greater confidence in what I say, they wouldn't sound like clichés to me and maybe even mean more to them."

We were back on the God question again.

"But they seem satisfied?"

"Oh, yeah. They think I'm a good priest."

"Are you?"

"Not very good, I'm afraid. I only wish I had deeper faith . . . there are times when I believe, as you well know, Marbeth, and times when I don't."

The electrical current bouncing back and forth between us was getting stronger. Part of me said that this was not a conversation I should be having with a priest the night before my wedding. Another part said that I was marrying the wrong man.

"What about you and Bud?"

"I'm not sure, John," I blurted out.

"Most people aren't the night before their wedding."

I wanted support and affection. He responded with a truism.

"He's been drunk for a week."

"He's frightened, Marbeth. Most men are more frightened at this time than are their brides. They show their fear differently, that's all."

"What's he got to be frightened about?"

"Marriage, life, you."

John was right. Poor Bud was afraid of all three. He should have married a woman he could have dominated.

If my conversation with John had continued, I might not have marched down the aisle of St. Luke's the next day. As it was, my mother dragged me away to face a new crisis about the floral displays. We never finished that conversation.

I was not surprised that John was unhappy in the parish. How could it have been any different? But the unhappiness was not because of his pastor. Or even because his career was sidetracked. He was unhappy because he had begun to suspect, I told myself, that he had made the wrong decision. Again I thought that he would have been much happier if he had accepted my offer. It was too late now, too late for both of us.

I wondered briefly about what had happened to Delia's influence. How long would it be before she freed him?

As it was, it took five years to persuade the Cardinal to send him back to Rome, two years longer than it would have taken, I was told by the priest at our parish after Bud and I came back from our honeymoon, if Delia had kept her mouth shut.

"The old man likes him and doesn't want to have him wither on the vine," the priest said, "but he can't stand that vulgar biddy that's his mother."

Delia, the pretty and adored second mother of my childhood, a vulgar biddy? Had she deteriorated that much?

Well, my childhood was over. There was nothing I could do about poor John McGlynn. He was a love from my childhood. I was now a mature woman about to acquire a husband and a family. Childhood dreams should be put aside as innocence is lost. At almost twenty, I could look ahead with clear eyes.

A conviction which shows how innocent I still was.

|| 26 || The next morning I woke up terrified. I'd been dreaming about sleeping with Johnny. I realized I was not as immune to his appeal as I had hoped. And making it worse still, this was the morning of my wedding day.

Despite my graphically passionate dream, I actually knew very little about sex. Oh, I understood the particulars, but having no personal experience beyond my furtive tumbles with Johnny, I was terrified at what would happen at the Drake Hotel that night, with good reason as it turned out—though I was not humiliated as poor Bud was. I had not drunk myself into a stupor so that I might be able to perform and thus guarantee that I could not.

I had been uncertain about the marriage for weeks. I had almost called it off two weeks before. I'd like to think I was prescient about Bud, that I had begun to see flaws in him that I would recognize in much greater detail on our honeymoon and in later years.

"Maybe I'm too young to get married," I had told my mother.

My mother was sympathetic to me in her words. "You don't

have to get married now," she said softly. "Maybe you should wait six months."

"The first banns have already been announced."

"Marriages are often postponed after the first banns, dear."

For years I blamed her because she did not stop me from marrying Bud. (I never accused her of it, however; I kept up the pretense with her and Dad that the marriage was working out fine.) Now I realize that she thought quite correctly that I was a nervous young bride who was frightened by imaginary demons.

One more sentence from me to her and we would have put the wedding off.

Why didn't I speak that sentence?

I hate to admit the truth. I was afraid of the embarrassment of a postponement or, worse, a cancellation after the banns had been announced. I brought everything that happened after that on myself.

I was a nervous wreck the morning of my wedding, mostly because of my dream but also because my mother's state of nervous exhaustion verging on despair had finally over-whelmed me too.

Mom wanted the wedding to be perfect—dresses, flowers, veils, music, ceremonies, photographs, ten bridesmaids in pink, two little cousins (scared stiff) carrying rings and flowers, nine priests and two monsignors in the sanctuary, everything.

Unfortunately, you can't have a perfect wedding, because humans make mistakes. So you have two choices: either you try for a perfect wedding and drive all the women to tears, or you decide to go for a happy wedding. Mom made the former choice. I was so worried about marriage that I did not have the strength to fight her.

"Mom," I would beg, "it doesn't matter."

"It's your only wedding and you're my only daughter," she would sniffle. "I want you to be the happiest bride in the world."

Which attitude, naturally, guaranteed that I would not be. She and Mrs. Quinlan had communicated through intermediaries for two weeks before the wedding because they were so angry at each other. I was in tears every day—Marbeth, who never cries. Bud was impossible, pretending to be nonchalant and casual. The goons who were his friends gave him a hard time about all he was giving up by acquiring a "ball and chain." He warned me repeatedly that he had no intention of giving up his "guys," and I had to get used to that fact. If I didn't like it, he sneered, I could call off the marriage.

I told him that he was a stupid pig and that if he was afraid of marriage, he could call it off, and then refused to talk to him.

It was like sticking a pin in a balloon that a kid has blown up too big. Bud was not used to women who refused to adore him.

Maybe I should have been more sensitive to and sympathetic to his fears—then and later. Maybe a lot of things would have been different later on. Maybe. . . . But I was an innocent kid with no sense of how much men feared women then. Later, I was trying to save what was left of my marriage.

It's useless to think back on those things. It's all much too late now.

So I walked down the aisle, conscious that everyone was looking at me and that they all admired the beauty of the radiant bride they were watching.

I also knew that my radiance was phony and that given the slightest chance I would have run. Bud looked like I felt, like he too would run if he could find an excuse. Poor dumb man, he couldn't cover up as well as I could.

There, watching it all, with a happy smile on his face, was John McGlynn, the man whom, I thought as I saw that smile, I should be marrying.

"Hi, Marbeth." He grinned at me as I walked up the altar steps, leaning against Bud. "Are you coming or going?"

The same greeting as I had heard on the Desplaines Street El tracks. Did he realize that? I wonder.

I mumbled something incoherent.

He was gorgeous in elaborate Gothic vestments. His smile

shone on me like the morning sun. His voice poured over me like the waters of a warm shower. His handshake after I was pronounced man and wife with Anthony Quinlan was a faint touch of bliss. His palm resting on my head during the nuptial blessing sent a current of excitement to the toes of my feet.

I was nervous, excited, and frightened. But now I was also confident. John thought I was a sweet and delicious gift. So I was. So I would be. I would offer myself completely to my new husband. If Bud didn't appreciate me enough, that would be his problem.

"Thanks, John," I whispered as we turned to walk back down the aisle after the final blessing at the end of Mass.

"Delighted," he said, as if he really meant it.

Did he see me as someone who might have been his bride? Even today I don't know for sure, but I doubt it. There was another drummer to whom John was listening, though one that beat both infrequently and inconsistently.

Yet John calmed me down that morning by his kindness and affection. His warmth permeated my body and soul, a promise of joy and happiness. I was filled with peace and serenity after Mass, and at the reception and even later on in our room at the Drake, I was as self-possessed as always.

Disappointed and hurt and angry and frustrated after Bud and I consummated our union—if that's what one should call what we did—but still, damn it all, Marbeth the woman in control of everything.

I was not the problem. Rather, the problem was a man who was too drunk and too frightened to be capable of arousal by a naked and willing bride on their wedding night.

What would I be like if I were not the kind of woman who was always in control? I'd cry more easily and more often. And I wouldn't be me.

But I did not lose the memory of those moments of peace and joy in St. Luke's church. Not ever. The memory gave me courage later in life when I would need it, which would be often.

27 I took charge of my marriage in Bud's office in Elmwood Park a couple of weeks before our first anniversary. As a coup d'état, it was simplicity itself. I had been planning it for some time and was merely waiting for the proper time to strike.

A few months of marriage to Bud convinced me that he was something less than a bargain. He was not a particularly bad man. He did not push me around physically, except once or twice, and I quickly put a stop to that. Moreover, for all his locker-room bravado, he wasn't much good in bed.

The honeymoon, in the best hotels in Europe as befit our station in life, was a mixture of misery and pain and frustration for me, and of diminishing self-confidence and arousal from him. Ugh. I still shudder when I think of it.

I discovered rather soon that he was, more than anything else, a weak and anxious man and terrified of me. He was also a prude, afraid of sex, and terribly timid in bed. Later on I would realize that many if not most locker-room commandos are cut from the same bolt of cloth. I put that knowledge to good use and began to make as much as I could of him, the best of a rather bad bargain.

Some young wives of my generation were content to complain and feel sorry for themselves when it turned out that their big-talk small-deed husbands were inept lovers. I decided that was not nearly enough. So I learned how lovers might "improve their performance" as it was said, and began to improve ours.

There are other women like me, I have since learned, almost all of them happily and blissfully married to husbands who adore them. But we tend to maintain a conspiracy of silence lest other women ridicule us.

The only thing I had learned during the honeymoon—and it was worth the misery of that trip to learn it—was that poor Bud was so much in awe of me that he would do whatever I told him to do so long as he could pretend to himself that it was his idea. I had no need to humiliate him, so I let him believe that all my ideas were his.

So that night, after nearly a year of marriage, I decided it was time to make my major move. Our sex life had improved, but now I was ready to take it to a level that would insure my permanent satisfaction.

I had promised to pick Bud up at his office after work. We were due to attend a Fenwick alumni dinner dance, so I was dressed to kill.

The office was empty; everyone had gone home. When I sauntered in, Bud was working over the books, his face twisted in bafflement.

"What's wrong?" I asked.

"Something seem to be missing here, but I can't quite see it."

I took off my mink coat. Not a word from him about how nice I looked in my black strapless dress. We'd have to change that too.

"Let me see."

"Women don't know anything about bookkeeping," he said, but passed the ledger over to me.

Despite my double major in English Literature and Philosophy, I could see in five seconds that a couple of his vendors were robbing him blind. Suitably led, he came to the conclusion that they were and that it was his discovery.

"Those bastards are robbing me blind," he announced proudly.

I realized then, though dimly that night because I had other things on my mind, that I would have to take over the business if I wanted our as yet unconceived children to be able to attend college.

As he began to see the pattern of theft in the book, he amused himself by fondling me.

I decided that I didn't need to wait until after the dance to put my plan for achieving full sexual satisfaction into effect. I began to take off my clothes.

"What are you doing, Marbeth?" he asked nervously.

"Taking off my clothes."

"Why?"

"Why do you think?"

"What if someone comes in?"

I laid my dress carefully across a chair and locked the door to his office.

"They can't come in now."

"What about the Fenwick dance?"

"Maybe we'll be a little late?" I continued my undressing.

"Marbeth!"

"Don't you like me?" I bent over and detached my nylons. I was standing only a few inches away from him so he could look down my bra—which any man in his situation would have done. I took a good long time to take off the nylons, so he could have a long look.

"Sure, but this isn't the place or the time—"

"It is too." I stood up and began to unhook my bra, black lace for the dance. "You're the one who turned me on."

That was all I needed to say to plant the notion that this was his idea. You didn't have to be very subtle with Bud.

"Yeah, but—"

"No buts, lover." I finished undressing and drew his hands to my breasts, holding them in place so he couldn't pull back without looking foolish.

"Gosh, Marbeth—I don't think we should—"

"Yes, we should." I started to undress and fondle him. His physiological response was instantaneous. No more protest or resistance. He was so aroused that he forgot his fears.

"Still worried about the dance?"

"What dance?"

I prolonged our game until he was out of his mind with passion and begged that we finish. I extended the match just a little bit longer. I was in control for the first time. It was a glorious feeling.

Despite my feeling of command, the sex itself wasn't great, but it was for me the best yet. Poor Bud never had it so good.

I wouldn't let him rest when we were finished.

"Isn't there a shower in there?"

"Marbeth," he protested, the prude again, "we shouldn't do that."

"Why not?"

"It's too—"

"Abandoned?"

"Yeah."

"Face it, darling. You married an abandoned woman. You might as well enjoy her."

I dragged him into the bathroom, turned on the shower, and pulled him into it. By the time we were soaking one another with hot suds it had become his idea. He even became convinced that he was the one who discovered that I was an abandoned and wanton woman.

Properly directed, Bud was an adequate sexual partner, so long as you didn't expect any deep love in the experience. Of that he was quite incapable. He didn't know what it was.

Could another woman, less fearsome perhaps than I, have seduced him into love? Maybe. But, on the whole, I doubt it. Bud was not a bad man. He was merely what he was, a product of a certain kind of family and environmental experience, a perennial fifteen-year-old.

We went to the Fenwick dance, at which he beamed triumphantly. Well, he should have. Not many of his locker-room buddies had a wife like he did.

Then we went back to our apartment and made love for a third time. For me that final interlude of our busy night was quite satisfactory. I'm pretty sure we conceived Beth that night, a nice touch.

Under my tutelage Bud grew into a more than presentable lover, though not as good a one as he liked to think. Because I knew that my husband would try anything—and I mean anything—I wanted, I developed into a practiced wanton. Our sexual life became the best part of a marriage which I slowly constructed out of my plans and his mix of docility and fear.

Our children would not have a mother who experienced deep love in her marital union, but they would have one who was sexually satisfied, which may be the next-best thing.

I controlled Bud with sex, not by denying him—a folly in which some women engage—but by overwhelming him. It put me in command of the marriage, not a role I would have wanted before our wedding day, but the only possible one if our union was to survive.

I managed the sex as well as everything else, including in due course the family firm which he inherited when his father died and of which he made a gosh-awful mess, as I knew he would.

There was not much left for Bud to do as the years wore on and I managed the company while raising the kids. So he was free to devote himself to his little-boy pleasures, especially golf, fishing, and hunting. As much as he enjoyed the role of paterfamilias, his greatest delight came in anticipation of, and celebration after, all-male fishing and hunting expeditions to Canada and eventually to Africa and golf expeditions around the country and then to Europe.

I was pleased to see him leave on these trips because it meant one less child of whom to keep track. He was exhilarated at the prospect of escaping from the world of women and children, which he did not understand and did not particularly like. When he joined the Ballybunion golf club in Ireland, I thought it was a crazy idea. But, poor man, he had to do something.

The all-male group—his teenage crowd continued into what passed for adulthood—was Bud's real world. There was no pretense, no self-deception required in that world, no woman to protect from the reality of family and job, no children to see through his artificial heartiness.

I drew the line only at golf clubs, shotguns, and large-bore rifles in our bedroom. I assigned a room in the basement for such toys.

He was never gone long enough for me to miss my sexual amusements. Whether he was faithful to me on his jaunts, I don't know. But on balance, it was a reasonably good marriage.

It was only when he died that I discovered that I had never really forgot about my other love, never forgot about John McGlynn.

LAURENCE

‖ 28 ‖ "Another miracle, Lar! This one live on TV."

"What time is it?" I was trying to orient myself. Where was I? Why did my back and arms hurt so much? What had I done to my body yesterday? Who's calling me at this hour when the bells are on Jamie's phone?

"Seven-fifteen"—the Cardinal's apologetic, nervous voice. "I'm sorry to have disturbed you, but I had to tell your, er, cook that it was an urgent matter."

"What's urgent?"

"The miracle. We're having a meeting at eight-thirty with Monsignor Albergeti of the Nunciature, who happens to be in town."

He paused as if I were supposed to be impressed by this information.

"So what?"

He continued with more good news. "Cardinal Ratzinger called me early this morning. He was most upset. The Holy Office, ah, the Congregation for the Doctrine of the Faith, wants us to dispose of this matter promptly."

"Good for him. Tell him to send a couple of Dominican inquisitors with thumbscrews. I'm going back to sleep."

"CNN carried the story all over the world." The Cardinal sounded like he was a hostage on a terrorist-occupied jet. "There's been an enormous reaction."

"Fine. I'm going back to sleep. I had a very difficult day yesterday."

Water-skiing, that's what I was doing. That's why my back aches.

"I really would like you to come to this meeting, Lar. It's most important."

There's enough residual respect for an archbishop in me that I didn't have much choice.

"All right, all right. I'll come. But, look—with the rush hour on the Congress Expressway, I'd never get there, even if I left an hour ago. Make it nine o'clock—and I may be a few minutes late."

"Monsignor Albergeti has an early plane back to Washington."

"Steve, three planes leave this city on the hour for D.C., four if you count Midway. Tell him to change his reservation."

I hung up, staggered through my early morning ablutions, and stumbled down the stairs to breakfast, almost killing myself as I collided with Nora at the foot of the spiral staircase.

"Damn bitch!" I informed her.

"Woof!" she responded happily, assuming as she always did that one of my complaints was a compliment.

Cook, God bless her, had prepared tea, and my resourceful associate was already at the table working at his wheat bran.

"Herself," he greeted me, "said that it was plainly a case of hysteria being cured and that you could quote her."

"Which self?"

His dreamy blue eyes widened. "Whatever self besides my mother? She saw it too and called me. By hysteria she doesn't mean the state that the Cardinal was probably in when he called you, but physiological symptoms caused by an emotional condition. The boy's doctor admitted on TV that there was no known cause of the paralysis."

"It must seem a miracle to him, nonetheless. He couldn't walk and now he can."

"Herself says it could be a permanent cure. His unconscious decided it was time to stop the hysteria and found the excuse it was looking for. It might come back, however, when the pressures in his life increase. You can never know for sure."

"This happened on live TV?"

"There was a candlelight service last night up at the Seminary in honor of Cardinal McGlynn's birthday, perhaps five hundred people."

"Shit."

"The reporter made it quite clear that the Church had not given any permission and discouraged the service."

"Which channel?"

"All of them, of course, and CNN."

"Shit."

"The cameras are focused on this kid, late teens I'd say, on crutches, his body all twisted in a knot, looking all the more terrible in the light of the flickering candles. He stumbles painfully up to the grave, touches the tombstone, screams wildly, his body goes through some apparently cruel contortions, then he throws aside the crutches and quite literally dances for joy on the Cardinal's grave. Do I have to tell you that the reporters jab cameras at him and he babbles incoherently, but quite clearly says the words 'miracle,' 'cardinal,' and 'saint'?"

"Ratzinger woke Steve up"—I put more jam on my last English muffin—"this morning with a complaint."

"CNN goes everywhere." Jamie smiled benignly. "Even to the Congregation of the Inquisition. . . . Mama Maggie says that you can tell them to say that they are investigating the medical background of the case but they have no reason at the present time to think there is any explanation other than a perfectly natural one."

"Did she say 'present time'?"

"I added that. . . . Do you want me to drive you to the train?"

I glanced at my watch. "I'd better drive. It would take an extra half hour to get across the Loop to the Chancery."

"Is the meeting only about a public statement?"

"Hell no." I swallowed a final gulp of coffee. "The Red Baron wants us to dispose of this matter promptly."

Jamie laughed. "Lots of luck, boss. What they have on their hands now is a popular cult. They can no more stop that than they can stop the Chicago River from freezing in the winter."

|| 29 || "Big night last night, Lar?" Bishop James Lane sneered at me.

The Cardinal, Don Price, Msgr. Albergeti, Bishop Lane, and Dale Foss, a "psychiatric consultant" who hangs around the Chancery, and Dolph Santini, the Archdiocesan Vicar for Liturgy, Spirituality and Art, had arranged themselves at the Cardinal's coffee table.

"I don't drink anymore," I shot back just so they'd all know what my mood was. "Which is more than I can say for you."

Jim Lane is an auxiliary that the Vatican imposed on Johnny against his will. He is a big, good-looking Irishman with white hair, red face, and a booming voice. He is also as phony as a three-headed nickel, and beneath his noisy good cheer, he's as mean and nasty and dishonest a man as it has ever been my displeasure to listen to at a clerical gathering.

He was doubtless at the meeting because Msgr. Franno Albergeti, a sleek little Sicilian criminal type with an even larger nose (not a Mafia hit man, but the guy who phones the hit man at the Godfather's instructions), is his close friend and stays at his rectory. Franno agrees with Jim Lane's unshakable convictions that (a) he would have been a better archbishop than Steve and (b) Rome expects him to monitor Steve closely so he will make fewer mistakes than he otherwise would.

Some priests will tell you that Steve shows enormous patience in tolerating Bishop Lane.

I tell them that Steve should toss Jimmy Lane out on his fat ass.

No, I don't like him at all. In all fairness to him, I should say that he detests me too.

"Lar . . ." Steve lifted his hands as if to calm me down. "Please—this is a very serious problem we have to face."

Sitting down at the empty chair and pouring my midmorning fix of Earl Grey tea from the Belleek pot that Don had arranged for me, I said, "First of all, I think it is perfectly safe to issue a statement in which you say that the Archdiocese is studying the medical evidence, but that at the present time there is no reason to think that there is not a perfectly natural explanation for the incident at the St. Mary of the Lake cemetery last night. I am assured by the most competent psychological and medical authorities that what we have is a case of hysteria, cured because the young man no longer depended on his paralysis and had been unconsciously searching for a pretext to end it. I'm sure Dale has already explained this possibility to you."

You see, even in a troublemaking mood, I was not above being helpful.

"Very good, Lar." The Boss was making notes as I talked. "We will omit the diagnosis, I presume?"

"Sure. His MD has already given it unequivocally last night."

"Will the paralysis return?" Albergeti asked Dale, not willing yet to acknowledge my existence.

"It might not," I responded.

"How unfortunate," he murmured.

"The young man might not think so."

"You are the one, Monsignor McAuliffe, who is responsible for ending this unfortunate affair?"

"I'm not a monsignor, Monsignor . . . and my only task is to make a discreet and informal investigation of the life and words of the late Jumping Johnny McGlynn to determine whether there are any positive reasons to exclude an eventual process which might lead to canonization. That's all I'm supposed to do, so I don't see why I had to be here for this meeting, with all appropriate respect for the Red Baron over in the Holy Office."

"Congregation for the Doctrine of the Faith," Jim Lane corrected me.

"How is your, ah, inquiry coming?" The Boss was almost trembling, he was so disturbed by the call from Rome.

"Look, Steve, I told you when I started that I never liked the guy. I've learned a lot more about him since then. I still don't like him, though I know enough now to begin to feel sorry for him. I don't think he was a saint. That's about it."

"This matter must be stopped," Franno said, "at once."

"Maybe we could have a study day about sanctity," Dolph suggested tentatively. He has study days in response to anything and everything.

"Close the Seminary grounds." Jim Lane, always one for the authoritarian response, insisted.

"Perhaps a pastoral letter from the Cardinal," Don Price suggested tentatively.

"You guys don't understand," I told them as I refilled my teacup, "what you've got on your hands here. It's a popular cult. You can no more stop that than you can stop the Chicago River from freezing in the winter."

Jamie's line, I admit.

"Closing the Seminary won't work. The roads are public highways, in case you've forgotten. You might get some of the local cops to keep order if the crowds get out of hand. Put a fence around the cemetery? They'd climb over it, or, worse still when the TV people find out, do their praying outside. Forget it."

"When they find the cure was of a hysteric?" Dale asked.

"He's still walking, isn't he? Anyway, the first miracle

would pass the Consulta Medica in Rome with flying colors."

"The son of a Jewish doctor," Albergeti mused. "An agnostic Jewish doctor."

"Who isn't an agnostic anymore. And, Franno, you've been here long enough to know that anti-Semitism doesn't fly in this country."

"People could come from all over the world!" Jim Lane thundered, possibly thinking of that result for the first time. "It was on CNN last night."

"Good heavens," the Cardinal groaned.

"That would doubtless help Chicago's tourism and make Mayor Rich very happy," I went on. "Come on, guys, let's talk reality for a moment. You're stuck with a popular cult and a wonder-worker. Thousands, maybe tens of thousands of people are going to stream into that little cemetery in the next year or two. That reminds me, Steve, you'd better make arrangements for sanitary facilities regardless. Sure as the sun comes up in the morning, there's a virtual statistical certainty that some of them will be hysterics whose unconscious is ready to change its needs. You might even get one or two cures that medical science cannot explain. You should be grateful that Mrs. Quinlan won't let anyone play around with the pectoral cross. That really seems to be magic."

"Ghastly." The Cardinal groaned again.

"Cardinal Ratzinger will be very angry," Franno murmured.

"Tell him to send the Swiss Guard, see if they can stop it. The cult of Johnny McGlynn is not about to go away."

"If they only understood what the Church really is," Dolph whispered. "An Archdiocesan program of instruction on the real nature of the Church perhaps. Something like the Rite of Christian Initiation of Adults."

"Maybe a personal plea from the Holy Father," Jim Lane suggested.

"If they won't obey him when he says they can't practice birth control, why will they obey him when he tells them they can't pray to Johnny McGlynn?"

"Why," the Cardinal groaned. "Why?"

"I'll tell you why, Steve. You won't like it. None of you will. Almost three decades ago the Church stirred up a lot of excitement at the Vatican Council. Since then all the lay people have heard out of the Holy See, as you like to call it, are complaints, warnings, prohibitions, and rules. In the meantime the liturgists and the theologians have taken away a lot of things the laity liked: processions, angels, saints, souls in purgatory, and the few old hymns they could sing. Then someone comes along who seems to fit the Catholic tradition they remember—a miracle-worker—and they're delighted."

"That's exaggerated," Jim Lane protested.

"The hell it is. I've got the wonder-cultists in my parish just like everyone else does. They're your ordinary, sensible, Sunday-contributing Catholics. Hell, Steve, you might have more on your hands than a cult. You might have a mass movement."

"My God . . ." The Cardinal seemed on the verge of collapse.

"What do you suggest, Lar?" Dale Foss asked. "What response?"

"The Gamaliel response."

"What is that?" Monsignor Albergeti demanded impatiently.

"Acts of the Apostles," Don Price explained to the Vatican diplomat. "Rabbi Gamaliel urged the Sanhedrin to leave the Jesus movement alone. If they were not of God, they would perish. If they were of God, it would be useless to resist them."

"Cardinal Ratzinger would not approve of delay." Monsignor Albergeti wrung his hands.

I finally had the chance to deliver the line I had been saving since breakfast.

"Fuck Cardinal Ratzinger."

As I was about to close the door behind me, the Boss recovered sufficiently to say, "You were a big help, Lar. There's nothing we can do at the present time, is there?"

I shook my head.

"You will keep us informed, won't you?"

"As soon as I have anything which looks definitive, I'll let you know."

"I expect to hear from the Holy Father himself about this matter, possibly before the day is over."

"Give him my best regards . . . incidentally, I may want to visit Rome soon."

"Is that wise?" The Boss was so frightened by the idea that one might have thought I had suggested plotting a papal assassination.

"I want to talk to some of the people at the Congregation— for Causes, not for the Doctrine of the Faith—and find out a little bit more about their criteria. You'll tell them that I'm on the level."

He had relaxed. "Of course. I'm sure they'll be happy to meet with you. They know about your inquiry, of course."

Do they now?

"I'll visit Vienna first, and possibly Warsaw."

He had considered me intently, weighing perhaps the dangers of revelations about the Solidarity money against the advantages of being able to whisper that there were certain financial improprieties in the late Cardinal's life which were most disturbing.

"That's an excellent idea, Lar." He squeezed my arm. "Send me the bills. We'll pay your way, naturally. I can't tell you how much I appreciate your help in this matter."

To be fair, I told myself as I traced the route of Johnny's nightly walk home from the Chancery on Erie Street up Michigan Avenue and Lake Shore Drive to the Cardinal's House on North State Parkway, all the money in the world couldn't buy most priests anything more than the purple buttons of a monsignor when they were still in fashion. You must have a product of some worth to go along with the money. Jumping Johnny was a good product, as his mother, Cordelia McGlynn, had discovered early in life—handsome, charming, brilliant, easy to market as an aspiring ecclesiastic. To give the devil his due, he might have made it on his own without her money.

In late summer the Magnificent Mile, the Beach, and the

Drive are crowded with men and women, a carnival of human-kind swarming to and from the Lake. Johnny McGlynn loved that walk to and from work every day, especially after Chicagoans learned his route and discovered that he would stop to talk to anyone who wanted to talk to him.

Toward the end of his life he would stroll through the underpass beneath the junction of Michigan Avenue and the Drive and wander up Oak Street Beach toward North Avenue. One heard that pictures of the Cardinal, in full clericals including pectoral cross and ruby ring, laughing with young women in bikini thongs, caused shock and dismay in Rome.

Some of those who didn't like him were prepared to give him full credit for mixing with people. I was content with the observation that it was a typical grandstand play. I'm sure his media mavens suggested the beach walk—not that Johnny would not enjoy talking to mostly nude young women.

Do you canonize that kind of man? Do you canonize a rich and ambitious son of a bitch who bought ecclesiastical promotion at the same time as he was carrying on a lifelong romance with another man's wife?

I had told the new Cardinal that I didn't think Jumping Johnny had slept with Marbeth, a stand I had taken when anyone had asked me about the relationship. Privately I was not so sure. How, I wondered, could he not have gone to bed with her, given the length and intensity of their love affair?

I suppose it says a lot about me that it was Marbeth's honor about which I was concerned, not Johnny's.

Does God permit a rich and ambitious son of a bitch who had a lifelong lover to work miracles?

I pondered that question as I ambled up the Gold Coast, the drive between the end of the Magnificent Mile at Oak Street and Lincoln Park, as the sun slipped behind the towers above.

Almost all of the private homes had long since been replaced by high-rise cooperatives and condominiums. But it was still the Gold Coast, still where the superrich lived. In a similar apartment farther north on Marine Drive, Cordelia McGlynn was living her final days, too senile to realize that her son was already an archbishop and on the highroad to his red hat, or that he had died.

Vanity of vanities and all is vanity.

I stopped in front of the Cardinal's house, a block in from the Gold Coast, restraint of sorts, though there was just enough of 79th Street left in me to resent a bishop living in a palace. I stood there contemplating the madcap Victorian pile that is the home of Chicago's Archbishop, the last home in which Johnny McGlynn had lived.

I recalled again that quick expression of pain in his deep blue eyes in the shower room at Quigley forty years ago, when I rejected his friendship. Jumping Johnny McGlynn wanted to be loved by everyone.

Now that he's a bishop and a martyr, maybe he finally has his wish.

My job is only to prove that the son of a bitch wasn't a saint.

|| 30 || My incomparable associate knocked on the door of my office. "I have Monsignor Carey here to see you, Father."

Ten years ago Len had probably been one of the attractive young men around Johnny about whom Maggie Ward had spoken. He was a little too short to fit the pattern perfectly, though a remarkable number of episcopal aides were well under five feet six. Now he looked like a sick old gnome, though he was younger than I was. Life had gone out of him when Jumping Johnny McGlynn had died.

"I intended merely to drop this off. Not disturb you. Your curate was very kind. Nice young man."

Jamie had evaporated. Charm the devil himself, would my young priest.

"Sit down for a few moments," I said to Len. "Something to drink? Coffee? Tea?"

"Have to run." He stood awkwardly at the doorway, frightened of entering the enemy's camp. "Don't want to give this to you, you know. Conspiracy against Cardinal McGlynn. Don't want to cooperate. Have to. Obedience."

I took the envelope from his hand. It slipped away like he was clinging to it at the last moment.

"I'll return it to you when I'm finished."

"Don't want it back. Have my own copy. Public record. Truth about the Cardinal. I'll release it if I must. Understand?"

A light had also gone out in Len's brain when Johnny died. The people at his parish in La Grange complained that all his sermons were about Johnny. They left in droves for other parishes. No associate could stand living with him for more than a couple of months. He needed a long vacation and counseling. The Cardinal would have to do something about him soon.

"I understand, Len."

"Should be canonized. You saw the cure on TV. There'll be more. Rome will have to act. I know."

Len had attended the North American too. He was slated to be a bishop like many of the others. Rumors had it that his name was before the Congregation of Bishops just before Johnny was shot. Instead we got Jim Lane.

I'd have preferred Len, even in his present condition.

"That may very well be, Len. We'll all have to wait and see. I can promise you that all I'm looking for is the truth about him, whatever it is. You knew him better than almost anyone else."

"Saint, saint. Definitely. Knew it all along. Must leave now."

Len faded away into the night, memories of the past swirling around inside of his poor head.

LEONARD

31 I can remember like it was yesterday the first time I heard his voice. I knew at that moment I was in the presence of greatness.

"I'm Johnny McGlynn. They call me the Assistant Vice Rector, which makes it sound like I'm one of the bad guys. In fact, I'm one of those with the white hats, which isn't hard to be around this city, because there are so many black hats."

The strikingly handsome young priest pulled the Roman collar out of his cassock and grinned at us first theologians.

We laughed tentatively. After the pompous talk of the Rector on our first night at the North American College, and the dull talk of the Vice Rector, we were not sure that we were supposed to laugh ever again.

"My job is to get you through your classes, which will be in Latin and spoken with an accent that none of you ever heard before. If this place seems terrible today, it's nothing like how terrible it will seem after your first day of class."

No laughter now.

"Forget it," he said. "This is one of the easiest seminaries which Americans attend, a pushover once you know how to play the game. My job is to teach you how to play the game. You know some older priests who studied here, don't you? Chancellors? Bishops? Did they seem very bright? Course not! If they could get by, so can you, right?"

Now the laughter was unfeigned.

"That's better." He smiled at us. "You make it through this place, through any seminary, by laughing at it. That's part of my job too—to make you laugh."

We began to relax. Here was a real man, a priest, a real friend. Maybe the NAC wasn't so bad after all.

For a half hour he entertained us with Roman stories in which he imitated the Rector, the Spiritual Director, Curial Cardinals, the Pope, the previous Pope, Madre Pasquelina, who had been the previous Pope's secretary (and would soon become our infirmarian), many of the professors we had yet to meet, and assorted typical citizens of Rome.

It was brilliant, hilarious, and enormously reassuring.

The Assistant Vice Rector, as is not generally known, was in fact a repetitor, a priest familiar with the Roman colleges, who coached the new students, many of whom were quite incapable of following the classroom lectures, which then were given in Latin.

We learned most of our theology from him. So great were the clarity of his presentations, the wit of his explanations, and the constant cheerfulness and patience of his disposition, that we actually looked forward to meeting with him late in the afternoon as darkness enveloped the college and the courtyard fountain bubbled—like a cow pissing on concrete he once said, causing all of us to laugh for many minutes.

Even more important than his intellectual assistance, Father McGlynn, as he was formally called, or "Johnny" as he was to all who knew him, provided tremendous personal support to those of us who needed it. While I had been through the two years of Mundelein and knew the loneliness of being separated from my family, the kind of loneliness that one experiences when one's family is across an ocean and far away is quite different.

Johnny spotted the lonely ones among us instantly. He went out of the way to help us, joshing us on the college basketball court, walking with us in the garden or on the Janiculum hill outside the college, encouraging us, cheering us, helping us to survive.

"It's going to be all right, Lenny," he told me one particularly gray and gloomy Roman winter day when I felt certain I would quit the next morning.

"How do you know?" I demanded.

"I've been there, my friend. I've been there. Promise me that you'll give it another week."

I promised. As he had predicted, in another week I was fine.

"How did you know?" I asked him.

"I can see it in the eyes." He chuckled. "It's all in the eyes."

I'm sure that John McGlynn understood our heartache, because he recollected how much he had missed his own beloved family when he was in Rome, and the pain of not being present when his father, Doctor McGlynn, was stricken with a fatal heart attack.

While he was to some extent alienated from his family, when he returned to Chicago as its seventh archbishop, by the regrettable conflicts which arose after his mother's health deteriorated, I know personally that he prayed for all of them every night and that they were never far from his thoughts.

During my last two years at the North American College, I saw less of John. He had been assigned to further study at the College of Noble Ecclesiastics, the institute which trains papal diplomats.

"No big deal, guys," he said when a group of us took him to supper to celebrate the honor. "When the aggiornamento ("modernization" or perhaps better, "updating"—the word Pope John used to describe the change in the Church begun at the Second Vatican Council) is over, the Church won't need diplomats anymore."

Despite his new program of studies, John still found time to participate in the work of the Council. He knew all the great Conciliar theologians personally—Congar, Rahner, Murray,

Diekmann, Schillebeekx, even Hans Küng—quoted them frequently, and explained their positions to us in words that made their insights clear and persuasive.

He was particularly close to Father Küng at the time and lunched with him often. He would delight us on the few occasions when we could meet with him—often after basketball games at the College—by quoting the latest witty statements from "Hans."

"Hans will be Pope someday," he predicted cheerfully. "He's smart, he's charming, he understands politics, he's good with the media, the Protestants trust him, he's everything the Church will need after the Council is over."

"Do you expect to vote for him?" I asked.

"I sure do." He grinned broadly.

"So you expect to be a cardinal."

"The next papal election," he said, "will be the last one at which the Cardinals vote. After that we will all have a vote."

In his exuberance, John McGlynn didn't foresee the problems and the disillusionment which would come after the Council. None of us did. Those were exciting days, and he was the most exciting person in Rome—or so it seemed to me.

I will never forget the kindness he showed to my family at the time of my ordination. He took them to supper when I was on my pre-ordination retreat and then celebrated the ordination itself with a meal in my honor at the Tre Scalini in the Piazza Navona, the most popular of the tourist restaurants in those days. My mother and father were astonished by the respect with which the staff of the restaurant treated him (calling him "monsignor" though it was not a title to which he was yet entitled) and the speed with which he found us a large table despite the long lines of waiting tourists.

I remember the surge of joy in my heart when, after bestowing my first blessings on my family, I found John kneeling in front of me.

Afterward he said, "Welcome in, Len. It's good to have you among us. There'll be great times ahead."

It was an accurate prediction, though neither John nor I

understood that the times would be all too short and would end in tragedy. I returned to Chicago to work in a parish for several years, a time which I have always said was the happiest in my life. John finished his course at the College of Noble Ecclesiastics and was posted to a small African country, a disappointing assignment, but, it seemed to me, what one would expect because of the anti-American resentment at that time in certain quarters in the Curia, the ones who began to undo the work of the Vatican Council as soon as the bishops left Fiumicino airport.

|| 32 || "Johnny McGlynn has found a home in Africa." My classmate, who will remain nameless even in these pages, was triumphant. He had always hated John from the first night that he had spoken to us in his role as Assistant Vice Rector.

"What do you mean by that?"

My classmate was already Chancellor of his Archdiocese; he had just returned from a tour of Africa with his Cardinal and had called me to tell me he was in town at a meeting of the American bishops and wanted to treat me to supper at the Empire Room of the Palmer House. I had never been inside that restaurant because I thought that its expensive luxury was inappropriate for a priest.

I had thought my classmate wanted to lord it over me because he was an important official. But as we ate I discovered he wanted to have the pleasure of telling me about John McGlynn's deterioration.

"He's going native. Likes Africa. He told me he gets all his work done before ten in the morning. Plays golf almost every day at the local golf course. Spends a lot of time staring at the river outside the Nunciature window."

"I don't believe it."

My classmate shrugged indifferently.

"It's true."

A slim, handsome man with jet-black hair, a narrow face, and vengeful eyes, my classmate was wearing a tailor-made suit and diamond-studded French cuff links. He was the most nakedly ambitious seminarian in Rome when we were there. I always felt that his dislike for John was based on his evaluation of John as a potential rival in the race for high ecclesiastical position.

"His term is almost finished there. I'm sure he'll be translated to a major post."

"If he wants one." He swallowed a large gulp of his Château Lafite-Rothschild wine—a hundred dollars a bottle in those days. "My boss says he doubts that John has the energy ever to become anything important in the Church."

"Indeed."

I presumed that by energy he meant the willingness to stop at nothing to obtain preferment, a characteristic which my classmate shared with his Cardinal.

"John admits his laziness himself. He figures he's done a good job straightening out the mess his Nuncio made of the post and that he'll become known in Rome as a third-world specialist. They'll ship him around Africa and Asia and finally make him a nuncio in someplace like Ethiopia before they move him to Europe and perhaps Lisbon and then bring him back to Rome for the Red Hat before he dies."

"Really?" If it were true, what had happened to John's enthusiasm?

"There are a lot of ifs in that scenario," my classmate continued. "But John seems confident, and I think that for now he's more inclined toward the pace of a third-world job. They told me that there wasn't a single third-world nunciature which could not be run before lunch. It seemed to be the kind of hours he was looking for. Not exactly the attitude of a man on the make."

"Indeed."

"Of course there's his mother's money, about which we all

know. She may be able to push him ahead the way she's always done. Personally, I find that sort of abuse despicable."

"Perhaps." It seemed that no matter how laconically I answered, nothing would stem the man's flow of venom.

"My hunch is that John doesn't belong in the priesthood," he continued. "I'm not sure that he believes in anything at all. I think he'd have a black mistress if he wasn't afraid of catching one of their diseases—it's really a sinkhole of disease and corruption over there."

He waved for another bottle of the expensive wine. And the main course of our dinner hadn't yet been served.

"John propounded a crazy notion to me while we were there—not in the presence of my boss, I hardly need note. He says that most of the African priests have women and that many of the missionaries back in the bush do too, all except the Irish. He says that the culture thinks a man is strange if he doesn't have a woman. You know how he was at finding things in history books to suit his purposes. He says the same thing was true when the missionaries went to work among the Germanic tribes fifteen hundred years ago. Unless he had a woman the Germans said he was a faggot. We hear all about the celibate monks like Boniface and Augustine of Canterbury, but most of the Roman priests in those countries took concubines like everyone else."

"I can't believe that John would propound such a shocking idea," I stammered.

"Well, I asked him if he thought those on nunciature staffs should do the same thing to gain acceptance in the local culture, and he just shrugged, saying that if they did—and he wouldn't be surprised that some of them were doing just that on the sly—they'd better be careful about disease. Then he went into a rather graphic description of the attractions of the young African woman. Can you imagine that!"

"That doesn't sound like John."

"Well, he always was a ladies' man, wasn't he? I said their careers would be finished if they tried something like that. You know what he replied?"

"I'm sure I don't."

"He said it was a long way to the Vatican from Africa, and," my classmate added, "I bet he doesn't pray from one end of the year to the other. If you ask me he's a hollow son of a bitch. He wants to get ahead in the Church but he doesn't want to put any energy into it. His mother spoiled him rotten."

It was an oddly disquieting picture. John had seemed on occasion indolent. He also had been a bit casual about prayer and other spiritual matters. I had wondered at times what, if anything, lurked behind his cheerful exterior. My classmate was saying that there was nothing there, nothing at all.

"Well, we'll have to see what happens," I said, covering up with my hand my half-filled glass of wine.

As we all know, John was transferred to Vienna and in the years after that disproved my classmate's theories.

"I gather I'm going to be Cardinal," my classmate had said to me at the last North American College reunion. He is indeed an archbishop of a city which normally is adorned with the Red Hat. "The only living Cardinal from our generation at the College."

He is fat now and pasty-faced and, if rumors are to be believed, quite actively alcoholic.

"Really?"

"Yeah. Your friend Johnny didn't last long, did he?"

"You may follow him into the Sacred College," I snapped at him, caring no longer about my career, "but you won't follow him into the ranks of the canonized saints."

"Oh?" he sneered at me. "Why not?"

"They don't canonize fall-down drunks."

|| **33** || When I was sent back to Rome for my own studies in Canon Law, John had been reassigned to the Nunciature in Vienna, an important post always, but especially at that time because of the influence of the great Conciliar Archbishop Franz Cardinal Koenig.

When we met at the Vatican, Johnny himself brought up the issue of celibacy. "Many of them don't believe that we seriously want them to practice celibacy. Men have wives, but priests are men, therefore priests have wives. They humor us by pretending that it isn't so, much like we pretend to children that there is a Santa Claus."

"Can't we stop them, Johnny?"

"Stop them, Len? You gotta be kidding. I'm not even sure that we can stop their bishops from practicing polygamy. A bishop, you see, is like a chief. If a chief doesn't have several wives, he can't be an important chief. They'll argue with you that polygamy is not forbidden by divine law. And the Church, they say, must adapt to African culture in every way it can. Just remember that when you hear the word 'enculturation,' what it means is married clergy and polygamous hierarchy."

I admit that I was shocked. I remembered my classmate's description of John in Africa and found myself wondering whether it might have been partially true.

While John never spoke of them, it was well known in Rome that he had undertaken risky and delicate journeys to the Iron Curtain countries as part of the Pope's efforts, through Cardinal Koenig, to open communication between the Church and the Communist governments so that some freedom might be obtained for Catholics to practice their faith.

"Do these abuses happen everywhere?"

"It's a big continent and there are a lot of differences among the various countries and tribes. In the big cities there's so much poverty that men are likely to have one wife at the most. In the countryside, the old customs still prevail. On the other hand, in the city, promiscuity, which is frowned on out in the village, is rampant. Everyone seems to be screwing everyone else. And the women are debased pretty early in life. I don't know, maybe the best thing would be to somehow combine the two attitudes. But we're not good at combining things these days, are we, Lenny?"

"That's a different view of things than what we're hearing from the Vatican," I said.

"Hell, the Vatican is so desperate to have black cardinals that someday soon they're going to make the mistake of appointing a man who has half a dozen wives they don't know about."

"Surely there aren't any of those," I said, astonished as much by the vehemence of his outburst as by its content.

"Probably not enough, Lenny." He winked at me, hinting that he was playing one of his little games. "I often think that the Church was better off when beautiful young women were awarding the prizes and passing around the toys than today, when withered old men control the goodies. There was more charm and brilliance in the Church in those days, anyway."

John's sense of history and his wide reading in the field always gave him excellent perspective in evaluating contemporary problems.

During the years he was in Vienna, Johnny would come to Rome often, on missions between Cardinal Koenig and the Pope. It was at this time, I believe, that Archbishop Benelli noticed Monsignor McGlynn's abilities and chose him to be one of his top assistants, a role in which he rapidly became one of the most powerful men in the Church.

Some of my fellow students, men of overweening ambition themselves, accused John of "sucking up" to Archbishop Benelli, but John was quite incapable of flattering anyone, and Giovanni Benelli was even more incapable of being taken in by an ambitious fraud.

At our dinners, in a small trattoria around the corner from the Gregorian, John would relax with a little group of friends and talk of the Church behind the Iron Curtain. He spoke of the great bravery of the "Church of Silence," which, he said, was suffering a slow martyrdom which could easily go on a hundred years. Naturally, he praised Paul VI's policy of trying to open communications with the puppet governments in these countries so that the Church could have some breathing room, especially in Poland.

Later I was convinced that those early trips of John's helped establish Solidarity and eventually led to the collapse of the Iron Curtain. When we know the full details of those trips, I'm sure we'll realize that they were the most important events in his distinguished career.

Many nights when I'd come home from one of those evenings out with Johnny in Rome, I would feel much more confident about the future of the Church. As long as we had churchmen with the vision and confidence and wit of Johnny McGlynn, there were still grounds for hope.

|| 34 || When our Cardinal finally died, there was the usual speculation about a successor. Johnny's name was almost never mentioned. He was too young, he'd never been a bishop of a diocese, he was out of favor in Rome. You can imagine, therefore, the astonishment in Chicago when we heard that he was our new Archbishop. The laity were delighted. He was the first native Chicagoan to be our Ordinary. He was an attractive man with a winning smile who could grin wryly at the TV camera and say, "I'm delighted. I thought I'd never be able to go home again."

His fellow priests were not nearly so pleased. John had been away a long time. Those who had not been in the Seminary during his time did not know him. He was not, some said, a Chicago native but a River Forest native. He was a climber, "jumping" up the ranks of the hierarchy. He knew nothing about administration and would make a mess out of Chicago. He would use Chicago only as a stepping-stone to the papacy itself. He would spend most of his time running for Pope, so we would never see him in Chicago.

Such talk was hopelessly unfair, but I soon gave up trying to argue with those who propounded it. They dismissed me as one who would curry favor with the new Archbishop because of my past friendship with him. I learned to keep my mouth shut. Moreover, I was careful to avoid contact with our new Ordinary during the ceremonies welcoming him. I did not want to seem to presume on our friendship, much less to be seeking preferment for myself.

In those days I was working in the matrimonial tribunal as an assistant officialis. In his first week after his installation, Johnny wandered into my office, apparently on a casual exploration.

"So this is where you are, Lenny?" He leaned against the door, hands jammed in his pockets. "No one seemed to know for sure where you were or even who you were. I thought you might be dead and buried. . . . Kind of small in here, isn't it? What the hell are you doing?"

"Matrimonial cases, Your Excellency."

" 'Johnny' from now on, or I'll suspend you from your priestly function." He smiled—that wonderfully radiant smile of his. "You like this stuff?"

He waved his hand at the pile of folders on a desk which I tried to keep as orderly as I possibly could.

"Someone has to do it, Your Excellency." I remembered to stand up out of respect.

"Last time, I warn you. And sit down, for the love of heaven . . . want to come to work for me?"

"Want to come to work for you?" I was so astonished that my voice cracked. "Doing what?"

"I dunno." He shrugged, as if that did not matter. "Administrative assistant, something like that."

"I know nothing about administration, ah, John."

"That will make two of us, Len, me bucko."

"Why me?" I could not gain control of my voice or my reason.

He grinned wryly. "Because I trust you, which is more than I can say for the other guys that are creeping around this building."

So began the happiest years of my life, and the most exciting. I should have realized then that they would not last long.

I should have savored them more. But we never know how short time is, do we?

Actually, the new Archbishop could not create any worse a mess than he had inherited. His predecessor had the reputation of being a shrewd and almost magical administrator. In fact, he was an incompetent and, toward the end, a senile incompetent. His advisers impressed us only because they were the wealthiest and the most important men of the civic and business elite. In point of fact they paid little attention to the Archdiocese and its problems. They managed its portfolio, which routinely lagged behind the Dow Jones average, entertained the Cardinal with jokes, often tasteless, over lunch at the Chicago Club, and arranged that their corporations made routine contributions to the Church's work. However, they paid little attention to the bottom line of Archdiocesan finances.

So financial control had slipped away. Expenses mounted and income declined. Records were not kept, budgets were not honored, accounts were neglected, bills were not paid, parish expenses were not monitored. There was literally no one Johnny could turn to for help and advice.

Moreover, the economies he attempted were stoutly opposed by the clergy, many of whom hated him and were determined to oppose everything he attempted.

It was in this crisis that Mrs. Anthony Quinlan offered him strong and able support. I will confess that at first I had grave suspicions about her. I did not think it proper that a cardinal be as close to a woman as he was to her, especially a woman who was as rich and powerful and, as it seemed to me, arrogant in her self-assurance and sense of power as Mrs. Quinlan seemed to be.

"Don't worry about me, Len," she said to me the first day she had lunch with us. "I don't have any evil designs on the man."

I felt my face turn red.

"I wasn't thinking of that, Mrs. Quinlan."

"I gave up such thoughts long ago." She continued to smile at me. "I'm here only to help."

I will confess that at the time I did not altogether believe her.

|| *35* || I assume that the late Cardinal's friendship with Mrs. Quinlan is the chief obstacle to his canonization. More than anyone else, I am in a position to assure the authorities that they were close friends and nothing more.

She is an attractive woman and—if I may use terms that I do not normally indulge in—very well aware of her erotic appeal. As I have said before, I did not like her. She knew I did not like her.

"Are you ever going to give me a break, Len?" she asked me one day.

"In what respect, Mrs. Quinlan?" I felt my face grow warm.

"I'm not a whore."

"I never suggested—"

"Nor am I trying to seduce your boss."

"The furthest thought—"

"Leonard!"

"I confess I do not understand the relationship, Mrs. Quinlan. But I am persuaded that it is a good one for him and perhaps for you."

She considered me carefully and then grinned.

"Looks like I'm making progress."

It was, however, a long time before I was won over completely.

I distrusted her expensive clothes, her costly automobiles, her assumption of superiority, and her unquestionable and well-tended attractiveness.

Moreover, she seemed to me to be an icy and even hard woman, one who had no respect for anyone but herself and no concern about any opinion except her own.

Finally I was shocked that she found time for John and the Archdiocese when her husband was under attack by the United States Government. Ought not she, I asked myself, spend all her time on her family problems?

Later, when her pregnancy became obvious after her husband's death, and the doctors warned her of the dangers of overexertion, I wondered why she did not remain at home as they had recommended. However, she did manage to help us while carrying the baby to term.

"When she makes up her mind to do something," the Archbishop said to me, "she does it. She made up her mind to help us and to produce a healthy baby, and she did exactly that."

I continued to be dubious about her. There was, I told myself, something fundamentally wrong about such excessive willpower.

However, in time, when I realized that almost by herself she had eliminated the financial and administrative crisis that John inherited, I came to admire her. In fact, she and I became allies in the cause of protecting John from those who would exploit and destroy him. She insisted on a firm of skillful public relations consultants who turned John's personable public image into an asset in dealing with the intransigence of many of the clergy.

"The question, John, is not whether you should or should not have a public image. The question is whether it will be a good or bad public image."

"I don't want to be a plastic man, Marbeth."

"You'll never be that."

Such comments, hinting at secrets between them, at first upset me. Then I realized that they were innocent.

I also came to comprehend how she had the intelligence and the energy to help us at the same time she suffered so terribly in her family crisis. I can only imagine the terrible cost in personal suffering these combined efforts must have required from her.

Late one afternoon, when John was at a meeting of the national hierarchy in Washington, I received a phone call.

"Monsignor Carey."

"Marbeth, Monsignor. I'm afraid I need some help."

She sounded like she really did need help.

"Of course, Mrs. Quinlan."

"My husband died this afternoon. I don't know whether you've heard about it yet. He was found guilty by the jury on all counts."

"How terrible!"

"I don't want to disturb John in Washington."

"I'm sure he'd want to know at once."

"The problem is that the pastor of St. Luke's is refusing him Christian burial."

"Incredible! Why?"

"I'm afraid my husband shot himself."

"Mrs. Quinlan, I'm so sorry."

"Thank you, Len." Her voice was strained, but yet she was in control . . . or sounded like she was. "Do you think you could explain to the Pastor that Bud has been under a doctor's care for acute depression."

"Of course, of course. I'll call him right away."

"Thank you."

"And I'll call the Cardinal too."

There was a moment's silence.

"Thank you, Len."

I punched the number for St. Luke's

"This is Monsignor Carey calling."

"Forget it, Len."

"Forget what?"

"Jumping Johnny himself is going to have to order me to bury that bastard."

"That is hardly charitable, Father."

"I don't give a damn. Tell him to call me."

"He is at the Bishops' meeting in Washington."

"Too bad for him. If he wants a Christian burial he will have to order me himself."

I was astonished at such gratuitous rudeness.

It took me more than an hour to finally reach the Cardinal. I told him, as briefly as I could, what had happened.

"Dear God," was all he could say.

"The funeral Mass?"

"I will say it, of course."

"The Pastor at St. Luke's?"

"I'll take care of it personally, Len." His voice was glacial. "When I come home in the morning. Straight from the airport. It will be a pleasure."

"Yes, Cardinal."

"Then I'll visit her. . . . How did she sound, Len?"

"Strained, but in control."

"It's an act, Len. The whole control bit with her is a façade. She gives a great performance, but it is still an act. She's really just a soft touch at heart. This must be tearing her up."

It was the first and last time I ever heard him say anything like that about Mrs. Quinlan.

Needless to say, her poor husband was granted Christian burial.

There have been rumors since the Cardinal's death that there was some sort of illicit love in his relationship with Mrs. Quinlan. I find such stories absurd and profoundly offensive. I was as close to the late Cardinal as any man could possibly be. I was present with the two of them many, many times. There was never a hint of anything illicit in their relationship. She was a childhood friend whom he greatly admired. She provided him with invaluable assistance when no one else was willing to do so. He respected her ability enormously and trusted her implicitly. They were very good friends and it is a terrible calumny to suggest that there was anything else in their relationship. As someone who was very suspicious of her at first, I am absolutely certain of that.

"Do you think I sleep with Marbeth, Len?" he asked me one summer morning at the breakfast table.

"When and where would you do that?" I replied.

The Cardinal laughed. "Always the practical man, eh, Len? Well, let's see. We couldn't do it here without your knowing about it. Or at her homes without her children being shocked, right?"

"Precisely."

"We could tiptoe in here late at night?"

"I'm a light sleeper."

I confess that I had no taste for this kind of conversation.

"Her condo in San Diego?"

"When have you been in San Diego?"

"True enough. . . . What about in an out-of-the-way motel or hotel?"

"The Cardinal Archbishop of Chicago would not be recognized and reported to the press?"

"I have a reputation for courting danger."

The Cardinal was enjoying his little game.

"Not that kind of danger."

He laughed merrily. "She's an attractive woman."

"I've noticed."

"Have you now? Well, I'm glad you have. And I love her, don't I?"

"Do you?"

Now the Cardinal turned serious. "Don't I?"

"I think you admire her as a loyal, lifelong friend who has been a great help to you and to the Church."

"I've admired her since she was five."

"That shows good taste on your part, Cardinal, but I don't understand the purpose of this conversation."

"I don't either. Maybe I'm only worrying about my public image."

One could not be indifferent to Mrs. Quinlan's charm once one knew her well. Beneath the surface coldness, she was a warm, sensitive, and kind woman. She was also uncannily intuitive.

"You don't disapprove of me anymore, do you, Leonard?" she asked me one day during our final trip, with a hint of a twinkle in her eye.

I felt my face grow warm. I hated to acknowledge that I had once been disapproving, but it seemed futile to deny the implicit charge. "No, Mrs. Quinlan, I certainly do not," I told her.

"I'm not a bad influence on the Cardinal?"

"Should I think you are?"

She laughed. "Sometimes I wonder myself."

"You keep him human," I told her. "Even keep him alive."

She nodded solemnly. "That's what I think too."

I fear that my denial of sexual involvement between her and the late Cardinal will not put to rest the terrible stories that malicious men and women have been spreading. All I can say is that these stories are lies, deliberate, ugly, evil, sinful lies. I will have no more to say on this distasteful subject.

In any event the Cardinal's reorganization of the Archdiocese was completely successful. Within eighteen months, financial control had been restored, the budget had been balanced, and the Ordinary was in firm control of all the institutions of the Catholic Church in Chicago.

"It's not just Chicago, Lenny," John would say dejectedly in the weeks and months during which we were struggling through the crisis. "It's a lot worse in most other places. We stay out of trouble because the people here are so generous. They pay for our mistakes and stupidities, so we don't end up bankrupt. Someday it will catch up and even their generosity won't be great enough to save us. Then we're going to be in deep, deep trouble. It will serve us right, I suppose, for giving power to so many idiots."

Then he'd grin boyishly. "And that includes me. What did I know about running a quarter-billion-dollar-a-year corporation, much less pulling such an organization out of a near-disaster? If it hadn't been for Mrs. Quinlan, we'd be far up the proverbial creek."

I could only agree with him.

||

The new Cardinal can barely speak in the presence of Mrs. Quinlan without stuttering. She gracefully withdrew from her always informal consultative role so that he would be spared the embarrassment of asking her to leave. The able men she had brought in as advisers were replaced by the same men who had advised Johnny's predecessors, or men just like them. They continue to take the Cardinal to lunch at the Chicago Club and give him "top-of-the-head" advice without paying any attention to the budgets or the financial structure of the Archdiocese. I strongly suspect that the current Cardinal has once again lost financial control and that a day of reckoning will soon be upon us.

I mentioned this to Mrs. Quinlan recently.

Her brown eyes flashed. "Don't worry about that, Len," she said tonelessly. "I know where the bodies are buried from the last administration and from this one. If they try to blame their cesspool on Johnny, I'll let the media know what really goes on. They'll be dead, all of them, I promise you that."

I would hope those in power understand that, as John used to say, Mrs. Quinlan does not bluff.

Verbum sat sapienti.

|| 36 || The worst calumny of the many that have been leveled against the late Cardinal was that he was not a devout man and, indeed, that his faith was weak.

I need say nothing about his public life as a cardinal, as that is on the record. His private life is not well known, much to my surprise.

"We're going over to the Charities Office," he said to me one day. "Scare the hell out of them when the Cardinal walks in, won't it?"

"I'm sure they'll be delighted, Cardinal. Might I ask the purpose of the visit?"

"I want to make a little contribution to them."

"Oh?"

He seemed embarrassed. "Well, uh, I will give the income from Doctor's trust for this year. I don't need it and they can make good use of it. They'll be charming and gracious while we're there, Len. Fall all over me—you watch. Then when I leave they'll complain about my family wealth."

During the last several years of his life, when his spirituality had grown more intense, he drew out the income from the

trust his father left him and donated it to the Catholic Charities of the Archdiocese. He did so with no fanfare, but with no
instruction that the contribution be kept secret. Such concerns about money would not have occurred to the Cardinal.
Yet I have had priests deny to my face the truth of his contribution. The men at the Catholic Charities office know of it, but
they have strangely conspired, as it seems to me, to keep it
secret since his death—perhaps fearful that revealing it would
offend his successor, who trembles daily in the shadow of
John's greatness.

Nor should his intense prayer life be a secret to anyone.

If his piety was an act, it was one that I witnessed every day,
especially in the last years of his life. I would rise at five-thirty
and join him in the chapel for Mass at six o'clock. He was
invariably there before me, wide awake and cheerful, no matter how long the previous day had been or how arduous the
coming day seemed likely to be.

I am often asked whether there was a sudden and dramatic
change in his piety a few years before his untimely death. I
cannot answer that question because I think of him as a man
who was always devout. If there ever was an intensification of
his spirituality, it happened in 1985. Some remarked at that
time that he stopped wearing the French cuffs that most of us
at the Chancery had always worn and adopted the black wash-
and-wear clerical shirts that most of the parish clergy wear.
I remarked on this change as gently as I could. Sartorially, it
did not strike me as an improvement.

"You're not wearing a rabat and French cuffs anymore,
Eminenza?"

"They're a nuisance," he said. "It's all right, Len, you don't
have to do the same thing."

Naturally I did not.

The late Cardinal, as everyone knows, was deeply devoted
to his poor mother, as great a Catholic laywoman as has ever
lived. Every day when he was in Chicago he would stop to see
her, if only for a minute or two. I know it wrenched his heart
that she did not recognize him most of the times he came to
visit. Her Alzheimer's was that advanced. It seemed sadly

ironic that she never realized he had become precisely what she had always hoped he would be: not merely a priest, but the Cardinal Archbishop of Chicago.

Sometimes his mother would mistake John for a high ecclesiastic. She would then launch into a big harangue through which she hoped to persuade him to promote her son to the position of responsibility and power to which she thought he was entitled.

John would smile his best smile and say something like, "Of course we will take care of your son. He is a most promising young man, but these things take time." He was very patient with her.

On a few occasions Mrs. McGlynn recognized John as one of her sons, though she wasn't sure which. When she thought he was James or Michael, she would demand that he remove the Roman collar which he was, as she saw it, not entitled to wear. The Cardinal would dutifully remove the offending collar.

The very few times she realized it was John, she would denounce him for his lack of ambition and failure to develop the friends he needed to facilitate his promotion. John would listen quietly and promise to try to do better.

I could not help but think that during these visits he was being nailed to a cross of agony from which he would never be able to climb down as long as his mother lived. Usually, I would maintain a discreet silence unless he said something, not wanting to intrude myself into his personal agony.

"Pray that such a fate does not befall either of us, Len," he would say on occasion. "It reveals what hell must be like."

Mrs. Quinlan has often confided to me her conviction that the Cardinal would have worn himself out eventually by his superhuman efforts to be everything he felt the Cardinal Archbishop of Chicago ought to be.

"It's a killer job, Lenny," she has said. "The only reason it didn't kill the idiot before him is that he didn't do the job."

But the matter is, after all, purely an academic question. He was killed at a muddy clearing in a jungle village in Nicaragua, a martyr to his commitment to peace and justice.

I will say little about our final sad pilgrimage to Central

America. All of us experienced a sense of doom through the entire trip, including the Cardinal.

When, cross in hand, he walked slowly into that clearing, wanting only to make peace, Mrs. Quinlan and I reached out to restrain him. Gently but decisively he shook us off and walked to his death, a death which he must have known at that moment was his destiny.

Some journalists have tried to make a hero out of me because, as they say, I rushed into the "teeth of the automatic weapons fire," along with Mrs. Quinlan. There was no heroism in that behavior. Every priest must minister to the dying, no matter what the risk.

It has been a painful task for me to record these words, especially because I fear that they will be searched with a microscope by those who are enemies of the late Cardinal's memory.

To recall these events, to see and hear, if only in my mind's eye, John Cardinal McGlynn again, is to realize what exciting years those were and what wonderful possibilities they contained for all of us. Now the wonder and the excitement are gone and the foolish and the mediocre are running the Church in Chicago again.

As John would say, "It was always thus, Lenny. Don't let it bother you. We'll give them a run for their money."

We surely did that.

LAURENCE

|| **37** || "A totally gorgeous woman in the office to see you, Father Lar. I mean like totally."

It was Jackie, the teenage porter who presides over the Rectory doorbell after school and in the evening a couple of days a week. I had been sitting dozing over a book in my bedroom.

"Mrs. Quinlan?" I asked.

Jackie nodded, urging me up from my chair with disrespectful haste. When I told her I must freshen up before going downstairs, she grumpily stomped off to tell Marbeth to wait in my office.

As I washed my face and put on a clean shirt, I thought back to a summer in the early sixties, when I had encountered Bud and Mary Elizabeth at my brother's house in Lake Geneva—yeah, some of us from 79th Street had made it after all. Motherhood had seemed to agree with her. She had been even more beautiful than I had remembered her.

Yet every time she had a comment on anything, her husband had put her down.

"What a dumb thing to say, Marbeth. Typical woman logic."

Or, "You just can't think straight, Marbeth. No woman can."

It had been an embarrassingly cruel assault. Bud probably didn't beat her, but with such endless humiliation, he didn't have to.

My brother Ed's massive fist clenched at every such put-down.

Mary Elizabeth said nothing at all. Indeed, she gave no sign of being troubled by his cruelty—or embarrassed by its impact on us. She had simply ignored him, as though he had said nothing. Indeed, as though he didn't exist.

Does she really love him, I had wondered, and hence doesn't notice? Or does she despise him and doesn't care? She knows that she's the one running the company and making it a success. Maybe that's enough.

She did not, it turned out ten years later, have quite as much control of the firm as we all thought she did—not enough to keep Bud out of trouble with the feds for bribery and kick-backs.

When her husband died, he left Marbeth pregnant again at forty-six and with the ruins of the company to salvage.

In the time since, she had delivered the child and salvaged the company and, more beautiful than ever, had become the traveling companion of the Cardinal Archbishop of Chicago.

At Bud's wake she had been dry-eyed and tense. Had she felt any grief over losing the stupid lug? You'd never find an answer to that question.

"What a sweet young woman, Lar!" Marbeth greeted me when I came into the office.

"Jackie? Kind of bossy, but that goes with being Irish and Catholic."

Though Labor Day had come and gone and the schools were open, it was still hot. Marbeth was wearing a light floral-print dress. She seemed to be in what was for her a positively vivacious mood.

"It's clever of you to have young women like her at the door. They make people feel welcome in the Rectory. Such an improvement over the crabby old housekeepers who used to answer rectory doorbells."

"Yeah, they even remember to write down some of the telephone messages too."

"I brought a memoir," she said, hugging the manila envelope she had been carrying against her chest.

"Are you going to give it to me, Mary Elizabeth? You don't have to, you know."

"I know." She hesitated. "I *will* give it to you . . . it's just that I'm kind of shy about it."

"I'll give it back to you. No copies."

"That's not the point." She hugged the envelope more tightly. "I've written it so people can understand how and why John and I were friends. I have to reveal a lot more about myself than I ever have."

"You sure you want to?"

"Yes, unless you tell me others shouldn't see it. Then I'll take it back."

She extended the envelope toward me. I took it. Our relationship was more relaxed now than it had been at Lake Geneva. The chemistry, if that was the right word, still remained. It was only more subtle.

"Might I ask you two questions I forgot at Lake Geneva?"

"Certainly."

She didn't seem troubled or threatened by my request, but how would one ever tell with Marbeth?

"Did you and Johnny ever talk about marriage, that is, to one another?"

"No." She seemed quite calm in the face of what was an outrageous question. "Not after he was ordained. We discussed it while he was still in the Seminary, or rather, I discussed it. Looking back on it, I think he was not all that much interested in either marriage or me as a marriage partner. After he was ordained and it became possible for priests to leave the priesthood rather easily, I was already married. Then, when Bud died and I would have been free to marry, he was already Archbishop of Chicago. To tell the truth, I have no reason to think that his interest in me as a possible wife had changed since that interlude at Clearwater Lake when I foolishly decided he should marry me rather than become a priest. John valued me as a close friend, not as potential wife."

Worse luck for him, I thought. What I said was, "Kate read me some of the correspondence between John and Delia. It's pretty terrible stuff, though not necessarily damaging to him."

"What a hateful thing for Kate to do."

"What happened to her?"

"Her resentment against Johnny became an obsession, I guess. Her husband doesn't seem to mind it. So why should I?"

"You became the scapegoat?"

"Our friendship did not survive my marriage. She thought—still thinks—I stole Bud away from her."

"Did you?"

"Of course not. She had not expressed the slightest interest in him until we began to date. Somehow I was supposed to know about fantasies she never shared with me. It may be that her mother put her up to it. You could never tell with the McGlynns when the words you heard might be the words of Delia. Poor woman. Kate, I mean. She never grew up."

Wealth, I realized once again, does not bestow by itself intelligence or sensitivity or health or taste. Or luck. I hadn't known that when I envied the Quinlans at Clearwater Lake.

"His ring?" I pointed at the ruby ring she was wearing.

Mary Elizabeth nodded. "I gave it to him when he was made a cardinal and took it back after he died. He was wearing the gold band when they shot him. I wanted this as a memory."

"Symbol of something?"

"Of love that does not die, Lar."

"Indeed, yes."

"There was a time"—she rose gracefully from the couch on which the Pastor's clients sit—"when you wouldn't have thought so."

In the hall outside my office, she said, "Take good care of him, Jackie. He's a very good man."

"I'll try, Mrs. Quinlan, but it's hard work for us all."

They both laughed—two biddies conspiring across generation lines.

As she left, she pointed at the envelope I still had gripped under my arm. "After writing that up, I've decided that while I made a lot of mistakes, on balance I have no regrets."

I watched her walk down the Rectory steps to her car parked by the curb and wondered how many other people, reflecting on their lives, could make such a claim.

MARY
ELIZABETH

‖ **38** ‖ I wished that I had a priest of my own when Nancy was born prematurely at Oak Park Hospital. Her delivery was hellish and she almost died because of a membrane in her lungs. Indeed, I wished that I had a man in the family to turn to.

My first three pregnancies had been easy. The fourth was difficult, from my initial bout of morning sickness through the twenty-eight-hour labor. I was terribly sick, depressed, angry at myself and my husband, and fully prepared to die.

Of course I wasn't going to die—women rarely do in childbirth anymore—but I had lost a lot of blood and was in no condition to leave the hospital.

The doctors told me that poor, tiny Nance was not going to make it. She had come into the world too soon. The possibility—the doctors were saying certainty—of losing her made me love her even more.

Bud was no help. He was proud of his three children, but he didn't like pregnancy and childbirth. They were too messy and too womanly for his tastes. So he tried to pretend that they really weren't happening. He resented the fact that his wife was taken away from him even for a couple of days and that he was deprived of the orderly course of his life.

Moreover, he didn't want another child this time around. He resented Nancy from the moment I told him that a new child was on the way. He especially resented her when we were both in the hospital.

"Hasn't it died yet?" he said on the fifth day after Nancy's birth—his first words as he came into my room.

I blew up.

"It's a little girl, Bud. They're normally called *she*," I screamed. "And she's still alive, no thanks to you."

"Gosh, Marbeth . . ."

"You're an unfeeling, stupid bastard!"

He sat silently at the side of my bed for a half hour, not hurt or offended by my rage, but baffled. Then he quietly left the room.

I was upset with myself for being angry. It never did any good. I also felt terribly sorry for myself. What good was it to be married if you had to deal with five children all the time, one of whom was your husband? And I was furious at God too, for so thoughtlessly messing up my life. I was just working myself up to a full-blown storm of self-pity when John Arthur McGlynn walked into my room.

"Marbeth," he exclaimed enthusiastically, "she's a beautiful little girl. Looks just like you!"

"She's going to die." Tears welled up in my eyes.

"No, she's not. Absolutely not."

"You're not a doctor."

"The kid is a feisty little bundle of life. She's too tough to die. I can tell it by looking at her."

Later, when I told Nancy about his confidence in her, she would smile and nod. "He had it right, Mom. Too tough to die."

There was always a special bond between her and John, an unspoken relationship of two very dissimilar people. He often called her "tough guy," an appellation of which she was terribly proud.

That evening at Oak Park Hospital, John held my hand while I poured out my rage and my grief. I knew that he would have been as sympathetic to anyone in the same situation. I was not special to him, but I needed sympathy so badly then that I didn't care whether he loved me as I loved him.

When I was cried out, he told me stories about his years in Africa, mostly funny stories, and I found myself laughing and happy again.

"I'm so glad you came, John. Just at the right time. God must have sent you."

He winked at me. "When I talk to you it's easy to believe in Him."

"Let's not go into that again." We both laughed.

Did he believe in God at last? I wondered. But I was not about to ask.

"Why are you home? Are you coming back to America to stay?"

"Afraid not, though after Africa, Vienna will seem almost like River Forest. I've been transferred to the Papal Nunciature in Austria. It would appear that I'm to assist Cardinal Koenig of Vienna in his work behind the Iron Curtain."

"How exciting."

He shrugged as if it didn't matter much. "It'll be interesting."

"I'm sure it will make your mother happy."

"She's overjoyed that I'll not be associating with the black folks anymore, that's for sure. I haven't told her yet I'll be talking to Communists."

We laughed again at Delia's bigotry.

"But you must be happy to get out of Africa."

John became momentarily serious. "To tell the truth, Marbeth, I'll miss it. I liked Africa. The country I was in is a terrible place—hunger, disease, corruption, brutality. Yet the people are magical. Part of me could stay there forever. I think I was on the verge of going native when this job in Vienna opened up."

"Nonsense, John—you'd never get like that."

"Well." He abandoned his serious demeanor. "I won't in Vienna."

That was the way John was—usually uncritical and transparent, but sometimes mysterious, occasionally revealing strange and enigmatic depths.

While what happened at the end of his life was not predictable, it was not totally surprising to me.

"I hope we see more of you now that you're closer to home."

"You bet. Only a nine-hour flight from Vienna to O'Hare. You'll see more of me, I promise you that."

He kissed me on the forehead as he left, a chaste kiss which was the turning point in my recovery—and my avoidance of postpartum depression.

I still loved John McGlynn as much as I ever had. But I began to see that night at Oak Park that my love for him was more than an obsession of which I could not let go.

John was right: Nancy was too tough to die. She began to win her fight for life the very next morning. She fooled all of us, including the doctors. She's been tough ever since, and yet so fragile, too.

Bud never could get over his resentment of Nancy for upsetting his life. She sensed it from the very beginning and resented him back—in spades.

I taught the older kids, as subtly as I could, how to deal with their father, doing my best to sustain their respect for him. I was successful, on the whole, I think, until his death. I even managed to put a positive spin on that event.

Nancy was the only snag. She is not only the youngest, but also the most sensitive, the brightest, and the closest to me. She resented Bud's constant and meaningless verbal assaults on my intelligence. I was never able to explain them to her.

"He treats you with contempt, Mom," she said when she was about twelve. "He doesn't love you."

"Yes, he does, honey. He loves me very much."

"Why doesn't he show it?"

I told her the truth: "He doesn't know how to."

"Then he's a jerk."

"Don't say that about your father."

"Even if I am right?"

What could I say?

|| **39** || Twenty years after my marriage I found my-
self sitting in Rome, across the table from my old love. This
time it was not a banquet, as it had been that night at the
Grand Hotel, but only a dinner with John and Bud and myself.
I was now a mature woman, confident of my sexual skills and
my ability to hold my own with men. I was also more power-
fully attracted to John than I had ever been before, as difficult
as that would have been for me to believe when I was an
eighteen-year-old at Eagle River.

We were in Europe on our mandatory twentieth-anniver-
sary second honeymoon trip. John took us to supper at Sabattini's after he had introduced us to Monsignor Benelli.

John was in his middle forties then, still trim and fit, though
his hair was going gray. His smile was as generous as ever, his
charm undiminished, and his concern for the other person,
whoever the other might be, as authentic as it had always
been.

Yet he seemed tired. He was edgy beneath the fatigue and
his eyes darted around, especially once we entered Sabattini's.
It was as if he were searching for someone who might be

watching him or checking up on him. He was, I thought, wearing thin around the edges. My compassion quickly turned into desire.

When Archbishop Benelli's deep brown eyes lit up in approval at the sight of me, I knew that my suspicion was right. I was still attractive. Not very many women, I told myself, produce that kind of reaction in the Pope's hatchetman.

I was, not to put too fine an edge on things, sexually aroused. And inexcusably flirtatious.

John and I had seen little of one another after Nancy's birth. He had eaten dinner with Bud and me at our home and taken us to the club for dinner. He and Bud got along fine—my husband was quite incapable of admitting jealousy, even to himself. Whatever his unconscious fears—and they were legion—it would have been unthinkable for him to acknowledge to himself that another man could possibly be more attractive to his wife than he was. I could have carried on affairs beneath his nose and he would not have noticed because his self-esteem would not permit him to notice.

At dinner that night in Rome we talked about Delia.

"She never did recover from Doctor's death, you know. Now she's not well at all. She has some odd . . . well, I suppose you'd call them obsessions. She thinks that she can buy me any office in the Church she wants. It's difficult to prevent her from trying."

"Can she?" Bud asked with his usual big laugh. "Everything is for sale these days, isn't it?"

"Not dioceses and archdioceses," John said, squirming slightly. I'm sure he never dreamed Bud could be so obtuse. "I go along with her to a point and then try to stop her. Sometimes I can't, and it's very embarrassing to have to explain to someone in the Vatican that your mother is not at all well—and that's to those who tell me about it, which not everyone does."

I had a brief memory of our shouting match at Eagle Lake, but virtuously dismissed it. Then I recalled stripping for him and thought that it would be fun to try again.

In the cold light of the next day I warned myself to stay away from Rome. Or at least not to drink four glasses of wine when there.

John was working for Monsignor Benelli at the time and wanted to introduce us to that man before our private audience (which he arranged) with the Pope.

I liked Benelli instantly. He liked women and he had the great good taste to like me.

"So, Signora," he said, "you knew this priest when he was a child? Was he as kind then as he is now?"

"He put up with little sisters and their friends, Monsignor. Is there any greater kindness?"

The Archbishop rolled his eyes and laughed. "You see, this is the way it works. I call an office and shout, 'Qui Benelli!' That document you were supposed to have on my desk two weeks ago? I want it tonight by five o'clock!' They are terrified, no? Then John goes to them and says, tomorrow at noon is OK. That way they don't lose their siesta. I am the bad guy and he is the good guy. Works good, no?"

We all laughed, but I knew it was more than just a joke.

"So they like you," I said at supper, "and they don't like him."

"They like me," John agreed ruefully, "but they remember who I work for. I won't last five minutes after they get him."

"Will they get him?"

"Sure."

"And you?"

"What difference does it make?"

"Does he know about your mother?"

He rolled his eyes in dismay.

"She hired a banker—not much of a banker—to come all the way to Rome to find out from Benelli how much it would cost her to buy me Denver. The guy had been authorized to pay whatever was the cost."

"What did the Archbishop do?"

"Hit the ceiling of course. Threw the man out of the office. Almost threw me out too. I brought over some of her letters and persuaded him that she was a little bit 'round the bend on the subject. He simmered down after a while."

"Women just don't understand, do they, John?"

"It depends on the woman. Mom's still all right in most other respects."

That wasn't true, but I saw no point in debating the subject with him.

John did not seem to notice the waver in my voice when I said goodnight to him. Certainly my husband didn't.

I had been more annoyed than usual at Bud's patronizing me during dinner. In fact, I was furious with him. I took out my rage as I often did—in passionate sex, sex in which there was little love, much anger, and a lot of self-pleasure. Very intense pleasure.

And all the time I imagined that John was my partner.

|| 40 || "John," I told the Archbishop of Chicago, "you are surrounded by mean-spirited fools, fossilized incompetents, and ambitious charlatans. Moreover, none of them even have the grace to be loyal to you. Get rid of the lot of them."

"I can't do that, Marbeth," he pleaded.

John looked terrible, haggard, worn, confused.

"Not only can you, you must."

"She's right, Cardinal," Monsignor Leonard Carey, John's secretary—a little man with angry eyes—agreed. "She's absolutely right."

I hadn't expected help from this quarter. Obviously I had overcome the Monsignor's suspicion of me. So we would be allies henceforth. Even if I was a woman.

When I read in the papers that Benelli had been sent to Florence, I assumed that John's days in office were numbered. Later, one of the priests at St. Luke's, too young to know of my friendship with John, told me with some satisfaction that John had been "given the sack and it serves him right too."

In the 1978 elections of the Pope, especially the second time, when Benelli was rumored to be a strong candidate, I prayed for him, both because I thought he would be a good pope and because I knew it would help John.

I also wondered whether, now that his mother was certifiably senile, the rewards of victory in the Church politics game would mean anything to him.

Then one morning I heard on the seven o'clock news that he had been named Archbishop of Chicago. The radio and TV people rejoiced. John made a good impression in his first interview from Rome, very good, considering how bishops usually muff such opportunities. He was diffident, charming, apparently forthcoming.

The priest at St. Luke's moaned to me, "We've been handed over from Annas to Caiaphas. This is a payoff."

I was too upset by the reference to the two crooked judges of Jesus to ask him what the payoff was for.

I decided not to attend any of John's installation ceremonies. We were already deep into our troubles with the United States Attorney for the Northern District of Illinois, and I had enough on my plate to keep me busy. Moreover, since I might be named an unindicted co-conspirator and maybe even a co-defendant, I did not want to be an embarrassment to the new Archbishop.

I'm not sure, incidentally, why they didn't hand down a true bill against me. I had done nothing wrong, but neither had Bud been guilty of any clearly criminal actions. The U.S. Attorney, as he cheerfully admitted, was experimenting with a "new theory" about white-collar crime. He could have just as well experimented with me.

I heard later that I was "given a pass" because they were afraid I would be too good a witness and they knew they could destroy Bud on the stand. Which is what they did. Literally.

I did call John after a couple of months and, following a long delay, got through to him.

"Marbeth! How are you! Where have you been? Why haven't I seen you? Let's have lunch! At my house! You gotta see it!" Same old John.

We had lunch. Len Carey came too. It took me all of thirty

seconds to see that he was a nervous wreck and another half minute to pry out the reasons: he had inherited an awful financial and administrative mess from his predecessor, and he didn't have a clue as to what to do about it.

I told him, and in no uncertain terms, "You clean out the deadweight around you in the Chancery. You bring in younger priests who are loyal to you. You hire young laymen from the accounting firms at higher salaries than they're receiving. You call in the best consultants you can find. I can give you a list of names. You ignore the pompous asses who patronize you at the Chicago Club and find some hard-nosed business-men who care about the city and the Church and not just about their corporation in New York or Los Angeles. I can give you a list of them, too. You have auditors go over the books. You hire Arthur Andersen to design a computer system for you. I know a little bit about that. You appoint a board of smart priests—if you can find any—"

"Whoa!" he said. "You're going too fast." He had been lis-tening to me. Len Carey was smiling, a rare enough event, heaven knows.

"These priests are to listen to what the auditors say. They can spread the word around about how bad things were."

That bit of advice was only partially successful. The board discovered how bad things had been under the old administra-tion, but were reluctant to spread the word because they were still hostile to John. It was only after he died that they began to praise his financial reforms.

"Why haven't I heard this advice before?" he demanded as he scribbled furiously.

"Probably because you haven't talked to anyone with com-mon sense."

"What is obvious to someone else is not always obvious in the Church, Marbeth."

When I told him, again, he had to clear out everyone, he protested. But Len agreed with me.

"All at once?" John asked, his face furrowed in an agonized frown.

"Not on the same day, but within the same week."

"It will kill some of the men on the staff."

"Personally I doubt it—but that's their problem."

"I don't know—I just don't know." He shook his head like a little boy who has been told that the castor oil is coming.

"I do, John. You're not doing anyone any favors by keeping the deadweight on a sinking ship."

"Will you help, Marbeth?"

"Help you? How? Fire them?"

"No, I don't mean that. I mean give advice now and then."

"I'm not sure that would be a good idea, John."

"With all respect, Mrs. Quinlan," Len interrupted us. "I think it's an excellent idea. Most people are reluctant to tell an archbishop the truth. That doesn't seem to bother you at all."

"Not in the slightest."

"Then you will give me a hand now and again, Marbeth?"

I hadn't thought that would be an outcome of my popping off about the administration of the Archdiocese. I was uneasy about seeing John too often. Archbishop or not, his erotic spell over me was still magic.

"There's the problem of Bud's trial, John. It might not look good if people knew that I was working for you. I might be indicted myself."

"Indicted? For what?"

I described our problems with the United States Attorney for the Northern District of Illinois. He hadn't been aware of the matter in any detail. He was horrified when I explained the extent of Bud's difficulties.

"I'll pray for you and the whole family, Marbeth." He shook his head sadly. "I wish I could do something."

"Don't try. It would only make matters worse for you and for us."

"Still, if you could find a tiny amount of time to advise me, I would be most grateful."

That seemed little enough to ask. So gradually I became adviser and confidante to the Archbishop and later Cardinal

Archbishop of Chicago. There were rumors about me at first. Later our friendship was no longer secret. In fact I actually had more power than anyone realized, not because I wanted to have it but because it was necessary for John that I have it.

He simply did not have the courage to make a tough choice unless someone held his hand (figuratively) and told him that it was not only the right choice, it was the only choice. Even then there were times when I virtually had to order him to do something he knew had to be done.

"I've become a confidante and adviser," I said to John one day.

"I hadn't noticed." He laughed. "Do you want an appointment with a title?"

"I wanted to make sure you knew what you were doing."

"I know, Marbeth." He grinned happily. "And I'll replace you tomorrow if you can find someone who is as good as you are and whose advice is less expensive than yours."

Mine was free, needless to say.

So it was arranged. That's all I ever was—and good friend too, I suppose.

|| 41 || "He may have to do time," Mick Whealan, Bud's defense attorney, whispered in my ear. "Poor damn fool."

My brother Iggy nodded in agreement.

"I know," I said softly. "I know."

"Maybe we can win on appeal," Iggy breathed softly.

"Depends on who the appellate judges are."

I had not realized until then how important the personality of a judge could be. Poor Bud was not fortunate. The judge who heard his case was a knee-jerk liberal appointed by Jimmy Carter. He believed that all businessmen were bastards. He had a grand time amusing himself at Bud's expense—playing the jury for laughs. As Iggy told me, he was smart enough to stay just within the limits of the law.

"A good lawyer on the bench," Mick Whealan had said before the trial began, "would dismiss this indictment out of hand. We were unfortunate; the wheel turned up a man who likes to see his name in the papers."

"But we can appeal, can't we?"

"A dismissal is rarely overturned on appeal. A conviction, on the other hand, has a good chance of standing up."

During the trial I had come to love my husband for the first time in our marriage. I'm glad I finally felt that love before the end came.

I loved him as an innocent, a man who, for all his bluster and his sometimes cruel words, did not have a mean bone in his body.

Iggy and Mick and I did all we could to persuade him to accept the plea bargain, pay a fine, and do community service as part of his probation. As much as I was able to manage everything else in his life, I could not talk him out of his stubborn conviction that an innocent man would be found innocent.

"This is America, Marbeth," he said in the tone of one explaining a self-evident truth to a child. "I didn't do anything wrong. In this country a man is innocent till he's proven guilty."

Maybe on TV, but not in the Northern District of Illinois and not in the courtroom of a Jimmy Carter liberal who enjoyed the jury's laughter at his cruel jokes.

New theory or not, the government's case against Bud was weak—a few dinners and golf outings for prominent politicians, some vague discussions of bids on government contracts. No proof that specific contracts were ever discussed or that there was a link between the golf games and the contract grants.

Sure we won a lot of the contracts. We were low bidders and we did good work; and we sold a lot of land in the process and made a lot of money. Those facts became prima facie evidence of conspiracy. Almost by definition, you couldn't make money without committing a crime—a fact that the majority of the appellate judges noted when they sustained the dismissal of charges against my son, Peter, after Bud died.

The testimony of Bud's friends to whom the government had granted immunity was not as devastating as I had feared. Mick Whealan destroyed them on cross-examination.

"Is it not true, Mr. Keane, that you are exchanging testimony against a man who has been your friend since you were both freshmen in Fenwick High School for your own personal freedom?"

"Objection, your honor."

"Sustained. We'll have none of that in my courtroom, Mr. Whealan."

"I beg your pardon, your honor. . . . Mr. Keane, is it not true that you often told others that the Quinlan Company was the most honorable development firm in the state?"

"Well, yes I did, I guess."

Lucky guess, Mick.

"You seemed to have changed your mind since then."

"Objection, your honor."

"Sustained. I will not warn you again, Mr. Whealan."

Defense council stared at the judge, then, after a moment's dramatic pause, said softly, "No further questions."

The implication was that despite the judge's interference, Joe Keane was not worth questioning.

It seemed to work, if one was to judge by the contemptuous expressions on the faces of the jurors. We still probably would have won the case if we could have kept Bud off the stand. But he absolutely insisted. "Some of my best friends lied about me," he said. "I want to explain to the jurors how it really was."

We spent hours trying to prepare him for the witness stand. He endured Mick and Iggy with the patient forbearance of a man who understood exactly what needed to be said.

"He's acting like an asshole," Iggy complained to me.

"He's an innocent, Ig. An infant caught up in a big-kids' game."

Iggy was startled. "That's an odd thing to say about your husband."

"Not true?"

"Perfectly true, I guess. Dangerously true."

On the witness stand, Bud ignored everything we had told him. He patronized the jury just as he had patronized me all through our marriage. The United States Attorney, hardly believing his good fortune, had a field day.

"Let me explain to you how things work in real estate," he would say, as if he was lecturing first graders about an interesting if slightly crooked world. Though he was still young and quite handsome, he sounded like an old-time Irish pol.

"You don't have to say anything explicitly about a deal"— he slammed a final nail into his own coffin—"people understand a wink of an eye or a nod of the head."

"No further questions," the United States Attorney announced triumphantly.

He frustrated every one of Mick's attempts to make him look good, not deliberately, but because he was convinced he knew better than anyone else how to explain his business in a way that revealed its innocence.

When he finally swaggered off the witness stand, he said to me in a stage whisper, "I told you I'd straighten everything out."

One of the women on the jury gasped at what seemed like arrogance. Mick Whealan winced. Iggy held his head in his hands. None of us had the heart to tell him that he had pulverized himself.

The jury was out for only an hour. Bud grinned broadly when they came back in. "See, I told you they'd understand."

Guilty on fourteen counts.

Bud was thunderstruck. We had to lead him speechless out of the courtroom. He tried to say something to the TV cameras outside the court, but burst into tears.

The United States Attorney told the media that he was going to ask for a ten-to-twenty-year sentence, "as an example to the young people of Chicago that wealth does not make white-collar crime pay."

Mick told the cameras that he was confident that the verdict would be overturned on appeal.

"Twenty years in jail?" Bud was incredulous.

"No way," Iggy reassured him. "At worst, you'll be out in eighteen months and we'll win on appeal."

"Eighteen months?" He burst into tears again. The difference between twenty years and eighteen months could mean nothing to a man who was serenely convinced of his own innocence.

The verdict had been brought in at eleven in the morning. Bud declined lunch at the Mid America Club and drove us home in silence—at the wheel of my Ferrari Testarossa.

"I should go over to the office and check up on things," I said to him when we had entered our house on Lathrop.

"Sure, fine," he said dully. "Whatever you want. I'll take a little nap."

I remained in Elmwood Park for several hours, most of them on the phone. Iggy and Mick were both confident that we'd win on appeal.

"If we don't?"

Silence.

"I'm worried about him. They've destroyed his world. Shattered it. All his illusions are gone."

"A man can't live by illusions," Iggy said pompously.

"Bud has."

"You shouldn't have let him."

"That's the way I got him. It was too late to change him."

"Well"—my brother signed heavily—"let's wait to see what happens."

Brilliant advice.

It had already happened by then.

I went home about four-thirty. Nancy, in her Trinity uniform, was sobbing on the couch in the parlor.

"It's all right, hon." I put my arms around her. "It's not as bad as it sounds."

"It will never be all right!" she screamed. "Never! He's deserted us!"

Nancy was not the hysterical type. I became concerned. What did she mean by "desert"?

I rushed up the stairs, past the dollhouse, and to our bedroom.

Bud had chosen a long nap.

He was sitting in the chair in front of my vanity, his beloved shotgun cradled in his arms. He had used it to blow off most of his head. His brain had splattered on the spread of our marriage bed.

The next days were terrible. The Pastor of St. Luke's—to whom we had given tens of thousands of dollars and hundreds of hours of work—sent one of his curates downstairs to tell us that Canon Law forbade Christian burial to a suicide.

I walked back to our house from St. Luke's, outraged, brokenhearted, and, of course, feeling guilty. I felt the same way the next morning when I went back to the church for eight-thirty Mass, at which I would pray for the repose of my poor husband's soul.

"Hi, Marbeth," said a familiar voice as I walked into St. Luke's. "Are you coming or going?"

I leaned against his chest and sobbed for the first and only time during those terrible days.

"It's all right," he said. "God loves us all. He loves Bud. He's brought him home."

"I could have stopped him—I should have stopped him."

He patted my back. "No, Marbeth, you couldn't have stopped him. You did the best you could, a lot better than most women would have done. He had many happy years with you. You were a grace in his life."

I might not believe that. I probably didn't fully believe it even then. Nonetheless, John's words helped me to survive the wake and the funeral and the harsh days afterwards. I would like to believe that there is at least some truth in them.

John overruled the Pastor and said the funeral Mass himself—and was savagely attacked in the press for doing it.

"Let him who is without sin cast the first stone," John said in reply. His homily was magnificent. Almost everyone in the church—except for Bud's family—was in tears.

"We'll be together some day in a better world, Marbeth," he said to me, holding my black-gloved hand in his at the cemetery.

"Do you really believe that, John?"

John hesitated. "Yes, Marbeth, of course I do."

He didn't sound too convinced.

The next months were terrible. I was sick every day with my new baby. I had to fight off the U.S. Attorney, who wanted my son as a substitute for my husband. John continued to need my help.

We finally beat the government. A new judge threw out the indictment. The Seventh Circuit promptly upheld the judge.

Reporters cornered me that morning at my office in Elmwood Park. I was dreadfully ill.

"Are you pleased that the Appellate Court has sustained the dismissal of the indictment of Peter Quinlan, Ms. Quinlan?"

"I would be more pleased if they had a chance to sustain the dismissal of the indictment of my late husband."

"Do you still blame Judge Learner for his death, Ms. Quinlan?"

"My husband was the innocent victim of the U.S. Attorney's political ambition and Judge Learner's need to have a jury laugh at his jokes."

"Will you oppose the United States Attorney if he runs for governor?"

"I guarantee you that he will never be governor. His political career is finished."

It was an empty threat but an accurate prediction. I didn't finish him off. He did himself in. But I received a lot of the credit.

There are tears of regret in my eyes as I write these final words about my husband. Unlike the children, I am not angry at his suicide, or at anything else in our life together. He was who he was, who his parents and his environment made him. He was a child, often an adorable child. He could never have grown up.

If I should marry again I would, I think, understand more about married love and do a better job of it. And I would choose a man whom I can't dominate and who, more to the point, doesn't need domination.

My present suitor would fill the bill nicely: a very attractive and genuinely nice man who does not need a woman to manage him and would not let a woman do so if she tried. Moreover, he perceives my reaction of both fear and delight for a man whom I cannot manage and is amused by it.

"You're afraid of me," he says as he envelops me in his arms.

"I am," I admit, as I feel emotions that no grandmother ought to experience. "That entertains you?"

"You have no reason to be afraid." He kisses me very gently. "You should give trust a chance."

"Who says so?" If I don't ease out of his embrace I will be undone. So I break the embrace. He does not pursue the issue, leaving me to my own damnable freedom.

He has reached my last wall of defenses. I must soon either send him on his way or yield everything to him.

"Mom," Beth, my eldest, says to me, though less often now than she used to, "Dad must have been terribly angry at us to have ended his life that way—and without a word of farewell."

"He was angry at the world," I reply, "because it had played such a vicious trick on him. He thought it was one kind of world and it turned out to be a very different kind."

But he died angry at me, too. I had failed to protect him from the viciousness of that world.

Alas, that was something which, love him or not, I couldn't do.

|| 42 || Between my topless act in the lodge on Eagle Lake during the rainstorm and his death in the muddy clearing in Nicaragua, the only dramatic event which John and I shared was his rescue of Caroline at Lake Geneva. That was, however, a sufficiently dramatic occurrence to last a couple of lifetimes—far more traumatic even than the cure of Brenny.

It was a hot night, dense with humidity. The Bears were playing an exhibition game on television. My brothers and their wives and kids and grandchildren had come to my house for a barbecue. I had told the servants to take the night off because I thought a party of our own would be the most fun. Thunderstorms were smoldering in the distance, farther up in Wisconsin. Young people were rushing in and out of the house and jumping in and out of the pool. Rock music was thundering in the background. The smell of mustard and charcoal and chlorine hung heavily in the air. Nancy and her Noah were supposed to be monitoring the pool, but at night with so much noise and movement, it was impossible for them to see everything, even in the bright overhead lights.

I had climbed out of the water after a brief dip, pleasantly tired, thanks to the success of what I thought had been an excellent multigeneration party. The Cardinal was walking by the edge of the pool, engaged in a heavy discussion with my brother Ignatius about abortion.

Suddenly, without a word, he plunged over the side of the pool and into its dark waters. He surfaced for a moment, but before I could say anything, he dove back down. Then he emerged again, holding above him what looked at first like a large doll. A few seconds later I realized that it was Caroline and that she was blue.

I must have screamed in horror, though my children later said that I was the only one around the pool who did not scream. Instead, they insist, I calmly took Carie from John into my arms and laid her on a towel.

"CPR," I am supposed to have said quite coolly to Noah. Perhaps that's the way I did act, sensible to the bitter end. At least I did not get in the way.

The next minutes were nightmarish. Noah began mouth-to-mouth respiration. Nancy was sobbing hysterically, just as she had after she had discovered her father's body after his suicide. Everyone else was screaming. I was paralyzed at the edge of the pool. John was slumped on his knees next to me.

My children also report that I turned to John and said commandingly, "The rosary, John."

"I don't have one with me.

"Say it anyway."

Then he began, in the calm, authoritative voice of a Cardinal Archbishop in his own cathedral, "In the name of the Father and of the Son and of the Holy Spirit. I believe in God . . ."

Someone thrust a rosary into his hands—Peter, I think.

The chaos ceased. All of us fell to our knees and began to pray. I know that I never prayed so hard in my life. As we prayed, kids and then adults from up and down the street poured into the pool area to join our prayers—scores of them. The word had spread very quickly.

"She's got to get better," a weeping ten-year-old whimpered next to me.

I put my arm around the little girl. "Don't worry, dear, she'll be all right."

Noah worked more frantically. Hope was slipping away.

I don't know how long we were on our knees. As time slipped away and our hopes with it, all of us prayed more fervently. I prayed for Nancy and Noah. It wasn't their fault. Yet they would suffer for the rest of their lives. Their marriage would be destroyed before it began.

Noah looked up at me in despair, about to give up. Then he tried once again.

Was her poor little chest moving ever so slightly?

Then Noah shouted and lifted Carie off the ground. She was coughing and choking but breathing. My baby was alive!

Everyone cheered. I rushed forward to embrace her. Noah and I somehow cradled her together as she vomited an incredible amount of water out of her poor little body.

"Mommy!" she wailed, "I drownded!"

The Rosary continued, now jubilantly with Peter leading the glorious mysteries.

"And Cardinal saved you!"

I looked around for John. He was still on his knees next to me, head in his hands, sobbing uncontrollably. I remembered that he had wept at Bud's funeral Mass—while we had all remained dry-eyed—but this was a different kind of grief, perhaps not grief at all. I put one of my arms around him, embracing my precious child and the man who had saved her.

Noah later told me that it was amazing that Carie had suffered no brain damage. "Almost a miracle," he had smiled. "If I believed in miracles."

Lar McAuliffe came rushing into the hospital in Elkhorn, prayer book in hand, and was greeted by my grinning daughter who informed him, "I drownded, but Cardinal saved me!"

"Then let's say a prayer for you and the Cardinal," he said, gasping for breath.

We joined hands and said the Hail Mary, each of us with our own fervor.

"I hope we didn't take you away from the Bears game," I said to him as we chatted.

"They were losing anyway," he laughed. "They've lost every exhibition game this season. One of the kids came in and said that this one"—he gestured at a grinning Caroline—"had drowned. It was an excuse to escape the game."

"All better." She waved her hands. "All better."

Lar and Caroline became instant friends. "All better," she said again and hugged him when he was about to leave. But it was to John she truly became devoted after this episode. Their relationship had always been special, but after he saved her it became all the more intense.

Later I phoned the house to see how John was.

"Still pretty much out of it," Beth told me. "It hit him harder than the rest of us. Tony is driving him home."

When I called him the next day, Len Carey told me that the Cardinal was in a state of shock.

"He couldn't quite explain it to me," Len whined. "Why would he be so upset if he saved the child's life? It would seem to me that if he hadn't then he would weep, but since she is alive . . ."

"He's still weeping?"

"Oh, yes."

"Let me talk to him."

Len had learned to do what he was told to do.

"I called to say thanks again, John."

"She's all right?"

"She's fine. We're taking her home this afternoon. The doctors are astonished that there was no brain damage."

"I called the hospital a couple of times and they said she was all right. I wanted to be sure."

He was weeping again. I became a little worried. Was this not an abnormal reaction? As Len had said, Caroline was alive.

"We will always owe the rest of her life to you, John."

"I was talking to Iggy." He didn't seem to hear me.

"Thought I saw something out of the corner of my eye, jumped without thinking, I don't know why, missed her the first time, got her the second, I knew it was her, somehow I knew it was her!"

"She's alive and well, John. You saved her life. She's fine."

"I know . . . I never prayed so hard. It was so close. If I hadn't seen her . . ."

"You *did* see her, John." I was growing more concerned. "And you did save her. It all worked out."

He laughed weakly. "You'll think I'm being hysterical. I'm all right, Marbeth. It was such a powerful experience. Caught up in the mystery of life and death."

"Life won this time."

"It's supposed to, isn't it?"

In a couple of days he was over it, same old smiling John, living, as it seemed, on the surface of events. But his reaction to the incident in 1985 at Lake Geneva is another proof, I think, that there were depths in him that none of us understood.

|| **43** || John and I had our worst fight right before he died. It was a fearsome argument, the only time in our lives that he responded to my anger with anger of his own.

We argued about the fact I'd let Nancy come with us.

"All I said was that you could send her home," he grumbled, "if you wanted to."

"She's an adult quite capable of making her own decision," I shouted at him. "This trip was your idea, not mine."

It was a difficult time. The three of us were tired, and irritable and constantly sick with some virulent form of the *turista*.

John was also worried—not about himself, not about me, but about Nancy's safety. His feeling was that we had lived our lives, I guess, and she had not.

"She has a husband and a little boy at home—she shouldn't be going up those mountains tomorrow."

"You tell her that."

"You're her mother."

"You're her special friend. You're the one who predicted her recovery when she was a dying little four-pounder."

"She came to take care of you."

"Bullshit, John. She came along because she doesn't think I'm capable of taking adequate care of you."

Actually, Nancy was taking care of both of us and all three of us knew it.

"Marbeth, that's the most stupid thing you've ever said in your long life of saying stupid things."

I realized that the comment was totally unlike John and that he was sicker than I had thought he was. What I said, however, was, "And that's a typically male chauvinist comment from an incurable male chauvinist."

"You're not going to tell her she has to stay here in Managua?"

"You've asked me that before and I already told you once that you should tell her. Has your intestinal difficulty affected your memory?"

"Goddamn it, you're her mother!"

"And you're her Archbishop!"

"Will you stop being unreasonable, for the love of God! We can't risk her life."

"She's risking her own life!" I exploded into tears and stormed out of the bar of the hotel and up to my room.

I knew enough about men in general, and about John in particular, to realize that what I should have done was to say quite calmly that I would have a little talk with Nance. I would then have the talk, Nancy would dismiss my fears, and I would report regretfully to the Cardinal Archbishop of Chicago that the young woman was as stubborn as her mother. I would have thus eased his conscience and soothed over the conflicts.

Almost any other time in my life I would have done just that. But I was sick and frightened and worried about all of us. So I acted stupidly on the last night of his life.

He called fifteen minutes later to apologize. Typical of John, blaming himself for my foolishness.

The next day I was even sicker and, if anything, even more scared. John judged by the look on my face that I didn't want to discuss our dustup.

I sulked in the helicopter and on the long walk up the mountain.

A few minutes before we entered the clearing where it all came to an end, he turned and essayed a tentative smile at me.

Thank God I could never resist that smile. The mists of the mountain disappeared and my sickness with them. I smiled back, my most beautiful smile.

He grinned happily in return. The storm clouds had been chased away.

That was our last communication before he died.

And that's the story.

What more can I say? Is he a saint? I've always said that I don't know the answer. I do know that he was always a good man and that in his final years he became a much better man, though he was still John. I'm prejudiced on the subject because I always loved him and always will. Yet, since his death, I have often thought that we didn't deserve to have him with us at all. Perhaps we were lucky to have him with us as long as we did.

LAURENCE

‖ 44 ‖ "He was the courier." The reporter glanced nervously around the busy restaurant. "There is no doubt in my mind about that. His appointment to Chicago was a reward for the risks he had taken and maybe insurance that he would keep his mouth shut. After all, he did bring stolen money, hundreds of thousands of dollars, maybe millions, across international boundaries. The Vatican couldn't afford to risk the possibility that he'd be afflicted by an attack of conscience, could it?"

We were eating lunch in a booth at Escargot, a French restaurant on the second floor of the Allerton Hotel on Michigan Avenue, right around the corner from the Chancery. Since I didn't belong to any clubs, I asked the reporter to choose a restaurant. Under the circumstances, we were perhaps too close to the center of ecclesiastical power.

"We had the whole story." She lifted a spoonful of watercress soup. "Everything. All we had to do was to prove definitively the source of the money and we could have tied it up. Then he died"—she curled her lip in disgust at Johnny McGlynn's death—"and my editors killed the story."

Marcy Rudolph was a woman in her middle thirties, thin, hunched-over, and fast-talking, with fading blond hair and darting green eyes, a bird of prey waiting to pounce on a victim for "investigative reporting."

"It sounds all very speculative to me."

She had written extensively about the Banco Ambrosiano affair, the disappearance from a Milanese bank of two billion dollars into paper Central American companies. The Vatican had been involved because it had offered support to the organizers of the operation. Legally, the Vatican had been absolved of responsibility. Now the conventional wisdom was that the Catholic Archbishop who had presided over the bank had, at the most, been taken in by the conspirators. However, rumors floated around Chicago in the middle nineteen-eighties that Marcy had been investigating Cardinal McGlynn's involvement in the affair. She had been quite willing to talk to me when I had called her. "The story is dead as far as I'm concerned, Father. You're welcome to it. The Church ought not to canonize someone who is guilty of grand larceny."

The way she said "Father" suggested that she was, or had been, Catholic. You can always tell. And once a Catholic, always a Catholic.

"Look." She put aside the soup and waited for her monkfish. "Put yourself in his shoes. He's a very ambitious priest, but he's passed his fiftieth birthday and he's still a plain old monsignor and his prospects don't look very good. The old Cardinal kept him in parish work for five years after his ordination. Four more years in graduate study in Rome. A couple of years at a nunciature in Africa, and then five years in Vienna, where he works with Cardinal Koenig on the Vatican's Ostpolitik. He's good with language so he's picked up German and French as well as Italian and he learns enough Polish to travel with Koenig into the East Bloc. Despite his late start he's moving up fast. Giovanni Benelli, technically the Under Secretary of State at the Vatican, but actually the man who makes it run for Paul VI, hears about him, meets him, likes him, and gives him a job in Rome. He's at the center of power, right?"

"Right."

"And his mother, who isn't senile yet, is delighted, which is what Jumping Johnny really wants. OK?"

She knew the nickname and she knew about his mother— the woman had done her homework well.

"This Benelli is quite a guy. He's no liberal, but he does believe in running a tight and efficient ship, which saves Paul VI a lot of worry about whether Curia people are going to do what he wants them to do. So he offends the hell out of the Curia. Benelli chews twenty asses for breakfast every day. No more midday siestas for the Roman Curia. We work American hours now, guys. Johnny is made his point man. He's supposed to balance Benelli's ruthlessness with his own charm. He's pretty good at it, but those whom he pushes around, ever so gracefully, have long memories."

"I guess."

"You'd better believe it. Hey, each of the last four Popes has found a way to cope with the entrenched power in the curial bureaucracy. Pius XII has this German woman who was his cook . . ."

"Madre Pasquilina."

"You know about her, huh? Well, she's his Prime Minister. John calls a Council. Paul has Benelli. The Pollack ignores them and runs his own little Polish government-in-exile up on the top floor of the Vatican. The Benelli strategy seems to work best of all. OK?"

"OK."

"But look what happens to Johnny McGlynn. Benelli's opponents finally do him in. Montini sends him off to Florence in disgrace, just like Pacelli had sent Montini off to Milano. . . . Tell me, Father, have you ever been to Florence?"

"Yes."

"How could that be a disgrace? . . . Anyway, Montini remembers how he felt when he was exiled, so he makes Benelli a cardinal in the hope that he will be the next Pope. In the meantime poor Johnny hangs around Rome, a minor functionary at the Secretariat of State with nothing much to do, a lot of enemies, and no patron unless and until Benelli returns from Florence."

"Bad scene."

"Decidedly." She was polishing off her monkfish with considerable efficiency. "OK, Paul VI finally dies. Benelli is a prime candidate. But he's only fifty-nine, too young, they all say. So Luciani is elected despite his bad health and dies in a month, mostly because the Vatican neglects his health. Then they elect the Pollack, who is even younger than Benelli, who returns to Florence definitely out of favor. Our friend Johnny is now on the margins, it looks like forever. To make it worse, Benelli dies, so his last patron is removed from the scene. He's finished, right?"

"Right." I sipped my iced tea.

"Then what happens? In a year and a half after the election of J.P. II, he comes to Chicago as its archbishop. A year later he's made a cardinal. From being a very old curial monsignor, he becomes a very young cardinal—even if his mother is now so out of it that she doesn't comprehend that he's made it big. Doesn't that strike you as strange?"

"Jumping Johnny always knew how to jump."

"Yeah. But at the same time money is disappearing out of the Banco Ambrosiano and money is flowing into Poland for the organization of Solidarity. Isn't that an interesting coincidence?"

"Interesting, but hardly conclusive proof."

"Yeah. But consider what else we know. Johnny is making a number of trips back to Vienna. He eats lunch with his old friend Professor Annemarie Hoffmann, a mathematics teacher, who has lots of contacts behind the Iron Curtain. He sees a lot of Koenig and, each trip, disappears from sight for a few days. Then he reappears and flies back to Rome."

"Maybe he's in the countryside with Annemarie."

"Nah." She waved her hand in dismissal. "We checked that out. He's flying to Warsaw and then taking a train to Cracow where he meets with a fellow named Roman Lezak, who is one of the intellectuals behind Walesa—guy is now a Solidarity member of parliament. The last couple of times Hoffmann goes with him."

"He travels as Monsignor McGlynn from Rome?"

"He travels as Michael Ulatowski from Chicago. With Annemarie as Mrs. Ulatowski on the last two trips. Someone has given him false documents."

"CIA?"

"Who else? When the Communists in Warsaw say that Solidarity is supported by the CIA, they are telling the truth."

"Couldn't it have been CIA money?"

"They don't have their own couriers? This Lezak fellow is a very devout Catholic. The Church wants someone who will spend their money the way they want it spent. They don't trust the CIA altogether and vice versa, get it?"

"They need couriers because what the Polish underground must have is hard cash, Yankee dollars."

"You got it. Mind you, McGlynn, alias Ulatowski, has balls. He could get caught and end up in a Polish jail. Or he could get shot. Or he could get the rest of his career ruined. But he's always been one to take the big risk."

Like pitching at the Villa without any practice.

"Why the woman traveling companion?"

"Part of the cover. Also, the last two trips are by car. They cross the border at Bratislava and drive through Czechoslovakia to the Polish border and on to Cracow. The woman knows both Czech and Slovak and has friends along the way. This part is risky. They're taking big chances. But apparently the LOT flight from Vienna to Warsaw every evening—LOT 226— isn't safe anymore."

"Shouldn't it be to his credit that he participated in the founding of Solidarity?"

She sat upright abruptly. "With stolen money?"

"Can you establish the link between Banco Ambrosiano money and the cash Johnny was bringing to Cracow?"

"Where else is the Church going to find a couple of million

dollars? It's broke at this time because of the cost of two papal funerals and elections and it's running each year a big financial deficit. Everyone in Rome knows that some of the Ambrosiano money is going to Solidarity. Johnny isn't the only courier, but he's probably taking the biggest risk."

"Maybe he doesn't know where the money comes from."

"Hell," she sputtered, "where does he think it comes from? Sure, he doesn't ask. Sure, he pretends to himself that it's money someone has found somewhere. But he knows the Vatican can't get its hands on that much cash unless there's something kinky going on. He goes ahead anyway."

The waiter came for our dessert order. Marcy virtuously declined. I ordered raspberry tart and more iced tea.

"Marcy, I don't think that you have a case with which you could persuade a grand jury to vote a true bill. What everyone in Rome knows is not always true. You haven't proved that the money which Johnny was smuggling into Poland came from the bank. Unless you can establish that connection, your case falls apart."

"You sound just like my editor. It doesn't matter what Johnny told himself. All we have to prove is that he actually carried the stolen money into Poland. What he thought is irrelevant."

"Have you proved that?"

"We were working on that when he got himself shot. My editors made me drop it."

"So all you really have now—Marcy, let me finish—all you really have is some highly informed speculation, some solidly grounded probabilities. Despite the likelihood that you're right, you don't have a smoking gun."

She looked down at her coffee, bit her lips, and said, "Do you want to canonize him? Do you believe he was a saint?"

"No, I don't believe he was a saint. I'm not an apologist. He was not one of my favorite people, but I'm supposed to get at the facts of his life."

"Would not even the solidly grounded probability—your words, Father—that he had cooperated with those who stole millions, even billions, raise an obstacle to canonization?"

"I can't dispute that."

"Do you think anyone in the Vatican will tell you the truth about the money or even about his involvement?"

"No. Maybe no one there even knows the truth anymore."

"So I'm stuck with a story that will never be written because it is incomplete and no one will let me complete it. You're stuck with a probability that you can never prove or disprove because no one can or will tell you the truth."

"That about sums it up."

"Nor can you prove that he didn't sleep with La Annemarie during their jaunt through Middle Europe."

"People are innocent until they are proven guilty."

"You don't believe that, do you?" Her lip curled scornfully. "Even if Johnny McGlynn didn't smuggle hot money, the fact that he traveled to Poland with an attractive woman should be enough to sink a canonization."

"Maybe."

She reached for the check. Laity tend to pick up the tab for priests.

"No way." I pried the bill out of her hands.

"I make more money than you do," she insisted.

"I'll bill the Cardinal."

She yielded with good grace.

"Thanks for the lunch, Father. I haven't talked to a priest for a long time. You're not like the priests at my parish when I grew up in Philly."

"I hope that is a compliment," I said, knowing damn well that it was.

"Hell, yes." She laughed. Then, turning serious, "Maybe I could talk to you again sometime."

Marcy, I reflected as I turned up Michigan Avenue, demonstrated a crucial truth, the crucial truth about American Catholics: It is impossible for them to really leave the Church. She was a tough, cynical reporter who knew more dirt about the Vatican than almost anyone else and who also remembered some bitter experiences with priests. Yet she was still a Catholic and now, perhaps because of children or perhaps because of maturity or perhaps a mixture of both, found herself drawn to Catholicism again—indeed, waiting for a chance to talk to a priest. So God sent a priest, not the best one on the bench maybe, but one who was available.

Johnny was right, perhaps more right than he realized, when he said the real Church was in the parish.

And what should I make of Marcy's story? Perhaps Johnny McGlynn had been a Vatican Scarlet Pimpernel. It fit the risk-taking part of his personality. Marcy was probably right that he saw such a mission as a way out of the corner of the Vatican in which he had been boxed. But no matter how courageous he might have been, Chicago was still a big reward. But, to the Pope, it would not seem an unreasonable request: Chicago as reward for Solidarity. Moreover, knowing Johnny, the request would have been so indirect and low-key that the Pope would not have taken offense. But as to the issue of the money used in Poland, Marcy was wrong. Johnny's trust in the wisdom and morality of Church leadership would make it unnecessary, indeed unthinkable, for him to ask where the money came from. That was perhaps one of the reasons why they had chosen him for the job.

His bravery for the good of the Church would be, from the Vatican's viewpoint, an excellent reason to proclaim him a saint. Alas, that would not be possible at the present time, they would say, because of rumors about where the money came from. False rumors, naturally, but they still had to be taken into account.

I would go to Vienna and Rome to learn as much as I could. Then I'd confront the Pope himself and ask what had really happened.

|| **45** || "Jamie," I shouted at my New Priest. "I'm going to Europe."

"Tonight?" he asked, pausing at the head of the steps. He was returning from the young people's session after the seven P.M. Sunday Mass.

My New Priest, as I have said on occasion, is a practically perfect New Priest. He does all things, including making travel arrangements.

"Oh, no," I said, deflated by his sangfroid. "Not for a couple of days."

"There's no problem, then. Where do you want to go?"

"Vienna, Warsaw, and Rome. In that order."

"Good. We'll put you up in the Imperial in Vienna—Wagner lived there for two years—the Marriott in Warsaw—that's the tallest building in the city—and, of course, the Hassler in Rome. Whom do you propose to see in these cities?"

Do I have to say that he wasn't taking notes?

"In Vienna, Professor Annemarie Hoffmann, a professor of mathematics. In Warsaw, Professor Roman Lezak, a Solidarity delegate to the Siejm."

"The parliament," he agreed. "And in the so-called Eternal City?"

"A couple of the relators at the Congregation for the Causes of Saints. I believe that your friend Steve will clear the path for me there."

"Right. You want to leave as soon as possible?"

"And get back as soon as possible."

"Precisely. Consider it done."

James is as smooth as they come. The next afternoon he caught me in the office.

"Everything is set in Vienna and Rome, Father. I spoke to Professor Hoffmann and she would be very happy to cooperate. She has apparently kept up to date on the saga of our late Cardinal through CNN and is most curious. She'll meet you for dinner at the Sacher where, I believe, she and John McGlynn ate. Father Kunkel at the Congregation will be happy to talk to you, and so will the Cardinal in charge. Roman Lezak was somewhat more hesitant."

"Was he now?"

How had my New Priest tracked down all these people?

"Wanted to know what the conversation would be about. I told him flat-out that it would be about the money that the perhaps Venerable Servant of God smuggled into Poland for Solidarity. That stopped him cold, as you might imagine. He said he'd have to check."

"Did he say with whom?"

"Sure—Lech. My guess is that they both will want to talk to the Church."

"The Church will say no."

"First they'll make a call to our mutual friend up on 1555 North State. And he'll be more likely to advise them to talk to you. Roman was a bit surprised that I could stumble along in Polish, what with me Irish name."

I didn't know that Jamie could stumble along in Polish, but nothing about him surprised me anymore.

"Keep me in the picture."

"Oh, I'll do that all right. So you leave tomorrow night at

ten to five on Lufthansa, Flight 431, nonstop to Frankfurt, change to Austrian Air 408, and arrive in Vienna at ten forty-five day after tomorrow morning. First Class, VIP all the way, like I promised."

"Tomorrow!"

Jamie seemed surprised. "You said you want to get it over with."

"I haven't packed."

He glanced at his watch. "You have twenty-five hours to do that."

"What about the parish?"

"Nora and I will run it, won't we girl? We do all the work anyway."

|| **46** || I decided to phone my doctor after I had polished off my second Sacher Torte.

I had spent the afternoon wandering around Vienna in the sunlight as Jamie insisted I do—as an antidote to jet lag.

"Two hours of direct sunlight in the afternoon for the first two days and you'll awake the third morning on Viennese time," he insisted. "I've scheduled the dinner with Professor Frau Hoffmann on the second day. You'll need a day to get over the trip."

I had walked the Ringstrasse, admired the Hofburg and the Stefansdom, and was relaxing in a sidewalk café in front of the Imperial Hotel, where I'd ordered tea and Sacher Torte. While I was consuming these delicacies, I read a plaque noting that Wagner had lived in this hotel while writing some of his operas.

It may have been an appropriate hotel for him, but it was too elegant for a parish priest with origins on 79th Street. I was not, however, about to check out.

Then I began to reflect on Mary Elizabeth's memoir.

If Marbeth was writing a cover-up, how would it be different from what I had read? In such a cover-up she would no doubt reveal enough about herself to make any reader think she couldn't possibly be hiding anything and therefore had nothing to hide. It would be a savvy use of candor as a dodge.

There was, of course, a good chance she was telling the simple truth: She and Johnny had never been lovers, though she had always loved him. I didn't have any reason not to give her the benefit of the doubt, did I? After all, she was quite frank, even when such frankness put her in an embarrassing light.

Even her portrait of Johnny was believable. I still figured him to be too shallow to merit her undying love, but that was her problem. I'd never denied that he was a charming man. She, for her part, did not deny any of the faults of which I was aware.

"Herr McAuliffe?" A Turkish bellman presented me with an envelope. Inside was a fax message, sent from the office of M. M. W. Keenan, Ph.D.

> *Boss,*
> *Cordelia Marie Meehan McGlynn died last night while you were en route Vienna. She seems to have set fire to the apartment while trying to light a cigarette in the middle of the night. The nurse who was sleeping in the other bedroom smelled the smoke only when most of the bedroom had been destroyed.*
> *The Cardinal will say the Mass of Resurrection tomorrow. May she rest in peace.*
> *Regards,*

The poor woman. I sighed. Perhaps she's found peace at last. I remembered the picture of that laughing young bride. What had gone wrong? What goes wrong in the life of so many happy brides?

Then I remembered the letters between Johnny and his mother. Had they been destroyed? Almost certainly they had. So my copies were the only ones. I'd have to decide what to do with them.

Burn them, probably.

If I believed Marbeth, Johnny had only humored his mother in those letters and was no more guilty of simony than any rising young cleric might be. I had no reason not to believe Marbeth's account. Why, after all, would she lie to me?

To protect his memory, that's why.

If her old chum Kate might try to deceive me in order to defame his memory, would not Marbeth also try to deceive me for the opposite reason?

You bet your life she would. Without a second thought. And she'd do a thorough job, too.

That's when I thought about something else in her memoir.

Let's see. A decade of the rosary, said aloud with a congregation, requires about three minutes. Let's assume that since they were already into the sorrowful mysteries, that they had said seven decades. That's twenty minutes, more or less. Could a child be without a heartbeat that long and still survive without brain damage?

I called my M.D.

"They said an overseas call," she said as soon as she was on the line. "Where are you?"

"Vienna."

"How nice. I'm glad to see you are following my recommendation about frequent vacations."

"Business this time. I'll explain next time I see you. I have a question now."

She was intrigued. "Must be an important question."

"A kid falls in a pool. No one sees her. By the time they pull her out, she's blue. It takes twenty minutes to revive her. What are the odds on no brain damage?"

"Zero, Lar. And the revival is unlikely at that point, too."

"She would not start breathing and then begin to talk to her mother?"

"Again, less than zero."

"Uh, huh. But suppose she did revive and did talk to her mother and did suffer no brain damage."

"Then you're leaving medical science and speaking miracles. Miracles or fantasy. I don't say it couldn't happen. I'm merely saying that we can't explain things like that when they do."

I decided I needed another Sacher Torte.

Another miracle. This one when he was alive.

47 Professor Frau Annemarie Hoffmann was a doll: short, blond, blue-eyed, she was a life-sized version of a souvenir you might buy in the gift shop at the Imperial Hotel, a carefully crafted and expensive doll. Age had apparently done no harm to her opulent little body and had touched her round face only lightly.

"Astonishing," she said often, as I recounted in detail the story of the changes in Johnny during the last years of his life. "Ja, simply astonishing!"

It had been, let's see, twenty-five years since Johnny had served on the staff of the Nunciature here. She was probably a student then, so that made her perhaps forty-five years old now. That seemed about right. She had been in her early thirties when Johnny came back for her help in smuggling money into Poland.

Physically she was the opposite of Marbeth. Intellectually, they were very similar, both sharp as they come and both quite capable of covering up for a man if they wanted to.

"He was a charming man." Her fair skin turned pink, as it would often do during our conversation. "We met at the opera, you know. I was sitting next to him in the very highest row. Very charming. And very kind. A martyr and a saint? It surprises me, and yet it doesn't. He was also very brave."

We were slowly working our way through a large and heavy Teutonic meal in the restaurant of the Hotel Sacher on the Philharmonikerstrasse, just off Kärnerstrasse. Its thick red wall hangings, ponderous waiters, and gleaming white tablecloths made one wonder whether it might not be 1910, and poor, lonely old Franz Josef might not be still living in the Hofburg and getting up at four o'clock in the morning to begin initialling documents.

At twenty, Annemarie must have been the kind of woman that a man would want to pick up and carry off as his own. Could Johnny resist the temptation? If I were to believe Marbeth, he could resist even more direct and appealing temptations.

"I'm interested especially in the trips he is supposed to have made to Poland some years after his term here at the Nunciature."

"Ja. It is important that they be described because they will confirm his willingness to risk his life for the Church and for religious freedom. He was a very brave man. I loved him very much. Please understand, Father, there was never anything improper between us, even before I married Herr Professor Hoffmann. My Ludwig"—she blushed again—"whom I love very much, was also quite fond of Monsignor McGlynn."

We paused while I inspected pictures of Ludwig and their three children. Ludwig was a solemn-looking fellow with a big mustache. The kids, two boys and a girl, were in their late teens.

Nothing improper? Everyone seemed to be insisting that Jumping Johnny never did anything improper. Well, maybe he didn't.

"I quite understand, Frau Professor."

"You see," she continued, "I am Polish on my mother's side. My aunts and cousins still live in Poland, in Warsaw. At the time, the Iron Curtain was very thick. When I found that he made frequent trips to Warsaw for the Church I asked him to bring little gifts to them. He always did so."

"Was that dangerous?"

"A bit, but the Polish customs guards usually didn't care. They were worried only about currency control—the removal of Polish money from the country. And Father McGlynn was an unofficial representative of the Vatican at a time when the Party needed the Church. So the guards would leave him alone."

"It was much later, was it not, after the election of John Paul II, that he made trips with money, large sums of money?"

"Ja," she replied, sipping her glass of red wine. "I accompanied him. Six times. As his presumed wife." She turned almost as red as the wine in her glass. "It was necessary."

"Part of the disguise?"

She might not know that I knew about this "arrangement." That she was telling me suggested that she was not trying to hide anything.

"That is right. This time he was not acting as an official representative of the Vatican. He was smuggling large sums of money for which he could be arrested, or if the Party was in a bad mood, he might have been shot."

"And you too?"

She waved a hand. "Year or two in prison, no more than that. But no matter the risk, it had to be done. Herr Hoffmann agreed. The money was for a Catholic trade union—it was still underground then and the name Solidarity had not been given to it. It meant freedom for Poland. I was proud of my role then, however small. I am proud now."

"Understandably. But why was it necessary for you to accompany him?"

"He needed a companion who could speak the language more fluently than he could—we were pretending to be American Poles from Chicago. Moreover, I knew the people he was to meet. My cousins. A different cousin with each rendezvous team. I also knew the customs officer in whose line we were supposed to stand. That was very important, as you might imagine."

"Johnny would have been in deep trouble if he made a mistake about the line."

"Oh, yes. So my cousins suggested that I be the, ah, should I say, accomplice?"

"Roman Lezak?"

"He is a friend of my cousins. You will see him too? In Warsaw?"

"Apparently. He was reluctant at first. I gather Lech told him it was all right."

"Only after approval by the Church, I'm sure."

"So tell me about the trips."

She shook her head, as if astonished at how reckless she had been.

"They were very simple. We would fly late in the afternoon from Vienna to Warsaw, carrying four suitcases, two for each of us, filled with packages of American dollars under a layer of clothes. We would check into an inexpensive hotel, a different one each time. The next morning we would meet our contacts in a small park on the outskirts of the city and exchange the suitcases for four which contained nothing but clothes. We would eat supper in the old city and spend a second night in the hotel. It would have been suspicious to leave too soon. Then we would take the two o'clock LOT plane back to Vienna in the afternoon. A three-day trip."

"A frightening three days?"

"Terrifying. Although it was a simple plan and we had problems only twice, I trembled every minute for the whole time. John was very different. He loved the adventure. He looked forward to our little pilgrimages, as he called them. He found them, how should I call it, exhilarating. He knew no fear."

"I'm not surprised."

"Even the fifth time, when our friend was not at the customs barrier and I was sure we'd be arrested, he was serene. He told me not to worry, that it would be all right. Fortunately, he was so charming that the man who did clear us thought it unnecessary to look beneath the top layer of clothes."

"He bluffed his way through?"

"But of course. I should have known that he would."

My blood ran cold. It was taking on Watersmeet without a couple of days' practice. Except that this time Jumping Johnny had won.

"A near thing."

"I trembled for a week. Our friends at the park were astonished to see us. They felt certain that we had been arrested."

"What had happened?"

"Our friend had been reassigned that very morning, so they could not send a warning to us. It was an accident. We had stirred up no suspicion."

"Didn't anyone think it strange that the same couple would come to Warsaw six times in the course of a year?"

"We had different identities each time."

"Provided by the CIA?"

"Presumably, Herr McAuliffe. I didn't ask. I didn't want to know anything more than I had to know."

"Understandably. And the final trip?"

She shivered. "I still have nightmares about it. It was necessary to drive through Czechoslovakia and cross into Poland at a small border crossing near Ostrava, where we had another friend, and then drive on to Cracow. There were dangers every mile of the trip. Especially at the Czech border posts. We had no friends there. Fortunately they were concerned only about those who were leaving Czechoslovakia for Austria and we did not have the money on our trip back."

"You mean you drove into Slovakia . . ."

"And across the bridge at Bratislava—such a lovely old town."

". . . with suitcases filled with dollars and no guarantee that you would not be searched!"

"It was necessary. . . . I still cannot believe that I did it. And I was not a wild little child then either. I had three babies . . ." Her eyes filled with tears. "I am proud nonetheless."

"Father McGlynn was not frightened?"

"Of course not. I told you he was very brave."

"How long did the trip take?"

"A week, Father. I trembled every minute of it. Especially when we crossed into Poland and were told that there was a change of plans because the police were suspicious. We had to meet different people at a different place than the arranged place. I would not know them. I thought it was a trap."

"How did you decide to trust the people you met?"

"John went to the rendezvous point, a rural church ten miles west of Cracow on a side road off the main road to Kantowice, and inspected it and the people who were waiting for us. He was certain they were not police. I remember his words. 'You can always tell a Polish intellectual by the sad frown on his face and the dejected cigarette hanging from the corner of his mouth.' That's when we met Roman Lezak, a great man."

"So you finally returned safely to Vienna?"

"Yes, and I swore that I would never do it again. Naturally, Herr McAuliffe, I didn't mean that. If John had asked me, I would do it again. Even today, though, thank God, it is no longer necessary."

"Solidarity should want to see him canonized."

"Oh, yes."

"Quite a story, Professor Hoffmann."

"You wonder about me, Herr McAuliffe? You wonder about a married woman, trembling with her foolish fear, lying in bed with some of her clothes removed, next to an attractive man of whom she is very fond. You wonder what this is like for her?"

"Exciting? Disconcerting? Troubling?"

"All of those, very exciting, deeply troubling. John's laughter would break the tension and make it possible. It was never easy. Especially that terrible week in the old Volkswagen."

"I'm sure it was very difficult for both of you."

"For John, I don't think so. He admired me, I know that. He would have liked to have enjoyed me. I know that too. But I don't think I was a very great temptation to him, not like he was to me. He enjoyed the danger of the adventure more than he would have enjoyed the body of a woman."

The perfect spy. The CIA would have loved him.

"As for me"—she sighed—"I was glad that it was over, but for a long time I missed his body next to mine in my bed."

The women in Johnny's life seemed to be coming through with more candor than I'd anticipated. But such frankness made me suspicious. By being so frank was she trying to win my confidence? Make me believe she wasn't holding back anything and therefore had nothing to cover up? Why tell me that unless she was covering up something?

"An astonishing story," I said as we walked to the lobby for our coffee.

"Yes." She sighed. "It is a story to remember always as one becomes old and as one's grandchildren grow up hardly believing that there ever was an Iron Curtain."

We arranged ourselves in comfortable chairs in the lobby.

"I presume the money came from the CIA?"

She shook her head. "No. John didn't tell me where it came from and naturally I didn't ask. But he did say that while the passports and identity documents were American-made, the money came from somewhere else."

"I see."

As we were leaving the Hotel Sacher, I asked one more question. "Is your confirmation name Lise?"

"How did you know that?" She was astonished. "Do you read souls?"

I explained about the "hat trick." I don't think she fully understood. But then, for all her charm, she wasn't Irish.

So I had eaten a pleasant, if large supper with a pretty woman and heard a stirring adventure story. I had seen an aspect of John McGlynn in action about which I had known little—though his reckless disregard of danger had not surprised me. I had discovered that he could trouble even a very pious and dedicated woman.

But I had not learned what I needed to know: where had John gotten the money?

Maybe they would know in Warsaw.

|| **48** || "The bravest man I ever met." Roman Lezak drew deeply on his cigarette, which did indeed hang dejectedly from the corner of his mouth. "Many of us took risks in those times—they seem so long ago now—but no one with more intelligence and courage and, how should I put it in English: flair?"

"Johnny had lots of flair, all right. But I wonder if it's bravery when you're really not afraid."

We were sitting in a smoke-filled coffee shop just off Market Square in the historic old city (reconstructed after the war) just down St. John's Street from the red brick cathedral and across from the gleaming white Jesuit church. Lezak also had the sad face of the Polish intellectual and wore the kind of worn tweed suit which seemed to have become the uniform of the Solidarity members of the Polish parliament.

Warsaw was a shabby city, the poorest city I'd ever visited during my limited travel experience. But the people did not seem depressed. And the shops were filled with goods—who, after all, had the money to buy them? Maybe there was a little bit of hope stirring that economic improvement would eventually follow political freedom.

"It is bad now," Roman had said to me, "worse in some ways than it used to be, although there is food in the shops for those who can afford it. However, it will get better, of that we are now confident."

I hoped so. I liked the people. They deserved a better hand than recent history had dealt them—and not so recent history, too.

"Johnny was afraid, all right," Lezak replied to my objection. "He was, after all, a priest in a very compromising situation. The Party would have made much of it if they had captured him. Rumors of adultery would have caused a grave scandal. The Polish Church would have denounced him. They knew the money was coming, though they did not know the route or the courier. He also had to worry about poor Frau Hoffmann. She is a very brave woman; the situation was extreme. She was holding up, but barely. John was afraid, I know. He told me he was afraid."

If he mentioned his fear, then he probably was not afraid, I decided.

"It was certainly courageous to take the chance that your group at the rural church were not the police."

"He had instincts, Father. Some men do, you know. We learned that in the underground. Sometimes your instincts fail, but it is still the best strategy."

"I'm sure it is. . . . How much money did he bring?"

"I do not know and neither did he. He said that he never counted it and I believe him. Millions, anyway. There were perhaps other couriers too, after him. No one, I think, knows for sure how many or how much money was brought. None of it was wasted, of that you can be sure."

"Then the Party's accusation that Solidarity was financed by the CIA had some truth in it?"

"Why not?" He lit another cigarette—there were no signs in Poland forbidding smoking, and everyone seemed to be smoking all the time. "Was there anything wrong with CIA money? But the money Jan brought was not American. It was cash that some people in the Vatican wanted to get into the hands of certain Catholic laymen."

"Ah?"

"The kind of laymen, like myself I suppose, on whose loyalty to the Vatican they could rely, but who would not be caught up in the conflicts of clerical politics inside the Polish Church. Some bishops would have much rather taken their chances with the Party than give money and power to men like Lech."

"I see."

"The CIA would not have been able to comprehend the nuances of such a transfer of funds. They perhaps would have thought that they were being asked to fund a factional fight within the Church. A much more sophisticated transfer of funds was necessary—simple in execution but elaborate in planning. No, it was not American money Jan brought to us when we so desperately needed it."

"Interesting."

"I myself do not know where it came from. I do not believe that even Lech knows with certainty, although sometimes he pretends to know."

"But John knew, didn't he?"

"Oh yes, he told us that he did. He found out, he said, quite by accident, and he could tell no one. Ever. He was quite firm in that."

That was the Johnny I knew: a show-off who'd tell the other kids he had a big secret that he'd never reveal.

"Did it seem to trouble him?"

"Not in the least. But very few things seemed to trouble your Bishop and Martyr."

I wondered a couple of times in the course of our conversation why Lezak was so forthcoming. It is not, I had been often told, in the Slavic soul to be candid.

Presumably Roman Lezak and those who lurked behind him had nothing of which to be afraid, and had been advised by their allies in the Church to answer all my questions. Even to answer questions I had not asked.

"I will admit," he continued, "that I was a little troubled by the fact that he was traveling with a woman, although the need for that was clear. I am"—he raised his eyebrows—"a reasonably sophisticated man of the world, but about priests

I still have some old-fashioned notions. Moreover, when I saw Frau Hoffmann I was even more, what should I say . . ."

"In America we might say scandalized."

"Perhaps." He ground out his cigarette and grinned at me. "My wife would not want me to travel with such a beautiful and fragile woman as a pretended mate. Yet one saw immediately that he was a father or a brother to her and nothing else. She was terrified, as she had every reason to be. Soaking wet from the terrible rain. On the verge of sickness. Longing for her husband and babies. A pathetic, woebegone little doll. He took care of her and protected her like she was his little sister . . . he did have a little sister, I presume?"

"He did. And he was always respectful and courteous to her and her friends."

"I knew it was so."

He lit another cigarette while I drank some of the thick coffee, which we might have used to scrub the corridors of St. Finian's school if we had run out of general purpose detergent.

"Were the police actually searching for them?"

"Oh, yes. They were not all that intelligent, but somewhere they had learned that money, in large sums, was being brought into the country and that there was a shipment destined for Cracow and that a blond woman and her husband were the couriers and that the rendezvous was outside the Cloth Hall in Cracow. The police cars were on every road between Cracow and the border. Somehow Jan was able to elude them. Instincts again. We were able to get a message to him to stay out of Cracow."

"Instincts can run out, as you say."

"Fortunately for all of us, his did not. And that was his last mission. He almost seemed disappointed when he said that to me."

I hadn't learned all that much: confirmation for Annemarie Hoffmann's claim that there was no intimacy between her and Johnny, confirmation that the money was not from the CIA, confirmation that Johnny did know who provided it. A few more pieces of the puzzle, but nothing startling, no breakthroughs.

"They will canonize him, do you think, Father Lar?"

"Not right away. Probably not for a while. Too many questions might be asked about both his life and death. My job is to sift through the facts of his life and find if there are any smoking guns, as we would say in American, any big reasons to forget about canonization now."

"Frau Hoffmann—would she be a smoking gun?"

"If there were witnesses who could be certain that they made love, then I suppose she would be a problem. But I will note in my report that there was no evidence to indicate lack of chastity in the relationship."

As I got up to say goodbye, it wasn't the question of Annemarie that troubled me. The people in Chicago so anxious to venerate Johnny might not inspect that relationship too closely. But they would want to know from where the money he had so bravely smuggled had come.

|| 49 || Vatican City makes me nervous. The Palace of Congregations, on the third floor of which one finds the offices of the Sacred Congregation for the Causes of Saints, reminds me of a hospital, a mental hospital at that. The men (and the occasional woman) who walk its corridors—grave, solemn, preoccupied—seemed far removed from the cares and concerns of folks out in the real world.

The Palace is on the Piazza del Pio XII, just beyond the colonnades of San Pietro. Outside is the hustle-bustle of the workaday world. Inside, the corridors are dark and threatening. How could a man like Johnny McGlynn, who it now seems was a lover of high adventure, survive all those years in a catacomb-like place like this?

Father Kunkel, the elderly Swiss Jesuit relator who had been assigned to me, seemed a kindly enough man. A little professorial perhaps, with his thin gray hair, broad forehead, and high-pitched voice, and somewhat dry, but perceptive and reasonably worldly.

"So, Father McAuliffe," he said in good American English, as he pointed to the only other chair in his small office, "you came here just at the time of another miracle for which your late Cardinal seems to be responsible."

I sat in the chair and tried to persuade myself that the news I had received earlier that morning had not upset me. "According to the account I received from the Cardinal this morning, it does not sound like a miracle that would trouble members of your Consulta Medica."

The phone in my room at the Hassler had rung at eight o'clock.

"I waited until I thought you might be awake, Lar." It was the Cardinal's anxious voice.

I hadn't been, but I didn't want to make an issue of it, since it must be one A.M. in Chicago.

"I am, Steve. Eating breakfast and preparing for my conference at the Congregation later on this morning."

"We had another miracle last night."

"On TV?"

"On a home videotape. They have one working all the time now at the grave."

"What kind of miracle?" I asked, trying to forget the little girl brought back from the dead at the side of a swimming pool.

"A blind young woman regained her sight."

"How fortunate for her. Medical background?"

"As far as we can determine at the present time, there was no physiological cause of the blindness."

"Another hysteria case."

"How many people are there like that in the world, Lar?"

"A lot, I guess. And they'll all be coming to Chicago in the next couple of years."

I could picture his shudder.

"We are following your advice to the letter. We said that as far as we know, nothing had happened which could not be explained by medical science and that the Archdiocese tolerates the devotions at the cemetery but does not approve of them. We are investigating the devotion but at the present time we have no comments to make."

"Sounds as if you made just the right comments."

"I presume we will have to learn to live with these phenomena."

"A couple more of them and they'll be so commonplace that the TV stations will lose interest."

"I fervently hope so. And, Lar, you will explain to the men at the Congregation that we are behaving most prudently here?"

"I sure will. In full detail."

"Aside from this, how is your investigation proceeding?"

"Slowly. No smoking gun yet. No conclusive evidence that he could never be canonized."

"That's a rather abrasive way of putting it."

"I'll be careful of the way I say it over at the Vatican."

So what I said to Kunkel, who seemed innocent of bullshit, was, "No smoking gun anywhere. Not yet." He understood what I meant.

"That would simplify matters, wouldn't it?" I said. "Eventually the popular devotions might ebb if people became aware of that smoking gun. Sometimes, however, God chooses not to arrange our lives so neatly."

"You realize, I suppose, Father McAuliffe, how important your work might be should there be a question of a further processus. If a future Archbishop of Chicago might eventually recommend to the Congregation that we prepare a positio, we would have to take very seriously even an informal report that was prepared shortly after the death of the Venerable Servant of God."

"I understand that."

"Have you reached any tentative conclusions yet?" He folded his hands in a bridge under his chin.

"I always thought he was a son of a bitch, Father. I still think he was, though I realize now that he was a more complicated son of a bitch than I realized. I can't see him as a saint. Gracious and charming, yes. Brave, yes. Kind and thoughtful, yes. But saintly or even holy? I don't see it. On the record, however, I have yet to find any evidence that would exclude the possibility that I may be mistaken."

"Admirably put, Father. And the woman?"

"All indications are that she was a friend and adviser—and a very able and generous one at that. She may have been something more, but I could find not the slightest bit of proof."

"I see. She is a difficult woman?"

"Only when crossed. If the Church should try to spread rumors that she was his lover, there'd be hell to pay."

"She is promoting his cause?"

"Quite the contrary. She holds completely aloof from it and does not accept the alleged miracle by which her grandson was cured."

"We have seen the videotape, Father. A very attractive and circumspect woman."

"She is indeed both."

"That is very fortunate. . . . What is your opinion of the alleged miracle, Father?"

"On the subject I'm an agnostic, Father. I think that God is the only one who knows for sure whether or not an apparent miracle is real. All the Consulta Medica can do is determine whether there is a scientific explanation. Although there are a few reported cases of remission of retinoblastoma, I think the Consulta would have a hard time explaining this one away."

"That would be my impression. However, we would need evidence of heroic virtue before we could consider the miracle."

"If you consider him a martyr, then the miracle wouldn't even matter."

"That's true."

Outside the dirty window of his office, clouds had gathered in the Roman sky, hinting at a rainstorm which might break the oppressive September heat.

"My feeling," I said, "is that he had no business being up there in a combat zone, and that he was killed by accident and not because of any desire to attack the Church. Ms. Quinlan, as you may know, took that stand at the time of his death and has not changed her opinion."

He rubbed his hands across his forehead. "You are direct,

Father, are you not? Well, there is time for direct talk, even here just outside the walls of Vatican City. At the present, the theology is not sufficiently mature for the Congregation to embrace martyrdom. But it would, at the most, be a small step to proceed in that direction, if Higher Authority should be sympathetic to such a step. At the present time I think it would be correct to say that such sympathy does not exist."

That's the way I read it too. So, my poking around in the ashes of Johnny McGlynn's life might make a big difference someday—once the theological and political climate had changed.

As I rode back to the Hassler in a cab, I cursed Jumping Johnny McGlynn. What the hell was I doing on this wild-goose chase when I ought to be back at St. Finian's getting ready for Oktoberfest?

The phone was ringing in my room when I returned.

"Father McAuliffe," a voice which considered itself very important thundered, "Cardinal Ratzinger would like to see you tomorrow."

The Red Baron himself. Cardinal Ratzinger, the Pope's right-hand—some would say hatchet—man. And he wanted to see me.

|| 50 || The Red Baron looked harmless.

He was a little man, thin, meek, diffident-seeming, with white hair, mild voice, and hooded eyes behind thick glasses, dressed in a plain black cassock. A nearsighted and perhaps absentminded professor. Hardly a Grand Inquisitor.

I was ushered into an alcove at the back of the trattoria. A big skylight and an open window made it seem like the alcove was a garden—a nice pleasant little place with wine bottles in straw cases and salami sausages hanging from the rafter and the busy voices of the Borgo San Angelo drifting in on the warm autumn air. No thumbscrews.

They knew who was coming, obviously, and where I should be sent. This must be the Baron's usual place for "informal discussion."

I had put on the Roman collar as a grudging nod to authority.

"Eminenza." The waiter bowed me into Cardinal Ratzinger's presence.

I reminded myself that this seemingly meek little professor had an absolutely first-rate mind. No playing games here, like I would at the Chicago Chancery.

He was courteous and cordial. He asked about my background and my parish, my opinion on conditions in America— small talk. My responses were terse and cautious. If he was not giving anything away, neither was I.

Finally, after choosing his wine and ordering me Pellegrino, he got to the point.

"I fear that this cult of your late Cardinal might trouble many American lay people. He was not, as I'm sure you know, a very deep man."

I remained silent.

"You think he is a saint, Father?"

"I very much doubt it."

"But the miracle? Do you believe it is a fraud?"

"There is no evidence of fraud, Eminenza, but, if I may say so, in the absence of heroic virtue, the question of a miracle does not arise."

"Precisely. Can you tell me about your investigation?"

I summarized it briefly. "So you see, so far there is nothing to refute the charges—but nothing to support them either."

"And your trip to Poland? What did you learn there?"

"As you doubtless know, Eminenza, he did indeed bring money to Solidarity in Poland, substantial amounts of money and with approval of Church authorities both here and in Poland."

"And?"

"None of his colleagues in the venture know where the money came from. Nor do they particularly care. John apparently knew, but he did not tell anyone in Poland. Or anywhere else, as far as I know."

"Do you have any ideas?"

"None whatever. I presume there are people whose offices are near here who might know."

He mulled my response and then ignored it. "In itself that adventure would not be reprehensible, would it, Father?"

"Quite the contrary. It would have been a sign of great courage, which I hardly need say is not quite the same thing as sanctity. It is only the suspicion that there might be something wrong with the money, a suspicion raised by American journalists, that raises the possibility of a smoking gun."

"If such a gun were found, it might well be more embarrassing to the Church than the cult of Cardinal McGlynn itself."

Was I being warned off that subject? Probably. Maybe they wouldn't even want my Cardinal to know about it if I did find out where the money came from.

"No one," he said confidently, "will ever be able to prove that the money came from the unfortunate affair at the Banco Ambrosiano. So the woman remains the pivotal issue—the one which would most shock the lay people, but, conversely, the one which would most likely end the cult?"

OK, I'd give him credit for being both terse and up front.

"If I should discover an illegitimate child somewhere, Eminenza, I would agree that it would do both those things. However, if I may say so, Ms. Quinlan's friendship with the late Cardinal was well enough known in the city. After all, he did die in her arms. Despite some nasty innuendos among priests, there is very little dismay about that relationship in the Archdiocese."

"I see. And, as I understand it, the woman is something of a mulier fortis."

"I'm sure if you wanted to question her, Eminenza, she would come to Rome. You would find her a very intelligent person, clear and concise in her presentation and responsible in her behavior—until someone attacked her or, more important, someone she loved."

"She loved John McGlynn, then?"

"She leaves no doubt about it, Eminenza. She merely denies that her love for him was ever translated into sexual relations."

"I see. You think she would persuade me that their love was entirely chaste?"

"She would, at a minimum, persuade you that if it was not chaste, it would be difficult to prove it."

He arched his eyebrows. "Perhaps. At the present time, it is a pleasure I have to forgo. . . . I am glad we had this conversation, Father. I see that, as my brother bishop in Chicago has told me, you are a man of resourcefulness, integrity, and honor. We need more men like you in the Church. I know that you will continue your investigation and bring it to a successful conclusion."

Why invite me to lunch if he already knew what I knew and perhaps more?

Maybe because he didn't trust Steve's judgment.

|| **51** || Back at the Hassler, I dashed into my room and I dialed Marbeth. Before going further, there was one aspect of Johnny's behavior I had to clarify for myself. And to do that, I needed Marbeth. I was surprised when she herself picked up on the second ring. After we had both discussed our mutual skepticism with respect to the latest miracle, I got to the point.

"Mary Elizabeth, do you remember the time when Jimmy McGlynn was in deep trouble at the Board of Trade?"

"You mean the time when Johnny made him quit?"

"Yeah. Do you know where Johnny found the money to cover his positions?"

"Are you worried about the rumors he took money from the Catholic Cemeteries Office?"

"Yeah."

"You priests!" She sounded amused rather than angry. "You have no financial sense at all. Johnny simply did the obvious. In his role as conservator of his mother's affairs, he lent some of her money to Jimmy, at normal interest rates, against the expected income the next year from his trust fund. It might have looked a little dubious, but no judge would have worried about it if it ever came to court. Micky and Kate would not have complained, if they found out, which wasn't too likely, because they might have needed a loan someday too. Besides, the money was paid back in a few months."

"That simple."

"I'm afraid so. I have records of the transactions. I was afraid John wouldn't keep them and someone might raise questions someday. You can look at them if you don't believe me."

"I believe you, Mary Elizabeth. However, I will look at them anyhow, just to be able to say that I did."

She hesitated. "What did you think of my little memoir?"

How could I have not thanked her for exposing herself with such openness? "It made me admire even more the author—a person for whom I already have an enormous admiration."

"That's very nice, Lar." Her voice choked. "But no smoking guns there either."

No, I thought, as I said goodbye. Just another miracle which no one seems to have noticed.

Hardly had I hung up the phone than it rang again. The man who spoke to me was solemn enough to be Saint Michael the Archangel. "Father McAuliffe, His Holiness has granted you an audience tomorrow morning at ten o'clock. You will come to the entrance at the Belvedere Courtyard at nine o'clock. A Swiss Guard will be waiting for you there. Do you understand?"

|| 52 || "So, Father McAuliffe, you visited Poland. What did you think of my native land?"

The name was pronounced as "Mac-owl-LEEF." I was not about to correct him any more than was the Archbishop who let the Pope think that "Looeyville" should be pronounced "Lewisville."

After all, it is Saint Lewis, isn't it?

Nor was I about to fall for that sucker question.

"I was only there for three days, Holy Father. I liked what little I saw. I hope to return. The people are very friendly."

Then the demon leprechaun in me took over and added, "Almost as friendly as the Irish."

"An interesting people, the Irish."

The Pope made a little expression with his mouth. Such expressions combined with movements of his frosty blue eyes were hints of what he was thinking, usually very opaque hints. This time, however, I think he meant that (a) he thought it was a pretty funny comment and (b) he kind of liked me.

That was fair enough because I kind of liked him.

Even as a kid, before the Second Vatican Council, I was not

much of a pope-worshiper. I figured that you probably had to have a pope and a Vatican and they were all right in their own way, but the Church was in the parish—the school, the yard, the priests hanging out with the kids or greeting the people after Mass on Sunday.

So I didn't go all starry-eyed when people came back from Rome and told me that they had actually seen the Pope— usually in an audience with ten thousand other people.

Hell, I'd shaken hands with Dick Daley once.

The only other time I'd been in Rome I hadn't bothered with the almost mandatory papal audience. I liked people-watching on the Via Veneto better.

Nonetheless, when this fellow with the square face and the strong chin in the white cassock reached out for my hand, I did feel a certain stir of excitement. He was, after all, the religious leader of seven hundred million people. Including me. As Packy Keenan says, "Given our beliefs about the presence of God in the world, if we didn't have a pope, we'd have to invent one."

Two things struck me immediately about the Bishop of Rome: he was not as tall as I expected—a good five inches shorter than I am—and he seemed frail and old. Having lead pumped into your gut, of course, doesn't do much for your health.

"Europe has not happened yet in Ireland," I said, continuing our small talk. "Yet Ireland formed Europe."

"They are also good with words, are they not, Father Mac-Owleef?"

"Talk a lot."

"Your late Cardinal talked very well."

That was a deft change to the subject that brought us together.

"He did indeed, Holy Father."

"He was a good archbishop?"

"I'll be candid, Holy Father. At first I didn't think so. Later on I began to be impressed. Now I think that if he had lived longer, he would have been one of the very greatest."

That gave him something to think about.

"So he is a saint, Father MacOwleef?"

"I don't think so, Holy Father. I could be wrong."

Another inscrutable little movement of the papal lips.

"He was a very brave man, was he not?"

"To the point of recklessness."

"Perhaps someday he will be canonized?" The frosty blue eyes bore into the depths of my soul.

"Perhaps. I believe that the matter should proceed slowly."

He sighed. "So we will wait and see, Father, will we not? Meanwhile you are interested in the money which went to Poland?"

"I am not a reporter. In my report to His Eminence, all I need say is that the rumors are not true."

"Or that they are?" He glanced at me sharply.

"If they are. I need not and will not go into details."

He nodded. "I believe you, Father. Many things happen here"—again the gesture toward Vatican City—"that a pope does not know about until after it is done."

"I understand, Holy Father."

"It is best that some of these things be kept totally secret." He waved his fingers slowly.

"Totally secret."

I was about to say that I would accept his word that the money for Poland was clean. Hell, if you can't believe a pope, whom can you believe?

He stood up and reached for my hand. "Your Cardinal is right, Father, you are a person of integrity. . . . A man named Roger will call you on the telephone tomorrow."

As I walked back down the steps to the Belvedere Courtyard, I tried to figure out what that meant.

Sure enough, the next morning my phone rang.

"Laurence? This is Roger."

"Good morning, Roger."

"We have an appointment, I believe?"

"So I gather."

"Would you find it convenient to meet me at the café across from the entrance to the Borghese Gardens in forty-five minutes? I will know who you are."

He spoke English with an American accent mixed with a slight hint of somewhere else.

"Big guy with silver hair and bright green eyes?"

"Precisely."

"I'll be there."

Roger was a tall, slim, dark man of indeterminate age, with implacable blue eyes, closely cropped black hair, and a neat mustache. He might have been a middle-rank executive in a large corporation. We shook hands. He motioned to a table. I ordered my tea.

"Langley, Roger?"

"Oh, no!" His mustache moved in a quick smile. "Tel Aviv. Mossad."

"Mossad?"

"That is correct, Laurence. Israeli intelligence."

I began to laugh. "Roger, this is the craziest thing I've ever heard of. You're telling me that twelve years ago some nut in Tel Aviv got the crazy idea that money to a liberal Catholic trade union in Poland might eventually precipitate the collapse of the Russian empire and thus free Russian Jews to migrate to Israel?"

Roger laughed too. "I was not part of that decision, Laurence. I quite agree with you that it was absurd, yet obviously it was one of our most successful ventures."

"Roger, this is one of the great stories of the modern world."

"Which, for obvious reasons, cannot be told."

"I've promised secrecy, Roger. I'll keep my promise."

"So we have been told. Too many people know now. One more does not make a difference."

"The courier knew?"

"Yes. Not particularly intelligent, but very clever. A man who could hold his tongue when necessary . . . incidentally, please don't think we were responsible for his death. Some of our people recommended it, I will admit. But they were overruled."

I hadn't thought of that.

"You would have done it more smoothly?"

He nodded solemnly. "Moreover, it was argued—effectively

I assure you—that our embarrassment was not worth the life of someone who had done us a very good service."

"I am happy to hear it."

"Some of us were relieved when he died. Others lamented the loss of a friend."

He didn't say which side he was on.

"How did he learn where the money was from?"

"I believe that he guessed. As you say, he had remarkable instincts. When we learned that he had discovered the source for the money, we insisted that the other party find a way to—"

"Buy him off?"

"Indeed. In their own way they rewarded him handsomely. I believe now that he was a man of honor who needed no such reward and was not aware that he was being rewarded."

"I gather he never knew the details."

"Deniability?"

"Of course . . . ten years from now it will be irrelevant."

"Even then someone else will have to disclose it."

He finished his coffee and rose.

I returned to the hotel to pack for my trip home.

It was only when I was in the air over Lake Geneva that I saw the real smoking gun. I sat up in my first-class seat when the realization hit me. My trip abroad had been unnecessary. Given what I understood so suddenly, I saw that I had not required a secret meeting with the Mossad.

Johnny McGlynn's secret had been concealed in the fact that while the Bears had won the Super Bowl in 1986, the key game took place at the end of the 1985 season.

Why hadn't I seen it before?

Maybe because I didn't want to. The implications of my discovery would stop any preliminary process toward canonization. If leaked to the public it would also destroy the popular cult and some people would be badly hurt.

But before I did anything, there was one other loose end I should tie up, though more for my curiosity than anything else.

|| *53* || Noah Epstein was cordial but guarded when I entered his office the day after I returned from Rome.

"I'm happy to meet you, Father McAuliffe. Nancy and her mother have spoken often about you."

"Yeah, I know. I'm sweet."

He flushed slightly. "Their very words."

"I'm not here to see you professionally." I nodded toward the couch. "At least not that part of your profession."

"Oh?" He frowned, trying to figure me out.

"I want to talk about miracles. Particularly the first miracle."

"Brenny's recovery."

"That was the second, Noah. You know that as well as I do."

The young man seemed to come apart. He exhaled sharply and then leaned back in the chair behind his desk, a man who was experiencing an enormous relief.

"I don't know how you know about it, Father Lar. But I'm so happy you do. It's been on my mind for months, and I can talk to no one about it, least of all my wife, who, in her enthusiasm, would instantly reveal it to everyone. The publicity would be brutal."

"It would indeed."

"The doctors in Elkhorn"—he began to recite his story—"simply didn't believe me. They said that in the excitement of the situation I must have miscalculated the time. The child had to have been breathing when we pulled her out of the pool to have made such a quick recovery."

"I see."

"My friends and colleagues told me virtually the same thing. They said that if my future sister-in-law had stopped breathing, which they doubted, she must have begun again almost at once. Perhaps I was so distraught that I did not notice slight respiration."

"Uh-huh."

"I was distraught, Father. Caroline was our responsibility, Nancy's and mine. If she had died, it would have been our fault."

I was not about to argue with Jewish guilt. We Irish have enough problems with our own guilt without worrying about other people's.

"But I was not so distraught as to miss something that obvious. She was not breathing, Father. I did mouth-to-mouth respiration for at least twenty minutes. In fact, I had given up. I was worried in the last few minutes that she might revive, because I knew that the brain damage would be terrible."

I nodded.

"Then she started breathing again, and in a few moments was talking to us. Theoretically, Father, that was impossible."

"I know."

"I paid little attention to the phenomenon at the time. I contented myself with the solution that there was probably a wider variation in response to drownings than my colleagues realized. I was simply happy that Carie was still with us and that was enough. Mind you, we were busy preparing for our marriage. There were many preoccupations. I think all of us relegated what had happened to Carie to the limbo of very bad dreams."

"With good reason."

"It took me several weeks after Brendan's recovery to link

the two events. Then I broke out in a cold sweat. The Cardinal was still alive when Carie revived. Perhaps I had witnessed a miracle worked by a living man."

My blood ran a little cold too.

"The Cardinal was right next to you saying the rosary when Carie started to breathe."

"More than that, Father Lar." The young man's face was ashen. "He had reached over and touched her just as I was ready to give up. It was a quick gesture. I hardly noticed it. Indeed, I had forgotten it till I remembered the incident in the light of Brenny's cure. I can only conclude with you that the first miracle Cardinal John McGlynn worked was not the cure of Brendan, but the revival of Brendan's beloved Aunt Caroline—and that while he was still alive."

"Do you think the Cardinal was aware of what he had done, or seemed to have done?" I asked, unwilling to concede the word "miracle."

"Not that I could tell, not from anything he said or did, then or later. He remained in a state of shock for some days, but I had no impression that he thought—what can I tell you—that he thought that the 'power' had come from him, that his touch might have, of itself, revived her."

|| 54 || Two hours later I was sitting in my Cardinal's office.

"We will make a Vatican diplomat out of you yet, Lar. Your work has merit."

That was as strong a compliment as the Cardinal could pay.

"I doubt it, but at least the Vatican seems content to leave us alone on this case. At the present time, anyway."

"And who did provide the money Johnny McGlynn brought to Poland?"

"Johnny never revealed the source to anyone, and neither will I."

"I understand. And the other issues?"

"He used family money to help his brother cover his market positions. The story that he used Archdiocese money is pure clerical nastiness."

"The woman?"

"As far as I have been able to learn, there is nothing to that either."

"Thank God."

"You want him to be a saint?"

"I don't want another scandal, Lar. I suppose I want him to have been a good man, too."

"In his own way, maybe he was. But not saint, Steve, no saint. Even though," I said, hesitating for a moment, "I seem to have discovered another miracle. A real one. One the Consulta Medica would probably approve. One he performed when he was still alive."

"Still alive?" he gasped.

"Yep."

"Is it likely to become public knowledge?" he asked anxiously.

"Not at the present time. A fair number of people witnessed the phenomenon, but only one person was sophisticated enough on the subject of miracles to comprehend its implications. He has written it up and I will keep the writeup in my files. Neither one of us will talk about it."

"Thank God for that, Lar. But are you absolutely sure that John McGlynn worked a miracle while he was still alive?"

"No, I'm not absolutely sure, Steve, because as you know, I'm not a firm believer in such forms of divine intervention. To be precise, I do know for certain that while he was still alive the late Cardinal was involved, directly and intimately involved, in a cure for which there is ample documentation and for which medical science can offer no explanation."

"What did he do?"

"Ah . . . he raised the dead."

"Raised the dead!" the Cardinal shouted.

"The person was not breathing. There was no heartbeat. The brain had been deprived of blood for some time. I assume that this person was not brain dead yet, but substantial brain damage had certainly been done. Then the Cardinal touched the person, so quickly that only one man, an MD at that, saw the touch. Almost at once the person revived, and with virtually full faculties. There were and are no signs of aftereffects."

The Cardinal was as still and silent as a statue in church— and as pale.

"Did John realize what he had done?"

"We're not sure. Probably not."

"How can you bring a dead or near-dead person back to life and not realize that you're doing it?"

"Have you ever done it?"

"Certainly not!"

"Me neither. So how should we know what it's like?"

"Does that truly make him a saint, Lar? Are we in contact with the direct powers of God?"

"We are in contact with the wonderful, the marvelous, the uncanny. Were the laws of nature suspended in this instance? We'd have a hell of a time proving it. All we can say is that as far as we know them, there are no explanations in the laws of nature. Does any of this make Johnny McGlynn a saint? I don't think so—and a whole host of other miracles wouldn't convince me. I want to see proof of heroic virtue too, just like our friends at the Sacred Congregation."

"Wonderful and uncanny, but not divine?"

"Right. A son of a bitch who works miracles."

I never thought I'd live to see the day when I'd admit that— even as a possibility.

"What should we do about it?"

"At the present time, Steve, nothing at all. Leave it in my archives and let it, as they say in Rome, mature."

"That suggestion is not without merit." He nodded.

"One more thing, Steve. If this really happened, and my witnesses to the whole event are extraordinarily reliable—"

"Witnesses? Plural?"

"Many saw the recovery. Only one man, as I have said, was close enough to see the touch. But the other witness who described it confirmed all the details without knowing their implications."

"Yes, I see . . . you were saying that if this incident really happened, then . . ."

"Then, Steve, there is no reason to think that other similar phenomena did not occur. We might hear about them eventually. Which is the point in my telling you this story. You and your staff had better be prepared for such claims."

"Good God!"

On Michigan Avenue, after I left the Chancery, I thought briefly about Nancy and Noah. They had crowded a lot of excitement into their young lives.

They seemed to flourish on it. She was as tough as Johnny had said she was when she was a dangerously ill neonate in Oak Park Hospital.

I stopped dead in my tracks, oblivious to the pedestrian crush pressing along the Magnificent Mile.

Good God!

I pondered the facts.

The doctors had said the little girl was going to die.

Johnny had seen her in the respirator before he visited Mary Elizabeth.

Johnny told Mary Elizabeth that the feisty child was not going to die.

She didn't die. In fact, the next morning, despite the doctor's predictions, and after a visit from Monsignor McGlynn, she was well on her way to recovery.

That was over a quarter century ago. Oak Park Hospital might still have records. There might be nurses or doctors who could remember the case. Someone might know what happened to the membrane in her lung which threatened her life. But we didn't need a third miracle. It would be one more embarrassment.

So I would keep any investigation secret.

Anyway, only two miracles were required for canonization.

It was a warm autumn day in Chicago. Yet, as I crossed Michigan Avenue, I felt a chill in my veins.

The uncanny seemed to be closing in on me.

|| **55** || Having disposed of Noah Epstein and the Cardinal, and having told Jamie about my secret file in the safe in case anything should happen to me, I knew that I should not turn to the smoking gun that was lying out there in the open.

I asked myself whether I was being vindictive toward Johnny McGlynn. Were my resentments so great that I wanted to destroy his memory? Or was I just trying to do my job?

The next day, happy that my motives were of the purer sort, I visited Oak Park Hospital. After I had found what I thought I would find, or rather didn't find what I thought I wouldn't find, I asked on impulse if the head of the OB department was on the premises. It turned out that he was.

Doctor McCafrey was a slim man of medium height, about my age, with white hair and a neatly trimmed white mustache. He wore a brown sports coat and chino slacks, and radiated the kind of genial good humor that would reassure the most anxious of expectant mothers. The smile lines around his mobile mouth suggested a man who enjoyed his job enormously.

"Nice to meet you, Father." He bounded out of the chair behind his white metal desk. "A lot of my patients are from your parish. They tell me good things."

"As they tell me about you, Doctor."

Hey, I can match any smoothy.

After a few more jousts at pleasantry, I got to the point.

"I am interested in a birth twenty-six years ago—a certain Mary Anne Quinlan, who came to be known as Nancy. I don't know whether you remember the case."

"I remember." His brown eyes continued to twinkle, but now with steady intelligence. "I was a first-year resident here then. New in Chicago. But one didn't have to be here long to learn about the Reillys—and the mother is the kind of woman you do not easily forget."

"Indeed."

"What would you like to know—within the bonds of professional secrecy of course."

"The little girl was quite sick, was she not?"

He opened a drawer of his desk and pulled out two files, almost as though he had been waiting for me.

"Decidedly." He flipped open one of the files. "We almost lost them both. Even a quarter century ago we didn't often lose mothers. Embolisms were the principal cause when we did. Mrs. Quinlan was lucky to be alive."

That she had never admitted.

"Tough lady."

"Oh, yes. Then, when she was out of danger, we began to lose the little girl. She was a preemie. Hyaline membrane. Now, we have a fighting chance in such cases; the neonatologist can save maybe sixty percent of them. Then"—he raised his hands in despair—"well, that was the cause of the death of the Kennedy baby, if you remember. The death rate was at least ninety-five percent."

"Yet the little Quinlan girl lived."

"Yes, she did."

"She began to recover after a priest said a prayer over her and gave her a blessing?"

He nodded slowly. "It gives me the willies, Father. I thought about it as soon as I saw Nancy, on TV with her son. I dug the files out of the archives in the basement of this place. I thought . . . well, I guess I thought that someday a priest might come looking for them."

So the priest came, a Devil's Advocate who was shivering on a warm autumn day. This could not be happening, it simply could not. It didn't merely shatter my theories about Jumping Johnny. Rather, it threw my whole world into a cocked hat.

"Can you recall any of the details, Doctor?"

"Sure. I was there."

"You were there?" The uncanny now pervaded his office, an almost visible mist of terror and fascination.

"At the nursing station, talking to a young nurse and a nun who was half keeping an eye on the two of us. This big, good-looking priest came up and said he wanted to see the little Quinlan girl. I took him into the incubator room. Sister and the nurse trailed along.

" 'Pretty little tyke,' he says. 'What are her chances?'

" 'Nonexistent, Padre,' I replied, shaking my head. 'She's not going to make it.'

" 'I'll say a prayer for her and give her a blessing. Then I'll stop in, if I may, to say hello to her mom.'

"I don't remember the words of the prayer. I suspect they were pretty conventional, but they were said with deep conviction. Then he blessed the poor little thing and went off to the mother's room. It was not by itself a memorable event. I suppose I would have forgotten it if Sister didn't rush into my room at three A.M. and say the little Quinlan girl was getting better."

"I see."

"Sister said it was a miracle worked by the priest. The nurse wasn't sure. I said something dumb about all life being miraculous. We agreed that we ought to keep it to ourselves. The kid's mother said it was a miracle, but she didn't mean it in the sense that we did because she didn't link it to the priest's blessing. I guess she thought we did it."

"A cure that medical science cannot explain?"

"Not the suddenness anyway . . . neonates sometimes fool us

all. We call a lot of recoveries miracles in the sense Mrs. Quinlan was using—happy surprises. This one was different. It happened so quickly. Mind you, there might be a perfectly natural explanation of the sort we haven't discovered yet. But the answer to your question stands: it was not a recovery that medical science, then or now, can easily explain."

This was absolutely impossible. Foundations were collapsing all around me.

"I don't suppose you've kept in touch with the nurse?"

He grinned. "In a manner of speaking, Father. I married her."

"How clever," I murmured.

"It turned out to be." His grin widened. "And Sister is still very much alive too. At another hospital."

"You could collect statements from them?"

"I already have my wife's." He gestured at his file. "I can get Sister's easily enough. When will this become public?"

"Not soon."

"Just as well."

"You've kept it secret a long time." I rose and extended my hand. "We want to protect the family."

We shook hands.

The cold mists trailed after me into Harlem Avenue.

Had it really happened? Did Johnny know what he was doing? Or was it an unconscious skill? How many other times?

I didn't want to think about the possible answers to those questions.

They were in a certain sense irrelevant to my mandate from the Cardinal. I would report the fact and tell him that I had the documentation. But I would also report my other conclusions. If the theory I was testing turned out to be accurate— and I was already sure that it would—then the miracles were irrelevant.

I made a few other visits, copied some material, called a few phone numbers, visited a photographer.

All the pieces fell into place, as I knew they would.

|| 56 || "Right on time, Lar." Mary Elizabeth opened the door to her house on Lathrop. "Not like most priests."

In the drive on the right side of the house, gleaming in the late September sun, her Benz and her Jag rested contentedly.

"A beautiful place, Mary Elizabeth. You must have put a lot of effort into redoing it."

"I wanted to re-create it the way it was when they built it just before the War—First World War, that is—keep it Edwardian and still make it comfortable for modern living."

She was wearing a simple dark gray suit and a white blouse with a light gray tie. Her only jewelry was two small gold earrings and the Cardinal's ruby. Businesswoman ready for an afternoon of work.

"This was the McGlynn house, wasn't it?"

"The house that Delia moved into when she and Doctor came home from their honeymoon. They were the second owners. How she must have loved it."

"I wonder."

Perhaps it was too much for her from the beginning. Again I thought, poor kid.

"Sad, the way she died, wasn't it?"

"Sad that her life was so sad for so long."

"I didn't buy the house from her. I bought it from the family to whom she sold it when she moved to the apartment up on Marine Drive. They thought it was too big and too old to maintain. I knew it had to be redone and I thought I'd like that. I wanted to be near my brothers. Iggy lives in our old home, just two doors away."

"That's the stained glass window?" I pointed up the staircase.

"It is. Tiffany almost certainly. In a fit of something or the other, Delia had actually painted over it, so I had to restore it."

We walked up the stairs. On the broad landing between the first and second floor stood a dollhouse, multihued in the afternoon sunlight which streamed through the window.

"Caroline's," she said simply. "Not the original."

"Not too much different from the original."

"As close as they could make it . . . my sentimentality surprise you, Lar?"

"I guess it does."

We walked down the stairs; she directed me into an immense parlor, ivory and gray, very expensive, very elegant, modern but with enough Edwardian touches so you could imagine that the year was 1910.

We sat down in two comfortable easy chairs in a corner of the room, small, low-slung table between them, the tête-à-tête site, doubtless.

"Here are the papers about the loan that John made to his brother from Doctor's estate."

"What?" I was momentarily surprised.

"The alienation of Church property." She sighed patiently as she passed a folder over to me.

"Oh, yeah." I glanced at the papers. Sure enough, everything was in order, including a signed agreement from James A. McGlynn IV to refrain from activity on the floor of any commodity market for ten years.

"Mary Elizabeth," I said, ignoring her offer of tea, "you did not tell me the truth. I can understand why you did not, but now I have a hard time believing anything you say about Johnny McGlynn."

I put the envelope I had been carrying in my briefcase on the table.

Her face was a frozen mask, her eyes cold, her body tense.

"I don't know what you're talking about," she said coldly.

"You do, Mary Elizabeth. The last thing I want to do is to be cruel to you. I've known you for too long and admired you far too much to hurt you. But we have to speak the truth to one another this afternoon. The whole truth. There is no other way out."

"What is this truth about which you're talking?" she demanded icily. "What nonsense do you think you have found?"

She would play the string out to the end. So I had to be blunt.

"Caroline is Johnny's daughter."

"That's a fantasy of your dirty clerical mind," she snapped.

I pointed at the envelope. "She was born ten months after your husband's death, not nine, as the baptismal records at St. Luke's state. And not at Oak Park Hospital either, as the St. Luke records also state."

"She was a late baby."

"No, Mary Elizabeth. In fact, she was born prematurely, a month early. At Lakeland Hospital in Elkhorn. You were staying at Lake Geneva at the time, probably hoping for a premature birth. She weighed a little less than five pounds. You almost lost her. Her birth is recorded in Walworth County, not Cook County."

"This is absurd. I don't have to listen to it. Please leave."

She did not rise from her chair, however.

"Pulling his own daughter out of the pool at Lake Geneva was the turning point in his life, wasn't it?"

She stared at me, hatred leaping out of her eyes. "What makes you think that?"

"That was the year he began to change. Even Len noticed that he turned down a Super Bowl ticket. Nineteen eighty-five was the Bears' winning season and the year he rescued Caroline."

"Life isn't a football season," she murmured.

I had hit home. Caroline's rescue, her miraculous rescue, had broken through to whatever depths Jumping Johnny had. Marbeth must have told him that night, her defenses swept away by the emotions of the moment.

"Please look at the contents of the envelope, Mary Elizabeth."

"I will not! I don't have to put up with this."

"Your wealth enabled you to pull this off." I opened the envelope. "I bet that even your daughters didn't suspect. But money can't buy permanent protection from the truth."

"I will not look at your goddamn documents! I don't care what they show!"

"Then look at this picture." I gave her the photo, which I had doctored a bit to make my case clearly. "Who's this?"

She glanced at it. "I suppose that it's a guess at what Caroline will look like in eight or nine years—beautiful and happy, if you leave her alone."

"No, Mary Elizabeth. It's Delia Meehan McGlynn at that age, a wedding picture shortly before she moved into this house."

She picked up the photo, from which the wedding appurtenances had been cut. "A beautiful woman, poor dear thing." All the fight went out of her. She knew the game was up and characteristically would not expend energy in a lost cause.

Then, astonishingly, she began to cry.

"All right, Lar, I underestimated you. I was afraid I might. I'm sorry I deceived you. I had to try. You win."

She seemed to have withdrawn herself completely from the room, leaving only a tearful, compliant shell.

"I don't like to think of it that way."

"What are you going to do with these?" She replaced the documents and photo in the envelope. "I'd like a copy of the picture, by the way. It's quite lovely."

"I don't know what I'm going to do. I simply don't know."

Her weeping was not hysterical. Rather, her tears were slow and gentle, a life of grief slowly escaping.

She nodded. "Sweet to the end. I will now tell you all the

truth, though you would have every reason not to believe a word I say."

"I'll listen."

"It was a very brief affair, a week at the most. I was devastated by Bud's death. I was trying to salvage the firm and keep the family together. The United States Attorney replied to my threat by indicting Peter. I . . . I am not making excuses. I knew what I was doing. I just fell apart. I am ashamed now. It was my fault. I seduced him"—she smiled bitterly—"more successfully than at Eagle Lake. Sympathy and tenderness are more erotic than a naked body. I don't even think he enjoyed it very much. I did, God help me. Then we both woke up. It stopped. It never happened again. As God is my witness."

I was inclined to believe her, but not absolutely certain. She spared me the need of an immediate comment.

"It was a terrible sin," she continued, "really it was. I was an occasion of sin for him. All my life I prided myself on being in control of my own destiny. I lost control. I was completely confident that I had outlived my teenage crush on John. I had not. It returned and I acted like a foolish adolescent. My state of mind was no excuse. I deserved to be punished. So what did God do? He sent Caroline. A reward instead of a punishment. Does that make any sense at all? Can I love the result and still repent the sin?"

"I'm not your confessor, Mary Elizabeth . . ."

"Not even my priest." She dabbed at her tears and tried to laugh. "No appointment yet."

"Regardless. I'm sure that whatever forgiveness you might have needed, God long since provided."

"I know that." She stopped crying, once more the woman who kept her emotions under control.

"Does Caroline know who her father was?"

"I haven't told her so far. I might when she's old enough to understand. I don't think it will bother her. She loved Johnny like a father anyway. She never knew Bud. . . . You're right about everything. I did fool even my own daughters. I knew from the beginning the birth would be premature. I didn't do anything to hasten it. I loved her so much even then."

"When did you tell Johnny?"

"I never did tell him. I wanted to protect him from knowledge which might worry him. That was foolish, but, as you see, I have always been very protective of him no matter what the risk."

"He didn't know?"

"Oh, yes, he knew. He figured it out. He saw his mother's face on Carie the night he pulled her out of the pool. I learned that only after he was dead. I suppose he wanted to protect me from worry." She grimaced. "Two of a kind."

"So he did love you?"

"Not that way. He would have protected anyone. He didn't want to hurt people if he could possibly avoid it. I suppose you think that's weak."

"It's better than being insensitive." I was desperately searching for a way to handle this time bomb I had uncovered.

"What are you going to do, Lar?"

"I don't know. What do you think I should do?"

"Give this to the Cardinal?" She touched the envelope. "Isn't that your job?"

"Maybe."

"You hesitate? Why?"

"I don't want to hurt you or Caroline."

"We'll survive."

"What if he is a saint?"

"Don't you dismiss that possibility?"

"Not as a possibility."

We were both silent.

"It was an interlude, Lar. We didn't let it happen again. Sometimes it was very difficult. We thought we had licked it but we hadn't."

"It's not up to me to judge either of you, Mary Elizabeth. God knows what I would have done in similar circumstances."

"But you must judge whether to tell the Cardinal that Johnny McGlynn has an illegitimate daughter."

"I wouldn't have to tell him her name."

"He'd guess. So would everyone."

"Do you have his private archives, Mary Elizabeth? Did you tell me the truth about them?"

She bit her lip. "Yes and no, Lar. There weren't any private archives in the strict sense of the word. He did have kind of a diary, scraps of paper. Some notebooks. At the end, drafts of handwritten letters he sent to the Pope."

"His memoir?"

"Kind of. I learned more about him from reading it than I did in all the years I knew him."

"Do you think I should read it?"

"If you do, will it become part of your files?"

"It might."

She hesitated. "I love him, so I was terribly moved by the story he told. I don't know what others might think. Some of it might destroy his reputation completely. I was not the only woman, you know. Most of them, maybe all but me, were before he was ordained. That's hard to tell."

"I have to ask you. Should I read it?"

She studied me carefully. "Nothing in it can do any more harm than what you already know." She rose briskly from her chair. "It's in my office. I'll give it to you to read. Both of us will then be in your hands."

"I'll read it here." I put the envelope with my documents back into the briefcase.

"That's not necessary." She led me into the main corridor and to her office at the back of the house.

"It is necessary. If I take the materials out of here, then I have possession. I'm not sure I want that."

She lifted a picture off the wall and opened the door of a safe. Then she reached in and removed a large manila envelope.

"It's all in here." Her voice continued to be flat, all the emotions inside her buried beneath her stoic exterior. "I'll turn on the copy machine. You may duplicate anything you want."

"Going for broke, Mary Elizabeth?" I glanced up from the still unopened file. Her tears began again.

"I'm sorry I didn't trust you from the very beginning. That's what I owed you—and it would have been the wisest course in any event. I won't do it again."

"Absolute condition for my being your priest."

She offered a smile through the tears.

"I haven't offered you the job yet."

"That may not matter."

She paused at the door.

"I want to say something more, Lar. For one of the rare times in my life, I don't know how to say it."

"Try."

"I guess it's this: I don't know what you will do. I trust you to do what is right. You'll hear no objections from me, whatever happens."

"That makes me free, Mary Elizabeth."

"That's how I want it."

|| *57* || The informal diary of John Arthur McGlynn
was more than I was prepared for. It was utterly frank, no
doubt since it was a genuine diary and not one made for private, if not public consumption, like Mary Elizabeth's and Len
Carey's memoirs. Mary Elizabeth had fooled me through what
read like completely honest revelations. It wasn't until I read
Johnny's diary that I realized that for all its revelations and
intimate details, her memoir was still quite deliberately con-
trived.

John's diary started with his days at the NAC in Rome. He
found Rome exciting, a refreshing break from Mundelein. It
was clear that he was relieved to be away from his domineering mother, though his love for her also shone through.
Marbeth was still very much on his mind. "I treasure her like
a sister," he wrote. But from the entries he wrote, she clearly
had an altogether different sort of relationship in mind. John
was obviously troubled that he could not convince her that his
vocation was genuine. He seemed to have no doubts himself,
although about his doubts about God's existence he was quite
frank. "I know it must sound crazy to Marbeth. It's hard for

me to understand, let alone explain it. But I have to be a priest and then let God, if there is a God, figure out what I'm supposed to do. For all my lack of belief in His existence, I still have an overwhelming sense that He has a purpose for me. And that purpose begins with my ordination."

What surprised me the most about Johnny's diary was the frank, even graphic detail about his women. To leave such a written record was risky at best; in the wrong hands it could have spelled the end of his clerical career. John seems to have recognized that danger, but he seemed to get some relief in writing his adventures down. For him, it seemed a form of confession.

Although he restrained himself where Mary Elizabeth was concerned, he didn't feel any compunctions about other women. Certain others, I should say. Johnny believed he could intuit the sort of woman he might harm through a tumble in bed (like Mary Elizabeth) and those who would be none the worse off for the verboten adventure. In Rome, he made love to an older woman, clearly reveling in the pleasure—both his and hers. He expressed a modicum of guilt after the contact and even a pledge to reform. But this pledge, if made in earnest, was short-lived.

Not long after making love to this woman, he picked up another woman, also in her forties. Just when I was beginning to see a pattern—were all his flings with older women? What would Mama Maggie say?—I flipped to a particularly graphic passage involving two sisters. "Very playful. They drove me out of my mind the way they teased me. Finally, I teased them back and drove them out of their minds. I can't believe that so much pleasure exists in the world. I want them again and again, but they're leaving for America in the morning."

I'd have to say that Johnny appeared as baffled by these sexual encounters as I was reading about them. It was almost as if he were periodically overcome by desire, the way epileptics suffer fits. What shame he expressed had more to do with his fear of being caught. He clearly believed—and I have no reason to believe otherwise—that all these women were quite willing and came to his bed with no expectations beyond a half-hour's pleasure. In that sense he was quite right to group Mary Elizabeth in a very different category.

When he was back in Chicago serving as a parish priest under that particularly splenetic pastor, John learned something about Doctor that gave him some insight into his own nature. He was having dinner with his brother Jimmy when Jimmy, no doubt in his habitual inebriated state, told Johnny that Doctor had died "in the saddle." Johnny pretended not to understand. "Do I have to spell it out for you?" Jimmy asked him. "The guy was a regular Don Juan. He had a real thing for the ladies, and they had a thing for him. Open your eyes, Johnny. Christ, do you really think he was working late night after night after night when we were kids?" Apparently Johnny had. But after that meal with Jimmy, he wondered if his fatal flaw might have been inherited.

Inherited or no, Johnny seemed to have put his desires in check after his subdiaconate and consequent vow of celibacy. His concerns, as expressed in his diary, take a clear turn. More and more he writes of battles within the Curia, news from home, and his mother's determination to see him rise to prominence within the Church. He aimed to please her. Fear of failing her remained close to his heart. John occasionally wondered why he felt so driven, but for the most part he didn't seriously question his nature; he accepted who he was and proceeded from there. Mama Maggie would have a hard time settling him down on her couch. If, indeed, Mama Maggie is the sort of psychologist who resorts to couches. Knowing her, no doubt she employs far subtler methods.

That Johnny resisted sexual temptation later in his life is clear. He writes with particular poignancy of his journeys across the Iron Curtain with the beautiful professor. She was clearly drawn to him, and he to her, and although they were often physically close as well as emotionally, their relationship remained chaste. But the temptation was great. Posing as husband and wife, they often checked into hotel rooms together and slept in the same bed. With the professor sleeping fitfully beside him one particular night, Johnny writes: "She is a delectable little prize. I am almost out of my mind with hunger for her. To turn away from Marbeth was much easier than to keep my hands off this woman. I hide my feelings as best I can so that I do not inflame her more." When it comes time to leave her in the morning, he says, "I will kiss her goodbye. Lightly on the lips."

Johnny was jubilant upon his return to Chicago as its Cardinal, but the jubilance was tinged with some sadness: Delia was already too ill to appreciate his triumph. And Johnny was nervous about the responsibility. He felt ill-prepared to run the Archdiocese. And he felt estranged from his family and from his fellow priests. Between his time in Rome, Africa, and behind the Iron Curtain, he had been more absent than present in their lives.

Mary Elizabeth quickly came to the rescue, not only through her role as financial adviser but also as a confidante and friend. That friendship also took an emotional toll on Johnny, as I knew it had on Mary Elizabeth. He found he desired her all the more, particularly so after Bud's conviction and suicide. "My lips yearn for your lips," he writes, addressing her in his diary in a way he couldn't in life. "My fingers are desperate for your breasts. I want you so badly. I tell myself that I must have you again and again. You stir the deepest part of my emotions. You set me on fire. You promise me light and love."

As to any action upon this desire, John is not forthcoming.

I was a little surprised to see myself in Johnny's diary. In spite of myself I was flattered to read: "Somehow I envy him a little, as I always have. He is a stalwart priest who has never had any doubts about his ideals or his goals or his principles. I wish I had a little of that determination and vision in me." I was even more surprised to read further, after what I consider our highly hostile conversation about my leave: "I had the feeling that we were friends at last." Go figure.

But the passages that held me transfixed were the somewhat erratic scribblings penned shortly after little Caroline's rescue from the pool. Clearly, the ensuing revelation proved the single greatest watershed experience in Johnny's life.

On what must have been the day after her drowning, he had scribbled in large block letters: O MY CAROLINE! CAROLINE! CAROLINE!

Then, a few days later, he added in a still shaky hand, "I am somewhat better now. Yet I cannot recover from what happened last Sunday night. Never will I forget my little girl's purple face and the face I saw in it for the first time, the face of the poor near-dead woman in the apartment on Marine Drive. I knew the child was dead when I found her body in the darkness at the bottom of the pool. I knew she was dead when I laid her body on the towel at the side of the pool. I knew she was dead when Noah tried to pump air into her poor little lungs.

"But she was not dead. As we prayed, she came back to life. She lives even now.

"Oh, how I thank God, not being certain that there is a God, that young Noah Epstein did not give up his efforts to revive her when it looked like he was going to quit. It took only a few more moments for her to come back to life. Yet we still almost lost her! Why is life so fragile?"

There was no hint that he was aware he might have brought the child back from the dead, just as in his earlier entry, after he had visited Mary Elizabeth in the hospital, that he thought he was responsible for Nancy's recovery.

Under that entry he wrote in a much more controlled hand, "How important life is. How I've neglected mine. I don't know what is happening to me. I feel that I am not the same man who drove up to Lake Geneva in the heat last Sunday afternoon, not the same man at all. Why am I so exalted?"

In the next few entries Jumping Johnny McGlynn turned mystic. I felt the uncanny slip into the room as I read those passages: "Who are You? What do You want? Why have You intruded into my life? Why don't You leave me alone? I don't want to know You! Go back into the blackness of the swimming pool where You belong! I cannot stand You!"

God? I wondered as I read that paragraph. Is that what God
is like when you really get to know Her?

The mystical entries continued for several days: "I don't
know You. Why do You care about me? Why do You enter my
life now? What have You torn apart inside me? What have
You stirred up in the depths of my soul? What do You want
of me? Can't You leave me alone? I am not worth Your trouble.
If You know me as well as You claim, You would understand
that."

But the One with whom Johnny was wrestling would not
quit: "Please go away. I can't stand the love which is bursting
inside me. Love for Caroline, for her mother, for her brave
family, for everyone in the world. Especially for my priests
and people. Such love is too much to endure."

So Johnny tried another classical technique to get away
from God, the Isaiah ploy. "I am an empty, hollow man. You
know that. I know that. It is too late for me to change. I have
never loved anyone unselfishly. Please go away. I cannot love
You. I cannot love anyone the way I love everyone at this
minute because of You and expect to live. This love will con-
sume me, burn me out, turn me to ashes."

It didn't work any better for Johnny than it did for Isaiah.
He would write in his next entry, "Are you God? If You are,
why are You unlike what I have expected God to be? Why do
You care so much about me, more than anyone who has ever
loved me? Why are You like the women whom I've trea-
sured—my mother, Kate, Annemarie, Mary Elizabeth, Caroline. They all needed me or thought they needed me. You
claim to need me the same way. You cannot be God. You're
someone else pretending to be God."

That gambit didn't work either. Then it began to dawn on
him, I think, what was happening: "A God who is like
Marbeth? That is impossible. I cannot believe it. Yet perhaps,
just perhaps, I could love a God like that. Perhaps."

The next day he was trapped. "A vulnerable God? I refuse
to believe it. I refuse to be seduced by You. All my life I have
striven to resist the temptations of attractive women. You are

not, cannot be, any more attractive than they are. I can resist Your allure too. If You don't go away I will lose my mind. Maybe I've lost it already.

"I don't believe that You have pursued me through all the loves of my life, even through those which were wrong, sinful. I don't believe that in those loves, in all my loves, I was seeking You and You were seeking me. That is preposterous. Go away. I am serving notice on You that this is all over. Finished. Done. I am returning to my normal self now."

Finally, as we all must when we become involved with the Lord God, he gave up. "All right, You win, as You knew You would."

And it is from that moment on that Johnny's diary becomes filled not with details of a successful Lothario or an ambitious ecclesiast's steps up the career ladder, but with simple yet elegant homilies delivered on subjects ranging from peace to love within the family. Also included are direct, impassioned pleas to the Holy Father himself, asking him at one point to encourage, rather than vilify, the faithful and, elsewhere, requested that he review the Church's position on the role of women in the Church. They are not the sort of letters an ambitious cleric would have sent. The Johnny seen here is far different from the insipid wit who penned the bland missives and sermons of the earlier part of his career. The changed Johnny was present, determined, and clear. What was as surprising to me as the change in him was the fact that his new Johnny was one even I could admire.

|| 58 || Quite a story, I thought, as I put aside the last page of the diary. Was he crazy those last three years of his life? Did the discovery that Caroline was his daughter unhinge him? He must have been crazy to think I was a close friend.

Smoking guns in those hundreds of pages? Enough to sink a couple of ships. His sexual escapades as a seminarian would be enough in some quarters to end all thought of his canonization.

And although he was as reticent as Mary Elizabeth herself was as to their ultimate consummation of their lifelong passion, he acknowledged the happy result of that union: little Caroline, whose uncanny resemblance to the young, radiant Delia was most pronounced when her features were relaxed in death.

I glanced out the window of Mary Elizabeth's office and across the lawns of River Forest. Trinity girls in their uniforms were already ambling slowly down the street on their way home from school. Kids from St. Luke's would soon appear. Time for me to leave.

There was no doubt that he had at least one illegitimate

child. I had the proof. The child's mother had admitted it. He had virtually admitted it in his diary.

In my letter to the Cardinal, I could say something like this: "I have found incontrovertible evidence, including admission by the mother, that the late Cardinal fathered an illegitimate child in the years since he was made an archbishop. No useful purpose can be served at the present time by revealing the name or the location of this child. However, under the circumstances, it could hardly be claimed that he is an appropriate candidate for the canonization process."

Maybe the popular devotion would continue despite the gradually leaked fact of an illegitimate offspring. I had no control over that. Maybe in some future era when an Archdiocesan commission examined the case, the information in my letter would not be as important as it seemed today. However, I would have done my job.

I would also protect—reasonably well—Marbeth and Caroline. Johnny had been Archbishop for several years in Rome on the staff of the Secretariat of State before he had been sent to Chicago. Perhaps he had fathered the child then.

The Cardinal could speculate as much as he wanted to. He'd not know where to look for the proof. Nor would it be in his interest to do so.

I removed several sheets from the big pile in front of me. I would make copies for my own secret files. I reached for the switch on Marbeth's copier and brushed against my briefcase. Ken Woodward's book fell out. I opened and read the last page again.

> Only God makes saints. Still, it is up to us to tell their stories. That, in the end is the only rationale for the process of "making saints." What sort of a story befits a saint? Not tragedy, certainly. Comedy comes closer to capturing the playfulness of genuine holiness and the supreme logic of a life lived in and through God. An element of suspense is also required: until the story is over, one can never be certain of the outcome. True saints are the last people on earth to presume their own salvation—in this life or the next.

"You son of a bitch," I muttered, looking skyward.

Even now I wonder: Did I mean Jumping Johnny McGlynn or God?

"You can keep these." I opened my briefcase and presented Mary Elizabeth with my precious documents.

"You didn't copy anything?" she said softly.

She was sitting in the same chair in which I had left her, reading glasses on and Jon Hasler's *North of Hope* in her hand. A Haydn concerto was playing.

"No."

She closed the book and took off her glasses. Eyes too tired for her usual contacts?

"Nothing of significance."

"Come on, Lar. There were tons of smoking guns."

"Nope. What he did as a seminarian is irrelevant."

"It could destroy his memory."

"Irrelevant to my assignment. The people at the shrine couldn't care less about his exploits before he was ordained."

"He fathered an illegitimate child," she said.

"Did he? That's one interpretation of his text, but it's not the only one. You'd have to read a lot into it."

I sat down in the chair next to her.

"But you know the only possible interpretation, don't you?"

"Do I?"

"You have your documents." She held up the manila envelope.

"You have them. Anyway, what do they prove? Only that your daughter was born late. Weight at birth? Who knows what that means? Besides, there is no evidence that, even if Bud was not her father, Johnny was."

"Delia's photograph?"

"All Irishwomen look alike. I bet you could find a picture of Bud's mother or grandmother that looks like Caroline. Or a picture of your grandmother or mother."

"I admitted to you that he was Caroline's father."

"Did you?"

"Yes."

"You be willing to testify in writing and under oath to that effect?"

She frowned. "I don't think so."

"Then all I have is hearsay."

"Lar . . ." She smiled, her little hint that I still amused her. "You're impossible. It's very sweet to want to protect me and Caroline, but you have your job to do."

I flipped open *Making Saints* and read her the passage.

"Look, Mary Elizabeth, we've all of us been used—Doctor, Delia, Kate, you, Annemarie, Bud, Caroline, me, and heaven only knows how many other minor characters. It's not you that I want to protect. It seems as if God, in effect, was determined to prove a point. You don't think I can turn a man like Jumping Johnny McGlynn into a saint? Just watch me."

"Why?"

"Because the Almighty felt we needed a story like his—"

"And those of us who were minor characters?"

"I guess God owes us some favors."

"What a marvelous Chicago answer." She smiled. "What should I do with this?" she asked, holding up the journal.

"Lock it up. Someday those who manage the formal process of making saints might be more willing to consider the whole story as one plot. Then they'd be impressed by the plotmaker. Or you could think about publishing a portion of it now. Why wait for them to be ready?"

"And the Cardinal?" she asked.

"I'll take care of him. Get him off the hook. I'll send you a copy of my letter."

"So all the loose ends are tied up neatly, just like a good story should end, is that right, Lar? I should have trusted you from the start."

"One more loose end."

"What's that?"

"Did you give your latest the wave-off?"

"Yes," was all she said, but from the hardened look in her eyes, I could tell what she meant was it was none of my business.

"Why? It wouldn't have worked?"

"Oh, it would have worked." She was about to explode at me. "Sweet man, very sweet. Strong, too. . . . But I don't need a man."

"I agree. Still, you'd be happier with one. You're a passionate sentimentalist, Mary Elizabeth. You've already admitted that today."

She watched me very coldly. "I have no right to be happy."

"You didn't listen to me, Mary Elizabeth. I said the story is over now. We all played our parts, you and I. All things considered, not too badly. We're free now. We must get on with our own stories."

She began to relax again, oh, but so slowly.

"How can you say that?"

"Didn't you understand your place in the story? Don't you see that you were the vehicle for Johnny's transformation? God's vehicle. You were the important grace in his life."

"I was an occasion of sin for him," she snapped. "How could I have been an occasion of grace too?"

"That, I think, is the Storyteller's whole point."

"I'll have to think about that."

"Great. But in the meantime I think you should call that suitor of yours."

"How dare you tell me what to do!" Her face flamed with anger. "What right do you have to give me orders?"

"I'm your priest."

"I haven't appointed you that yet."

"Doesn't matter. I've appointed myself. Call him. Now."

Her smile expanded to a broad grin.

She walked to the other side of the room, picked up the phone, made a face at me, and dialed a number.

She was, for a few moments, a teenager again, calling for a prom date. Her facial expression and body language changed rapidly from embarrassment to contrition, to expectation, to relief, and finally to joy.

"A woman my age," she said as she walked back slowly toward me, her face glowing, tears pouring down her cheeks, "should be ashamed to be as hungry for a man as I find that I am."

She leaned her head against my chest. Then the tears came, body-racking, liberating sobs.

"I never wanted to always be in control. But I had no choice. Bud, Johnny. They both needed . . ."

"It's over now, Marbeth."

She nodded and produced a tissue from somewhere.

"I'll try to believe that."

"Now get ready for a whole new story, in which you'll have a different role."

She gulped and dabbed at her nose. "Did you think I could cry so much?"

She breathed deeply.

"Probably you'll cry a lot more before the weekend. Then you'll stop crying and begin the new story."

"You'll do the wedding?"

"Sure."

She became limp in my arms, a surrender not to me, but to the Grace which had enveloped her life and which she was only now recognizing.

"And always be my priest?"

"Do I have a choice?"

Fortunately there are many different kinds of love in the world.

"None whatever."

On my way down the front steps, the ebullient Caroline bounced up to meet me with her standard hug and kiss.

"All *better!*" we exclaimed together.

Good ending.

EPILOGUE

St. Finian's Parish
Forest Springs, Illinois

November 1—Feast of All Saints

Your Eminence,
  To summarize a report I will send you later, I find no grounds for rejecting the possible cause of Cardinal John McGlynn as a candidate for canonization. He used family money to help his brother out of financial trouble. The funds he smuggled into Poland were not stolen. Mary Elizabeth Quinlan was a friend, adviser, and confidante. I found no conclusive evidence of anything else in their relationship. I have documents from her and from Monsignor Carey in my files, should you wish to peruse them.
  Ms. Quinlan also possesses the only material which was ever in "secret archives," a collection of notes and letters which the late Cardinal assembled in his final years in Chicago. She intends to publish them. Before publication, she will send a copy to you. I'm sure you will find the material very moving.

While the book will unquestionably be controversial, it will contain nothing that will call into question his personal holiness.

I know it does not fall within the limits of my assignment to recommend policy for the Archdiocese in this matter. However, I think no great harm will be done if you state a public position that (a) the Archdiocese is not opposed to an eventual process for canonization but that (b) you believe the process will be aided and not hindered at the present time by approaching it very slowly.

I have gathered documentation for two more miracles which I believe might someday be acceptable to the Consulta Medica. At the present time, however, I believe no useful purpose will be served by making these materials public or by burdening you with them.

Finally, as to whether John Arthur McGlynn is really a saint in heaven, as part of some wonderful, if slightly kinky plot on the part of God, all I can say is that if he is a saint, he is the only saint who understands how tough your job is.

It would not hurt, therefore, if you began to pray to him. As, God help us all, I have.

Faithfully yours in Our Lord,

Laurence O'Toole McAuliffe M.A. (Trin.) D.M.
Pastor

NOTE

My suggestion that the Mossad funded Solidarity in its early phases is, of course, pure fiction. Nonetheless, as it turns out, it would have been a good idea.